# STRIKING TERROR

By

Denis Lipman

*Striking Terror*



Cover images: Shutterstock/Weerachai Khamfu, D. Virtser
Greater Jerusalem map: Kira Masi
Author photo: Frances Erlebacher

Published by Piscataqua Press
An imprint of RiverRun Bookstore, Inc.
142 Fleet Street | Portsmouth, NH | 03801
www.riverrunbookstore.com
www.piscataquapress.com

ISBN: 978-1-944393-19-9

Printed in the United States of America

*For my daughter, Kate*

# GREATER JERUSALEM

The West Bank
Palestinian Territory

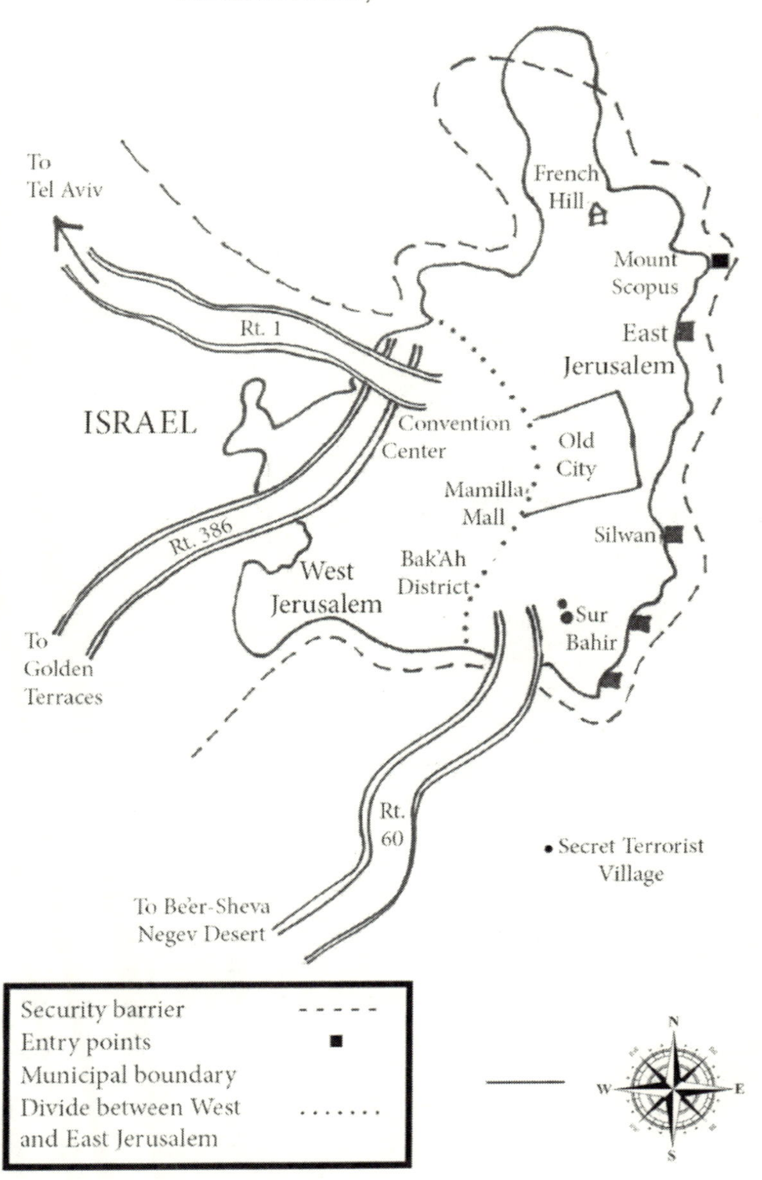

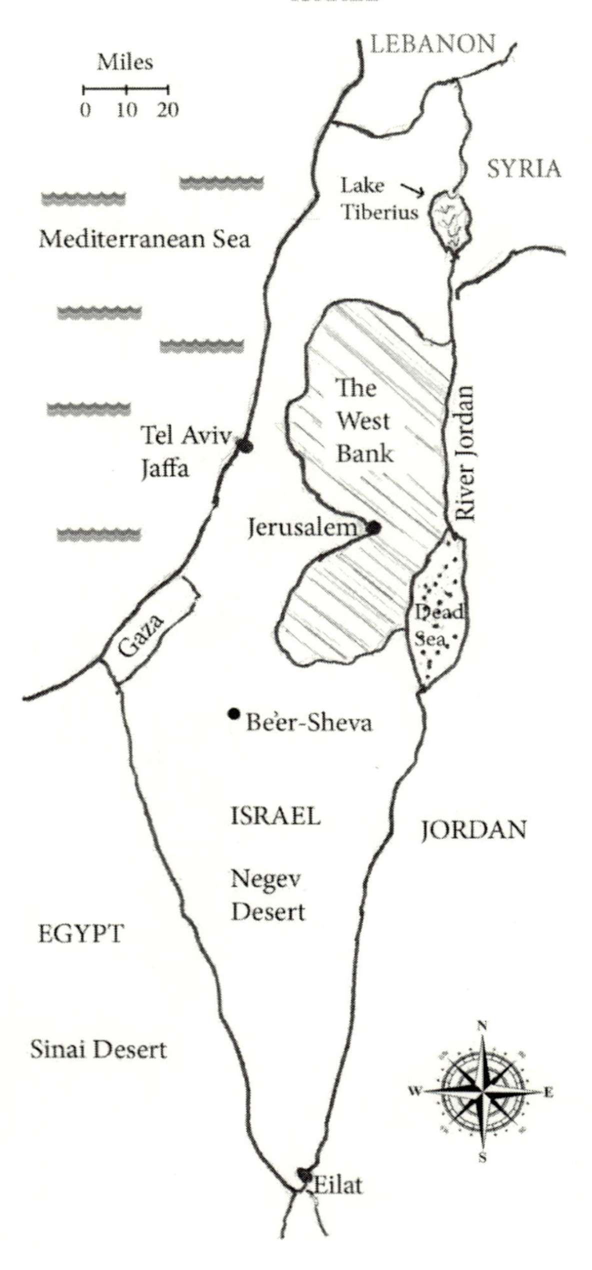
ISRAEL
LEBANON
Miles
0 10 20
SYRIA
Lake
Tiberius
Mediterranean Sea
The
West
Bank
River Jordan
Tel Aviv
Jaffa
Jerusalem
Dead
Sea
Gaza
Be'er-Sheva
ISRAEL
JORDAN
Negev
Desert
EGYPT
Sinai Desert
N
W
E
S
Eilat

# CHAPTER 1

MICAH MONTSEES HELD UP HIS HANDS and showed them empty. He reached toward the sun, a difficult feat considering there was so little about. Micah was in a forest and, after all, this was England. He grabbed a fistful of air and held it above the unlit campfire.

"Magicus, Solaris," he shouted out the incantation.

Unclenching his hand, he clicked his fingers and the smoldering newsprint burst into flames.

"It worked," Micah said to himself. Producing silks and flowers out of a tube was okay, but to take ordinary stuff and do extraordinary things, well, that was more like it. The trick used a purple compound and glycerin, separated in a gelatin capsule hidden in the paper. A safety pin puncturing the capsule started the reaction.

Having missed the last Scout camp, Micah was trying to catch up with the others. He had trudged out on a cold winter's day to earn a campfire cooking badge. The test was to build a fire then cook something without utensils like pans or even oil. Micah had set another challenge for himself: he would start the fire without matches. And he had succeeded brilliantly.

The kids in his troop would have been so impressed. Never would have figured how the trick was done. If only they'd come. But one by one they had begged off. They had said it might rain. Might! Twerps.

Their loss. And so what? Just kids in the troop. They were not really his mates.

Micah wrapped a fish in wet newspaper. As he shoved the briny package into the embers, he caught a headline: "Tensions flare in Jerusalem. Side by Side Accord on hold." It made him think of his relatives in Israel. The paper burned away before he could read more.

Ten minutes later, Micah pulled out the charred bundle and peeled away the hot, blackened newsprint. The skin of the mackerel stuck to the paper, revealing clean, cooked flesh. It was like a trick, Micah thought. He snapped a picture of himself and the campfire dinner, then grabbed his bike and pushed off for home. Luckily eating the bone-ridden fish wasn't part of the challenge.

Riding back, Micah was already thinking about his next goal—the entertainer's badge. He had told Skip, his troop leader, that he could swallow real razor blades and pull them back out neatly joined up on a piece of thread. Skip had been so impressed by the description of the effect that he said Micah could perform the trick, along with the rest of his act, at the next social. And, according to Skip, it would be a real show, with stage lights and curtains, even a band.

The trouble was, Micah had lied. He could not do the trick, and had no idea how it was done. Panic.

From what Micah could see, the Magic Place on the Tottenham Court Road sold more plastic vomit pats and plaster-of-paris doggy-doo than just about anything else. After hanging about looking at moth-eaten tricks behind glass, Micah plucked up enough courage to ask for a demonstration of the razor blade trick. The old man behind the counter, with sideburns, a paunch, and an unbuttoned sweater, stared at him sideways and tried not to smile.

"You what? You want to buy it or are you just wasting my valuable time, chick?"

"No, I'm not. I do. Honest. I mean, I really want to buy the trick."

"Then what's the point of seeing it done, chick, if you're so set on buying it?"

Micah caved. "All right, I'll take it."

The old man swiveled about with amazing agility, a small brown paper bag in hand.

Micah ripped open the package in a café nearby. The effect was not as expensive as Micah had expected. Not a good sign. Cheaper tricks were usually harder to do. The supplied props consisted of a gimmicked spool of thread that concealed a set of blunt razor blades strung together with cotton. And that was it. Micah pored over the instructions.

First off, he had to take real safety razor blades (not supplied) and put them in his mouth one at a time. No trick there. He then had to spit the blades into a glass of water, under the guise of washing them down his throat. Micah was not convinced this ruse would fool anyone. And the alarming idea of sharp blades churning around his mouth was…well, alarming.

Micah decided to practice in front of his parents first.

Two days after buying the trick, he was ready. Sort of. He scampered around the garden to make an entrance through the French windows. Showtime. Throwing back the curtains, he sent his table and props flying. A rubber chicken oozed out from a secret hole in his props table.

Paul and Lori Montsees fell about laughing. Dressed in a slightly too-big tuxedo, a velvet cloak, and a pre-made bow tie, their son was quite a sight, a slightly pudgy-faced kid with dark toffee eyes and a mop of curly blond-brown hair.

"You may laugh, but never before have so many wonders been revealed to so few," Micah intoned with Churchillian confidence, hoping his innate streak of chutzpah would make up for a lack of practice.

Micah sliced a piece of paper with a razor blade. Dad still asked if it was real. Micah nodded while pretending to chew and swallow the blade. He glanced at Mum, saw her eyes close. Dad hadn't noticed. It wasn't the first time Lori had dozed off during a trick since she'd gotten sick some months before, but that was okay. He stopped chewing. The razor blades could wait.

"Ladies and gentlemen. Welcome. Let's begin the Tenth Epping Troop Social with a little mystery and legerdemain. A round of applause, if you please, for Micah the Magician!"

Skip bounded from the stage, barely keeping pace with the curtains as they swooshed open.

The spotlight dazzled Micah's eyes. He blinked and froze in a weird kind of pose, his mind a blank. He heard slight applause, probably from his dad. Get on with it, he told himself, just get on with it. He picked up a silk handkerchief as he palmed a plastic egg. In one half of the egg was a compartment filled with glycerin and a round yellow disc. The idea was to push the silk into the hollow part of the palmed egg, then reveal the egg—and the handkerchief would appear to be gone! Micah would then expose the trick by showing how the silk went inside the egg. He would repeat the trick, but this time, the audience would be *really* fooled. From even a short distance away, the glycerin and yellow disc would look just like a real egg.

Without much fanfare, Micah tucked the silk into the prop's unseen hollow. When he opened the egg and the handkerchief had apparently vanished, the audience unexpectedly burst into applause. Amazed, Micah decided to quit while he was ahead. Why expose a trick just to fool them again?

So he simply "cracked" the egg into a glass and got on with the rest of his act. Time for the razor blade trick.

The first blade glinted in the stage lights. Slowly Micah placed it on his tongue and closed his mouth. He appeared to chew, then swallow. For added effect, he sliced a piece of paper with the second blade before popping it into his mouth.

The audience became very quiet. Only a faint brushing sound on the drums could be heard, like in movies when people were going to be executed. Another blade was tested and eaten. Then another. And another. Micah puffed out his cheeks and waggled his jaws, as if chewing. Then he pretended to swallow. While getting a sip of water to wash the "meal" down, Micah had to spit the blades out into the glass, unseen by the audience. It had worked in practice. Not that night.

Micah reached for the water and, as the blades came out, so did a mouthful of blood. One of the blades was lodged in the top of his mouth. The audience saw the water in the glass turn pink. There were gasps, stifled murmurs of concern. Was it part of the act? No one was sure. Micah was bleeding but he drank more. The water finally dislodged the blade, which shot into the glass along with the others. He opened his mouth. No blades. The applause came and so did more blood. His tongue and gum had been nicked. Don't quit, Micah told himself, don't quit. He forced himself to swallow, to go on.

He brought the spool of thread to his lips and propelled the hidden blades into his mouth. He bit off some thread, rolled it into a ball and brought it back up to his mouth. Although he didn't swallow thread, he did swallow blood. But he went on.

As the drummer began an insistent roll on the snare drum, Micah reached into his mouth and grabbed the end of a piece of black cotton. And pulled. One by one the blades appeared, threaded together, glinting in the light.

The first ripple of applause turned into a wave of cheering. But when the lights went up, Micah noticed his dad was not applauding.

Amid the noise and hoopla, Paul had a phone pressed to one ear, a hand pressed to the other. Mum, thought Micah. It must be mum.

✦ ✦ ✦

The weather was gray and sullen. A perfect day for a sad occasion. Micah peered over at the hole. His grandmother, his Nanny, was in a pine box, dead at ninety-four. Micah was very sad for his Nan, but part of him felt relieved it was not his mum.

The service droned on. Micah looked around. Only men were present. Nanny had wanted an Orthodox service.

Lori's brother had flown in from Israel for the funeral. Micah had never met his uncle before. Uncle Bernard Rothner didn't look one bit like Micah's mum. His face was framed by a red beard, and his eyes looked as if they were trying to pop out of their sockets like jawbreakers. And it's Ber-*nard*, he was told. Ber-*nard*. Micah tried to remember.

The grave was filled in quickly and without further ceremony. Micah was told that in a year, a stone would be laid, but that was it for now. The worst was over.

Or so Micah thought.

# Chapter 2

"See the way I hold the rifle? Barrel down. Even unloaded. Always handle a weapon as if it is loaded." Farouz Obeid looked around expectantly. "You understand?"

His sister Shireen understood. Only too well. She went on reading, trying to ignore the lecture on gun safety.

Farouz cradled the model gun, an exact replica of the infamous AK-47 assault rifle, and added, "Unless you mean to use it. You understand me? Boom! Boom! Boom!"

Muzzle up now, he shook the gun at the ceiling of the small house as he made sound effects, then handed the lethal-looking toy back to his youngest brother, Amir. The slightly older Hisham tried to grab it. Farouz laughed as they tussled for ownership.

Shireen saw Alika, their mother, glance up from shelling peas. Perhaps this time she would speak out? But Alika returned to the chore at hand. Better to pop peas than pop the ego of her eldest son. Shireen hated her mother's silence. The only other girl, eleven-year-old Suray, was indifferent but she paid attention. Played the game. Shireen had no intention of doing that. Defiantly she tried to read again.

"Stringy. Pay attention. You're not listening. Stringy! You have to learn these things."

That's what Farouz called Shireen. Stringy. At fourteen, his nearest sibling in age, Shireen was thin, a bit awkward, but almost as tall as Farouz. Stringy was not an affectionate nickname. Shireen looked at her brother, just as annoyed as he was.

"Boom, boom, boom. I heard," Shireen said flatly.

Farouz snatched the village newsletter from her lap and popped her on the head with it.

"She does not pay attention," Farouz said for the benefit of their mother.

"Pay attention, Shireen," Alika said. "Do as your brother says."

"I do not want to learn about guns." Shireen stared pointedly at Farouz. "Even toy guns."

Again he swiped her head with the newspaper, harder this time, but Shireen did not cower.

"I see hate in your eyes. Good. That is good. We need that hate," Farouz said. "Turn your hate from me, sister, turn it to our enemies."

Fool, thought Shireen. He thinks I hate him, but I hate myself for not speaking up.

Shireen had long been aware of her brother's activities. At twelve, he had joined a street gang, then became a stone thrower. Within a few years, he had traded stones for bullets. His behavior was never checked, his rhetoric never questioned.

Shireen assumed the Israelis nurtured similar feelings and fears, embedded deeper than wisdom teeth. Even so, she had the measure of her brother. He was more thug than freedom fighter, and he knew how she felt about him. It did not make for an easy relationship.

If only Farouz were like Father, thought Shireen. Omar Obeid had tried to live between two worlds with the aid of lots of sweet tea and a cigar or two, which Shireen would light for him. He wanted his children to understand the world beyond Sur Bahir, their small village just south of Jerusalem and just north of the Palestinian-controlled West Bank.

Shireen's father had dreamed of taking his family to a quieter, more peaceful place. Sur Bahir had changed over time. The village had turned into a politically charged area since the construction of a new Israeli settlement. Settlements. They were fulfillment of a prophecy for some, salt in the wound of unhealed history for others.

Shireen knew the settlers had good views of the valley below, where the sheep grazed and gnarly olive trees clung to the earth as fiercely as the people who lived there. *I wonder if the settlers know how we feel about them.* Shireen thought about it, then smiled to herself. *At least they do not have to live with my brother.*

# Chapter 3

The plane passed over the Swiss Alps. Shards of white snow appeared to drip down dead-looking peaks like ice lava. A few minutes later, Micah glimpsed the softer tops of the lower Italian alpine range. Then the deeper blue of the Mediterranean. No more land.

He stared out the window, remembering how he'd ended up on a plane bound for Israel.

His parents had dropped the bombshell the day after Nanny's funeral. Micah's mother, Lori, had been accepted into a medical trial in America. So, amidst the sadness and loss of Nanny, his parents had seen a silver lining and grabbed for it. Micah had wanted to remain in England, but there was no one to stay with. Uncle Bernard, their only close relative, had generously offered to take Micah back with him to Jerusalem while his sister and her husband were in the States.

Paul and Lori were grateful and relieved. Micah felt torn. Of course, he was thrilled that his mum might get well again. He wanted that more than anything. But even so… He was being pulled out of school, pulled out of England. Pulled from home. It would be the first time the family had been apart. He already missed them.

"Landing soon. Your cousins Jakey and Zeke can't wait to meet you. And Aunt Gilly. You must show them your conjuring tricks. Use coins. The twins collect coins. Avid, they are." Then Uncle Bernard sucked the air from Micah's throat. At home, he said, the family only spoke Hebrew.

"You mean no one speaks English?" Micah was shocked.

"Oh, yes, everyone does. But at home we speak Hebrew."

"I know hardly any bloody Hebrew. Bloody hell." Micah did nothing to conceal his anger.

"There's no need to flare up," said Bernard quietly.

"I'm not flaring!" But Micah knew he was. Why do I do that? he thought. I always do that; why can't I count to a million first. Short-fused, quick-tempered—Micah had heard it all before. He shot a quick glance at his uncle.

"Sorry," Micah said. He smiled awkwardly.

"Don't worry," said Bernard, smiling back. "You'll soon get the hang of it. Hebrew, you know—a smart boy like you, you'll catch it like a cold. The twins will help you. Just have to try. You'll try? Yes? Good!"

Micah looked out the window. He didn't know what to say. At least it was sunny. A golden pirate cutlass of sand held back a light-blue sea. Beyond the beaches was a flat sprawling metropolis. Tel Aviv.

An hour later, Micah and Bernard were driving to Jerusalem. It was now midafternoon, and Micah could see the opposite side of Highway One was jammed. Arab women in traditional garb and Arab men in Western suits waited for buses at shelters shaped like giant question marks.

"Afternoon rush hour is always like this. Commuters leaving Jerusalem to return home to Tel Aviv. And to the Territories. But the checkpoint clears up. Eventually."

The terrain changed. Irrigated plots of land gave way to stony desert, less flat, more rugged. Trees on distant hillsides seemed stuck in the gold, parched earth like green lollipops on elongated sticks. Micah saw a donkey on a rocky ledge. Very biblical, he thought.

Bernard pointed out a new town. To Micah, the buildings and houses looked like endless white Lego pieces plunked haphazardly on top of a hill.

"What do they do there?"

"Sleep." Bernard smiled. "People who live there work in either Jerusalem or Tel Aviv."

They sped on, heading east. In the far distance, the setting sun was dusting the Judean Hills in pale orange. Then the fences started. Bernard explained they were passing through the Territories. High concrete walls fringed with rolls of barbed wire snaked across the undulating ground on either side of the highway.

"The villages are both Jewish and Arab. But they are connected. Never any trouble here."

"Then why the high walls?"

"Just to be sure," said Bernard. "Here's the Jerusalem checkpoint."

Micah could not see the city, only concrete barriers, single-line traffic lanes, and fences. Bernard rolled down his window. Several bored-looking soldiers idled in the shade. One approached, nodded, and waved them through, barely glancing in their direction.

"Sometimes they look in. Sometimes not. We've got yellow license plates, the Palestinians have green ones. That's what they look for first. It only takes one crazy guy…" Bernard shrugged.

The walls on both sides of the highway became lower. Some parts even had murals. Then the barricade sank away and the barbed wire was rolled back. Bernard said they were now back in Israel. Within moments, the boxy buildings of Jerusalem appeared in the distance.

After the relative flatness of Central London, Micah was unprepared for the hills on which Jerusalem was built. As they drove east, an old-fashioned windmill came into view. Beyond it, Micah glimpsed the honey-hued stone crenellations of the Old

City, built atop a steep hill skirted by a narrow valley. They drove down a wide, busy street past a huge YMCA building, the King David Hotel, then up another incline, heading north to Mount Scopus.

Bernard parked in the shadow of a silo-like building near the light-rail train station. They walked to a small cluster of stepped houses built of Jerusalem stone. All the window boxes were brimming with colorful, lush plants.

"Welcome."

Even if it was in Hebrew, the greeting was warm and genuine. Aunt Gilly gave Micah a big hug and he hugged her back. Then he smiled and said, *"Boker tov,"* Hebrew for good morning. Gilly and Bernard laughed. Micah had meant to say hello.

Jakey and Zeke appeared. The twins. Jakey mumbled something in Hebrew, and then looked away. Zeke was all smiles and made a big deal of saying hello. Micah responded in English. The boys appeared to understand, but replied in Hebrew. At least they seemed friendly. When their parents left the room, however, Micah noticed how different Zeke became, almost cold despite the ready smile he could flash like a headlight. Micah tried a phrase in Hebrew, something about the weather. Jakey responded. At least he sounded encouraging. Micah tried to smile, not understanding, feeling like an idiot. Zeke laughed without humor.

Micah thought it odd that twins could look so different. Jakey had a round, open face and red cheeks, with a snub nose and black hair flopping over his forehead. Zeke's face was pinched, with narrow, almost sunken cheeks. His hair was a mangle of brown and ginger, and his complexion was completely white, as though he never spent any time in the sunshine.

Dinner was ready. Micah was handed a black yarmulke, which he dutifully wore. Bernard said a prayer, bread was passed, and the evening meal was served. After dinner, Bernard motioned to Micah to follow him upstairs. He explained, in English, that the house was Arabic in style: high roof, narrow windows, and rounded doorways.

Bernard opened a door. Micah's bedroom was small and smelled of sneakers. He wondered whose room he had gotten. Then Bernard yelled goodnight from the hallway. In Hebrew.

# CHAPTER 4

A CHAIR SKIDDED ACROSS THE STONE FLOOR. Shireen blinked, tried to focus. She was waking up in a nightmare. Her mind was a blur. Everything was a blur.

"Are you responsible for that atrocity? Are you? Stringy, do not lie."

Shireen stared up at Farouz, inches above her face. He dragged her out of bed and into the front room, trailing a blanket. He shook her shoulders, then let her go. Farouz circled her threateningly. He smelled of sweat and the harsh residue of cordite. Shireen wondered if he'd been on another secret training exercise. All she knew was that his anger and frustration had turned once more on her.

"No, no, no," was all she could think to say. She needed to buy time. Had to think. What had she done? By his lights, her sin was a stain upon the approaching morning itself. Then all became clear. He had seen Uncle Samil's old home. Painted green. Oh. That. Oh.

It had started months ago when Shireen started reading Shakespeare and playing scenes in Miss Jezar's English class. Shireen had been totally bitten by the theater bug. A bug that had taken a huge chunk of her brain. Or so her friends had said.

Shireen had read every bit of Shakespeare she could get her hands on. And the more she read, the more she thought about her life. Apart from Miss Jezar's class, everything she learned in school was set in stone. The way of things unchangeable. But Shakespeare's plays were filled with people who, for good or for ill, made their own way. The Bard's characters lived their lives unshadowed by fate, and they inspired Shireen to create her own destiny. No more standing in shadows for her.

That's why she had decided to turn the shell of her uncle's ruined home into an outdoor theater where she and her friends would put on plays. Her best friends, Hameeda and Nahil, had grabbed some of Shireen's enthusiasm, if not her grasp of old-fashioned English. And unlike some of her other wild schemes, like building boats or virtual malls, Shireen had stuck to this one. All three girls had worked hard, removing rubble until the site was cleared.

Then Shireen had summoned Nahil and Hameeda to the spruced-up ruin for a special meeting. From behind a broken wall, she produced a can of blue paint and two cans of yellow. Plus big paintbrushes and a very charming grin.

"We shall create a wood near Athens, beyond the coast of Bohemia..."

"Oh, no," Nahil groaned.

The broken walls soaked up the paint like cloth. It took three coats. Finally one wall was painted in various shades of green. They stood back.

"Still looks like a painted broken wall to me," Hameeda sighed wearily.

Not to Shireen. She felt a bush had grown among the stones. Not exactly the forest of Arden, but perhaps the edge of a magical glade.

She never expected Farouz would understand, but somehow she had to make him. Once he calmed down.

Farouz was in full rant. The family woke, drawn to the edge of his tirade like reluctant moths to a flame.

"This was the home the Jewish destroyed, and you paint it—you desecrate it along with Uncle Samil's memory. Or did you forget what happened?" Farouz asked sarcastically.

"Uncle Samil tried to ram the checkpoint at As-Sawana. I will never—"

"They killed him." Farouz talked over her. "The Jewish, they killed him. But who cares? Not you. You have moved on."

How could she move on from an event that set such terrible things in motion?

After Samil's death, the family had learned that, a week earlier, he had been detained at the Israeli–West Bank border while on his way to work in Bethlehem. He resembled a terror suspect. Samil had begged to contact his employer, but no calls were allowed. Although an apology was offered when the mix-up was discovered, the damage was done. Samil lost his job. But rather than telling his family, he continued to cross the border as he had always done.

Until the day he stole a truck and drove it at the border wall. The border guards had shot him dead as he accelerated towards them at high speed.

Shireen had stood with her father as Samil's wife and children were forcibly removed from their home and placed on transport bound for a refugee camp. Together they watched as the house was bulldozed down to its foundations, knocked from the scarred earth like teeth broken by a hammer.

Shireen remembered leading her father away from the dust and the noise and the gathered crowds. He was inconsolable. He spent the next day wandering the village streets, grieving quietly. Words of revenge rang hollow in his ears, but words of comfort hurt the most. Shireen believed her father's heart had been crushed along with his brother's home.

Three days later he was dead. All that remained was a ruined house—and ruined lives.

Farouz sniffed the air as if it smelled foul, but when he spoke again, he was calm. Unnaturally calm. "You will put it back as it was."

"It is but a little tree," said Shireen quietly, trying to sound meek.

"Do not defy me on this, Shireen. Or you will suffer. And you would have no one to blame but yourself—this act of vandalism will not go unpunished."

Farouz often yelled at his family as if they were members of a jury. Across the street, neighbors cracked doors open to hear better.

"I did it for our uncle, our father, and all Palestinians—" Shireen faltered, thinking wildly, then began again with certainty. "You think you alone feel hatred? I feel it, too! So I turned that decaying symbol of hate into a symbol that will only grow strong."

He let her go. Shireen fell backward. The pain began to subside. One or two neighbors, overhearing, applauded. Shireen watched her brother as he assumed a contemplative pose.

"You speak a truth, little sister, an immutable truth to all the wrong that has befallen us."

"If only you had let me explain, dear brother…"

Shireen patted her brother's back reassuringly. Over his shoulder, she smiled mischievously at Suray, who had been watching with fearful admiration.

Farouz stood upright. He spoke to those gathered around the doorframe. "From the rubble of our despair, Shireen grows the tree of hate."

There followed a general muttering of *"Inshallah."* Shireen sighed with relief as she realized her brother would make a better actor than she ever would. Moments later, she heard his old motorbike sputter into life and he was gone.

"You provoke him, Shireen. Why do you do this?" her mother was fuming.

"I did not mean to. That place, that old ruin, it could come alive again. My friends and I can turn it into something special. Something special for the entire community. It is my dream."

"We all have dreams, child. Your father and I had dreams to leave this stony place, to live in the mountains."

"You did?"

"This is just a dwelling. A shell. This place was nothing to us. It was always filled with hatreds. I know this. And your father, he knew… If I could, I would take you, Shireen, you and your brothers, your sisters, far away from all this, from the settlements, the barriers, the endless resentments. Oh, Shireen, what I would give to live in some kind of peace with our neighbors."

"The Israelis?"

"Why not them? I would do it."

Shireen hugged her mother gently. Suray was still there, saying nothing but taking it all in. Shireen beckoned her over and hugged her, too.

"George the Third," said Micah. "History is about the only thing I'm good at. What's that one?" Micah pointed to a disc of bronze in the coin tray. "Can I look?"

Jakey handed Micah the heavy two-penny piece dated 1797, as round and thick as a cookie. Zeke had deigned to show a sampling of his coin collection. Both twins collected, but Zeke's horde was definitely more impressive. He showed Micah a gold sovereign dated the same year as the two-penny piece. Micah tossed it hand to hand. He then closed both hands. When he opened them, the sovereign was gone. Everyone but Zeke laughed. Reaching behind Aunt Gilly's ear, Micah pulled out the vanished golden coin and gave it back to Zeke.

"Want to see another?" asked Micah.

Zeke shook his head, then took off. Grinning, Jakey leaned protectively over his coins. The adults chuckled. A moment later,

Zeke returned with a small chest. It was two feet wide and a foot deep. He placed it on the coffee table in front of Micah and muttered something in Hebrew with knowing anticipation.

"Could you open the box?" Bernard translated.

Micah examined the chest from all sides. There was no lid, no hinges, no drawers, no slats, and it was completely seamless. It looked like a large, solid block of polished wood. Strange. Bernard explained that the chest housed the rest of Zeke's coin collection. A birthday present from an uncle, and only Zeke knew its secret. Everyone in the family had tried to open it and failed. Zeke insisted it could be opened without any tools. If you knew how. Now Micah was to be put to the test.

Zeke started to grin his rat-like grin as he watched his cousin turn the giant puzzle over and over. Then Micah recalled a trick using a smaller box with a lid. Zeke's coin box might open the same way. He placed the narrow sides of the chest between his knees and, using the palms of his hands, held it at catty-corners. He pressed and pulled up.

As the box slid open, so did Zeke's mouth. There was a small roar of amazement from the other three Rothners. They even applauded. Micah put the coin chest on the table and looked up. Zeke's face had crumpled and he seemed to be crying, but no tears came. He grabbed the open box and fled upstairs. The adults suddenly stopped applauding. Bernard rolled his eyes, Gilly shrugged. Micah stood up, no longer grinning. He looked around.

"Let him be. He's highly strung. He's young; he can be..." Bernard ran out of words.

Gilly said Zeke would get over it. This was nothing new. Jakey looked at Micah and gave him a thumbs-up.

# Chapter 5

School that day was completely different. Shireen noticed it immediately. The teachers, the principal, everyone seemed tense. Miss Jezar stood at the head of the class with the principal and a tall, robed man. He wore a rounded red cap and was introduced as a sheikh, a respected leader.

Shireen noticed that he spoke through his smile, and his words sounded as fake as his gleamy teeth. "There are to be changes in your beloved school. Your beloved principal and instructors will help me implement these changes. We shall filter out the putrid waste of Western life…"

On and on he went. Shireen shot Hameeda a glance. None of this sounded good. The principal and Miss Jezar said nothing. Nothing. Shireen rolled the sleeves of her shirt above her elbows.

Nahil noticed and touched her arm. "Pish!" she said, as though burned by hot coal. "Oh, you'll get in trouble, curdy deep trouble," she whispered playfully.

"Tuk, tuk, tuk." Shireen smiled uncaringly.

"You, girl!"

The robed scholar barreled down the aisle, yanked Shireen's arm, and pulled down her sleeve. Shireen turned red in humiliation.

"This is what I talk about. The looseness of the West, their lack of order, of discipline, must be filtered from this beloved school. And we shall do it, together." He smiled coldly.

In a blink of an eye, Shireen's school had become a waqf school, a religious institution. The Palestinian curriculum would remain but the Western focus would not. The sheikh handed out instruction sheets detailing Islamic-approved clothing, hobbies, and reading material, along with new codes of behavior. The instruction sheets were to be handed to parents, signed and returned the following day. The guest scholar issued a blessing, bowed to the class, and walked out. The girls looked at their teacher expectantly. Questions cracked the brittle silence.

"What about field trips?"

"What about the e-pal project?"

"Can we rehearse our scenes from the play?" Shireen asked carefully. Then she looked up and knew something was amiss.

"I am going to retire," Miss Jezar said. "I have longed for this. To do things I've always wanted to do. Imagine…"

"You cannot leave us!" Shireen expressed in those few words what the entire class felt. No answer. Shireen looked into the face of her beloved teacher, but Miss Jezar did not return her glance. She was staring ahead, imagining nothing.

✦ ✦ ✦

Light poured into Micah's bedroom; it was as bright as noon. Micah looked at his watch, couldn't believe how early it was. He blinked the sleep out of his eyes and sat up. Zeke was lolling in the doorway, smirking for some reason. Micah propped himself on an elbow and stared at his cousin. Neither said good morning.

"Got any money?"

Micah was surprised by Zeke's sudden switch to heavily accented English.

"Yeah, I've got some money, why?" Micah said, unsure what Zeke was up to.

"This is my room. Rent. Okay? For me. Pay me. Figure it is fair. Okay?…*Aaaaaw!*"

Jakey had peg-legged his brother in the thigh with his knee. Zeke crumpled into the doorjamb. He swore, which sounded to Micah like clearing a week's worth of snot from a throat. Zeke hobbled away. Jakey hooked a thumb toward his brother.

Micah nodded and smiled. He got the picture. Then Jakey handed him a yarmulke to wear. Micah held up his Gunners cap instead. Jakey nodded as if to say okay. And it was.

At the breakfast table, Micah pretended to bend the spoon he'd used for his cereal. He made the spoon look wobbly, like jelly, before straightening it up and replacing it on his plate. It looked convincing enough for Gilly to gasp with delight. Bernard applauded and Jakey seemed to acknowledge the stunt was pretty cool. Zeke wanted to know how it was done.

"Got any money?" asked Micah.

Zeke scowled, swept the air dismissively, got up, and left the room. Jakey tried not to smile. Bernard shouted after Zeke, who shouted back. Gilly sighed.

The trip to school took about twenty minutes. Uncle Bernard parked the Volvo and came in with the boys. The twins took off. Micah followed his uncle into the main reception area. Bernard said quietly, and in English, that tomorrow Micah would be taking the bus with the twins.

When the head of the school appeared, Uncle Bernard shot up and started pumping his hand, talking a mile a minute. The elderly rabbi listened patiently. Moments later, a younger man appeared. Bernard carried on talking to the principal as Micah was shunted off to a classroom.

Micah spotted his cousins. They did not sit together. Then a bell rang. The class broke up quite suddenly. And so did the room.

Sliding panels that hung down from the ceiling were pushed

aside. Chairs were stacked against the farthest wall. Everyone piled out and Micah asked Jakey what was going on.

Jakey pointed as three robed rabbis, one carrying a large and shiny copper holder containing the Torah, moved with quiet solemnity into the converted room.

The students filed back in after the elders. The container of hammered copper and brass was opened. Prayer books suddenly appeared and a bunch of rambunctious boys quieted down, looking old beyond their years, no longer children. Micah felt part of a profoundly religious event. The room seemed to smolder and glow with a quiet ritualized fervor.

The service ended just as suddenly as it had begun. The Torah was carried out by the rabbis. Silence. Then pandemonium. Kids started talking, pushing, and shoving. The room was re-divided into three classrooms, and textbooks were redistributed. The school day began in earnest.

# Chapter 6

"'NOW THE HUNGRY LION ROARS, and the wolf behowls the moon...'" Shireen sounded flat.

"What's the matter?" Hameeda asked.

"I don't feel like it." Shireen let the play book fall to the ground.

"Things may not be so bad." Nahil tried to sound encouraging.

"They won't let us do plays anymore. No more Shakespeare. Certainly not in English. And you won't be able to wear that anymore." Shireen indicated Hameeda's jean jacket.

"I shall still wear it," said Hameeda, smiling defiantly. "Under my abaya."

"An abaya? That's like wearing a smelly Bedu's tent," said Shireen dismissively.

"Will you not wear the hijab, Shireen? If you have to?" asked Nahil.

"The veil? I will not take the veil. I will not." Then Shireen changed her serious face into a grin and suggested all three run away, join the circus, maybe wear pink burkahs and become clowns. Her friends weren't sure if she was joking or not.

One afternoon, Mr. Bahjar, the new principal, came into the class with a visitor he introduced as Jamal, a learned scholar. Jamal was very plump and sported a keffiyeh like Arafat used to wear, and Ray-Ban sunglasses, which Arafat did not. He also wore a Western-style suit with a shirt that flapped down over his tummy. And the more he smiled, the more he sweated, or so it seemed to the three friends. Shireen immediately nicknamed him The Oily One.

Jamal began a lecture and slide show. Horrifying pictures of death and carnage. Bulldozed homes, barbed wire, refugee camps, and the concrete walls that divided the territories. Walls that tore up farmland and olive groves as easily as they tore up communities. Then he showed pictures of Palestinian funerals.

Afterwards, when the shutters were reopened and afternoon sunlight seeped back into the classroom, Shireen realized this period used to be Miss Jezar's English class. She gulped a bit and squeezed her eyes shut.

On the way home Shireen stopped as usual by the Everything Sold shop, where she had a part-time job stocking shelves and occasionally serving. In return, she earned a little money and had use of the computer. Most importantly, she had her mail delivered there.

Shireen couldn't wait to go through her customary stack of magazines from all over the world. She loved them all—the glossier, the better. Much more fun than getting e-mags. Couldn't get perfume testers with e-mags. She sent in every coupon she could find, and every month, trial issues came her way via the shop. These provided the base material for her dreams, along with the growing pile of scrapbooks she kept in the back of the shop. Shireen could spend hours flipping, sorting, cutting, and pasting. She was always amazed at what girls in other countries wore, and how expensive it was to wear so little.

As Shireen entered the musty, sweet-smelling shop, she headed for the back room, but the owner came out to stop her. Shireen could see how nervous and jittery he looked.

"Listen to me, it was a mistake. The postman, he was here. And your brother, well, he is never here, but this time he was, and the postman handed him your mail—"

"No!"

"I was serving someone at the time—"

Shireen flew out the door and up the hill before he could finish.

She burst into the house to find the kitchen table bare of the plates and utensils normally laid out for the evening meal. In place of food, the tabletop was covered with magazines. The glossy pages were eviscerated, laid out as evidence of a nameless crime. Her older brother and mother sat together. Her younger sister and brothers gathered in the shadows, bystanders to an accident waiting to happen.

"You have opened them. They were mine." Shireen spoke defiantly.

"I had warned you. It is written of the Prophet: Blessings be upon him, that 'a woman should only be struck with a handkerchief.' So be it." Farouz walked toward her.

He wound a cloth handkerchief around his fist. Shireen knew what he was going to do. *The brush of the hanky*. As proscribed by law. But not if she could help it. Not this time. As he swung his covered fist at her face, she ducked and sprang for the door. Too late. An open-handed blow turned her head and then the fisted handkerchief pounded into her cheek.

Shireen reeled yet remained standing. But another juddering blow sent her sprawling across the floor. And then another ground her teeth into the fleshy part of her cheek. Blood filled her mouth. She did not get up. Farouz unwound the red-speckled cloth from his hand. Then he scooped up her magazines and barged into her bedroom. He began ransacking the tiny room for more offensive material. And he found it. Along with more magazines and cut-out photos for Shireen's scrapbooks, he found her Shakespeare Folio.

And then he was gone.

Shireen forced herself to get up. Wiping blood from her mouth, she staggered to the open door of the house. Ignoring pleas from her family, fighting every instinct to run and hide, Shireen followed Farouz. He was walking down the hill with her world under his arm.

And a large plastic can.

The little theater! He was heading for it. By the time she got down to the converted ruin, an eerie yellow light was already starting to fester. Fire.

The magazines crumpled and writhed like living things. The Folio smoldered and charred, as if trying not to succumb. Farouz poured on more accelerant, which splashed beyond the burning book pyre. Within minutes, the wooden planks and pallets the girls had used as a stage were consumed by the flames. Shireen stood there, no longer dazed or even scared, just aware of what Farouz had done. She could see it all. Yet within the bright, revealing light of the fire, all she could see was a sorrowing darkness.

Shireen awoke to the sound of the household getting ready for the day ahead. Her jaw ached and her cheeks still felt hot and painful. It was difficult to swallow; her throat hurt with every breath. She drifted into the kitchen. It was like watching a movie—people were getting on with life, ignoring her as if she wasn't there.

Shireen sat at the table unable to eat or drink anything. But the family busied themselves with breakfast as though nothing was amiss. Perhaps nothing was, thought Shireen. Perhaps, she imagined, this is how it should be.

Everyone was pleased to see Shireen wearing the hijab. She didn't know if they approved of her newfound propriety or were just happy they did not have to see the livid bruises on her face. Or feel the remnants of the hurt that burned through her soul.

At school, Shireen saw how shocked Hameeda and Nahil looked when they saw her. The girls were brimming with questions—why the long robe, why the hijab? Why, why, why? She did not tell them. The scarf-like headdress covered up most of the damage. Just as well; why upset them? Her pals chirped away like sparrows. They only fell silent when Shireen brushed past them and took her seat. She looked up from one to the other but the ice-blue of her eyes froze them out. Without another word they went to their seats.

Shireen wanted to tell them what had happened, but what difference would it make? What could they do? It was hopeless. Her face would heal but the charred remains of her life would not. The theater was gone, her Shakespeare had been burned out of her life. Farouz had even found and destroyed her scrapbooks. She was no longer allowed to work in the Everything Sold shop. Even school had changed; the computers were gone, the Western studies were no more. Instead, they were being taught propaganda by rote, like multiplication tables. Shireen didn't care. Her life—her old life—was over. She willed the bell to ring, hoping her friends would one day understand.

After the roll was taken, Jamal, The Oily One, appeared once more with the head of school. With ill-concealed pride, he announced that he was a member of the Rafah Martyr's Brigade, the elite group of freedom fighters everyone had heard about. There were murmurs, some of approval, some of shock. One girl applauded. Another praised Allah.

"People know of us. Some think we are heroes. But some think the worst of us. They think we condone taking one's own life. And yet it is written in the Book, suicide is not permitted. So how could we condone such an act, condemned by Mohammed, peace be upon Him? We cannot. And we do not. But martyrdom is different. Is it not worthy to give of oneself for others? My children, it is the greatest gift to give. And many of you hold the key to this gift. It is a Jerusalem resident identity card. How many have it? Let me see."

Most students lived in the Municipality of Jerusalem, so virtually everyone held up one of the picture IDs issued to Arab residents. Jamal looked around the room and clasped his hands together. He smiled.

"And this, dear sisters, this little card is the key to a glorious future..." he droned on.

Shireen kept her head down. She felt Hameeda looking at her, probably wondering why she was not rolling her eyes or misbehaving. But Shireen had to tread a more mature path now; school stuff and play projects were things of her past, not of her future.

"Why do we tell you these things? You have seen what our enemies have done. Imagine what you could achieve as a member of the Rafah Martyr's Brigade. You could help unshackle the yoke of oppression and humiliation. And when you lay waste to our enemies, you will be rushed to Heaven on the heroic wind of triumph. Who are these heroes?"

Silence.

"I will show you two such heroes. Two young men who became immortal soldiers of faith as young and pure of heart as all of you."

The homemade film showed two teenage boys saying good-bye to their families. Both wore vests, mustard green in color, with explosives stitched inside. After the farewells, the boys brandished guns they would never fire. Shireen looked into their happy young faces. She was saddened by what she saw but also strangely elated by it. Lights went back on.

"The one who volunteers to be a martyr will receive special courtesies. Her family will receive a pension for life. They will be relocated to a beautiful new home. The boys will go to university, their education will be funded. No expense will be spared, all wishes will be granted."

Suddenly Shireen saw a way forward for her mother, her family.

And a way forward for herself. She had felt she had nothing left, nothing left to live for.

Oh, but I was wrong, she thought, there *is* something left to live for. The thought exhilarated her. It was all so simple. She realized it had been there all the time. Her life.

*For my family, the ones I love, my life will be my gift to give. Yes,* she thought, *yes!*

"Who among you is brave enough? Who will stand for her people? Who among you is the one?" Jamal cried out, his voice breaking with emotion.

"Who among you is the one?" the new headmaster yelled with mounting fervor.

"Who among you is the one? The one!" the men chanted over and over.

The one, the one, the one! Who would it be? Shireen felt herself smiling with secret knowledge. She felt as if she was bursting with excitement. For she already knew the answer. She was now chanting too, in her mind, *the one, the one, I am—*

Shireen was on her feet.

Silence. The chant was done. Shireen saw faces squirming, looking around at her. No one spoke. Shireen stood alone. Jamal spread wide both his arms and his smile in a kind of embrace. Shireen tried to smile back. And then, as if in one voice, the entire classroom erupted into a frenzied celebration. Everyone swarmed around her, cheering and shouting. Except Nahil and Hameeda.

Avoiding their bewildered, frightened stares, Shireen just looked straight ahead and, without a word, was led out of the classroom and out of her friends' lives.

# Chapter 7

THE PROCESSION, FOR THAT IS WHAT IT HAD BECOME, led from the school into the village. Shireen pointed things out to Jamal as they walked the gravel paths.

As they all walked up the hill to her house, Jamal acted as if Sur Bahir, made of concrete and corrugated iron, was the prettiest village he had ever seen. They both ignored the still-smoldering ruin of the little theater.

Shireen's mother welcomed them. She already knew. Someone must have phoned. Shireen saw pride in Alika's eyes. Jamal spoke of the day and how momentous it all was. Shireen reached down and kissed the smiling faces of her youngest siblings. Tears welled but were caught in time. Some of the kids from school peered through the windows as if watching a play unfold. Shireen was told, in no uncertain terms, not to lift a finger.

"No, no, no," Alika scolded her oldest daughter ever so gently. "Now you sit at the head of our family. A place of honor."

Shireen smiled to herself. She was thinking of the new family home, the compensation her mother would receive, the education for her brothers. Even her sister Suray would benefit. Yes, yes, she thought, it will all be worth it, and I will be remembered and honored.

"And your tea, Mother," Jamal said as he sipped the hot beverage, "perfect. Not too sweet. Now Shireen must pack. We have a training camp where Shireen will be residing prior to the day of vengeful release and heavenly emancipation—you understand?"

He paused. Said nothing. Shireen saw him looking patiently at

Alika, waiting for a response. The older woman looked uncertain, hesitant. She turned to Shireen, as if seeking guidance.

"It is the will of God. It is my gift. My gift of life, for you all." Shireen stared back at her mother with iron determination.

Alika said nothing, but Shireen could see in her eyes a little sorrow, or was it gratitude? Shireen was not sure. But the awkward moment soon passed.

"Our blessed journey will continue." Jamal smiled warmly at both mother and daughter. He appeared relieved, then stood up and bade Shireen to do the same.

Shireen gasped when she saw Farouz in the doorway. She almost recoiled when he touched her shoulders. But his touch was gentle. He seemed different. Almost loving. She felt the warmth of his hands on her arms and no longer felt scared. All she saw was the joy in his eyes, the pride he felt.

That night, Shireen walked out of her home. Everything for the journey forward, she was told, would be provided. Except her bar-coded Jerusalem identity card, the one with her photograph. She was to bring that. She also took her Quran and an old picture of her father smoking a cigar. As she boarded the Jeep, Suray came running up, a drawstring bag in her hands.

"Not as good as yours, but—" she said with a brave smile.

Shireen took the cloth bag. By its size and shape she knew it was a book. Shireen smiled and gently touched her sister's hair. Then she swung the car door shut. Abruptly, the Jeep took off, scattering a rash of gravel. Stone dust coiled up.

Jamal told Shireen they were heading to a new facility. They crossed an unmanned part of the security wall that was still under construction. The Jeep was soon speeding through a town with narrow, twisting streets cut deep in the ground. They headed east.

Always east. Shireen looked out the window. She had never been so far from her village.

When the Jeep came to a halt, she was escorted to a large, sprawling villa of stone and brick, with a flat roof and curved archways. They walked to the inner courtyard, and Shireen heard the soft, yielding sound of a water fountain in the most verdant garden she had ever seen.

"This way, Shireen."

"Thank you, sir," said Shireen. She could hardly call him The Oily One, she thought.

"Call me Jamal, dear child," he said.

They walked along a pathway lined with tiny carnival lights. An ornamental pool of black lava rock shimmered with fish. They passed beneath a grape arbor and came to a huge wooden door.

Just inside was a foyer. Jamal asked Shireen to sit and sat beside her. They were served by a young man who did not speak. He brought a damp, cool cloth for Shireen's face.

"For the swelling. It is anointed with special oils. Our medical knowledge reaches beyond the Jewish," Jamal said with pride.

So The Oily One acknowledges my bruised face, Shireen thought, but does not inquire how it happened. Because it is in the past, she realized, an impediment to the way forward. *Her* way forward.

Shireen followed him into a suite obviously prepared for her. Nothing was missing. She peered inside the well-appointed bathroom. She took it all in, hardly believing this luxury was hers.

Jamal bowed and left. Shireen sank into the large double bed. The pillow billowed up around her still aching cheek like a cool, soft breeze. She closed her eyes and slept.

# Chapter 8

"How about an outing? The Old City. Just the three of you. You're old enough not to get into too much trouble. Any takers?" Gilly looked from one boy to the other, her face bright as the morning. Micah looked up from his cereal. The twins kept on eating, ignoring their mother.

Gilly thought letting the boys go out together without any adults might be just what Micah needed to spread his wings and get to know the twins better.

"I'll stake you all train-fare money," Uncle Bernard happily volunteered. "This is such a marvelous idea—I might come along with you myself."

"No!" For once the twins agreed in unison.

Less than an hour later, Micah and his cousins were at the light-rail station. The train was sleek and looked like a stretched-out cyclops with a clown mouth. They headed down Mount Scopus, skirting the university campus, into the older Arab neighborhoods. Graffiti was splashed on the dirty gray concrete walls. Micah couldn't understand the words, but he could tell they looked angry. They stopped a few times, crossing busy intersections where cars waited impatiently for the train to pass.

*Beseder! Boh hay na!* Jakey mumbled something like that to him. *Beseder* was "okay." Micah got that one, but *boy hay na?* Was that even Hebrew?

Damascus Gate wasn't much of a train station, it was virtually level with the ground, with just a few seats and a couple of ticket machines. Micah followed the twins down a crowded sidewalk.

Vendors were selling food and coffee and tea along the curbside. The boys crossed a small, busy roundabout, jumping between stopped cars. In this predominantly Arab neighborhood, the men wore Western clothes, but the women wore traditional robes or long dresses down to their feet. They were accompanied by young girls, teens mostly, in long tees and scarves. Two Jewish scholars in wide-brimmed hats and thin black overcoats walked purposefully down the median strip, reading to themselves, intoning or praying, completely oblivious of the traffic and people crisscrossing their path.

"Is this it?"

"*Lo,*" said Zeke.

*Lo* was "no." Micah knew that one too.

Directly ahead, he saw the castle-like Damascus Gate. The large cobbled forecourt was crowded with vendors selling fruit and sticky nuts and vegetables. And the biggest carrots Micah had ever seen in his life, over a foot long!

Micah followed the twins inside the gate, past a couple of green-clad Palestinian policemen. He was momentarily overwhelmed by the denseness of the ever moving crowd.

"*Zuh-hee-root!*" yelled Zeke. At least that's what it sounded like to Micah.

"Come on. Keep up. You must not get lost here," said Jakey, also in a hurry.

The twins pointed the way. Reluctantly Micah followed, but at a slower pace. Everything looked so ancient. The walls were high and seemingly in a permanent shadow. The ground was laid with cobblestones as big as bricks, smoothed down by thousands of years of use, glowing in the occasional shafts of sunlight like tiny shields of polished pewter. Micah picked his way down the bustling thoroughfare. Smells of ginger and cinnamon seeped out of a dingy coffee shop. A knick-knack store sold belts and beads. Mirror-splattered jewelry hung like glittery webs across an awning. Micah watched someone frying bits of dough. It smelled great and he was almost tempted to—

*"Oi ee! Oi ee!"*

Micah turned and jumped, almost slipping on the silvery stones as a boy on a small handcart whizzed past, narrowly missing him.

*"Oi ee! Oi eeeeeeee!"* Another kid sped past on a blue-green handcart.

People yelled at the boy but he ignored them. He semi-squatted in the colorful cart with one leg over the side, using his foot to scoot along. Micah wondered how he could scoot along the steps so smoothly until he noticed the alleyway was cut with ramps on either side and one in the center.

Two Israeli soldiers stood casually near the next intersection, where a thick crowd of tourists moved in sluggish procession across their path, up a steep, extremely narrow street streaked with gold light and shadow. The Via Dolorosa, the Way of Sorrow. Tourists stopped and gawked at everything from street signs to hewn rock walls Jesus might have touched.

"Where are they going?" asked Micah.

"It's just alleys with Arabs selling stuff. This way." Jakey tugged at Micah's coat sleeve.

They turned into another steep alleyway and climbed more platform steps. The boys swung into an even smaller alley with buckled arches and more steps leading to a level stretch of path. The place smelled old. The air was tangy and woodsy and sweaty, like a long-closed cupboard opened by someone who needed to wash badly. They entered a kind of market; shops spewed onto the pavement. The alleyway was festooned with blazing light bulbs, even though it was still morning. Micah could see why. The rooftops almost overlapped. Above him, lines of sunlight streaked in as if it were being rationed.

The boys sidled around a barber cutting a man's hair and past a tailor turning a collar on a shirt. He worked the foot pedal of his old sewing machine as if it were a grand organ. More smells. Barbecue smoke billowed up like a half-formed genie. At one open doorway, Micah was hit by pillows of hot air and the smell of bread. He peered in. The bakery was old and dark. The baker was putting the salami-like bread loaves on a rod. Just outside, Micah could see that the oven was fired by two large gas canisters. He didn't see any no-smoking signs.

And cats! So many cats! In the crease of the alley Micah saw a kitten with its mum, sidling between the gas cans. He wanted to stop, but yet again the twins hurried him on.

Eventually they came to a tiny shop with fading green shutters and a thick, impenetrable glass window congealed with wire. Iron bars grated the door. Micah read a small sign in Arabic and English: "Alim-Alim's Antiquities. Coins. Medals. Collectibles."

The small counter inside was made of glass. The top was covered in dried rings from tea and coffee cups. Hardened dust in the corner added to the overall dinginess of the place. The shop was no bigger than a large walk-in closet with a very tall ceiling. A very tiny man in late middle age appeared from behind a filthy plastic-ribboned doorway. Presumably Alim-Alim. He removed a sweat-stained red fez. Strands of hair were carefully positioned across his forehead like rigging on a sailboat. He wore an old suit, a red tie, and a nylon shirt.

"Yes?" Alim-Alim asked in English, his slightly ingratiating smile heavy with condescension. "May I be of assistance, gentlemen?"

"Have you got anything for under ten?" Jakey asked, also in English.

"Well, young man, we have a few sundry treasures—"

He gestured with his hands, never once taking his eyes off the boys. Then he produced two old shoeboxes filled with coins.

"In this box, ten each. In this box, five each." He pointed with casual indifference. On his pinky was a silver snake ring, and on his middle finger a greenish-silver coin was mounted as a signet ring. While the twins rummaged through the boxes, Micah looked around. Alim-Alim watched him carefully while smoking a cigarette with studied care.

"And you, young man, are you, too, a numismatist?"

"No." Micah shrugged. "I'm just with them."

"Good investments, coins... Gold, silver, such rarities. And so beautiful. Well, gentlemen—" He turned back to the twins. "Anything catch your fancy?"

"Yes," said Jakey. "Can I see those coins on the third shelf down?"

Alim-Alim stubbed out his cigarette in an overfilled ashtray and looked where Jakey was pointing. Meanwhile Zeke was turning slowly, ambling toward the exit. Micah blocked his path.

"Put them back," he said quietly.

"Whaaaa?"

"Put the coins back. The ones you nicked. Put them back." Micah was angry now and loud.

As he pushed Zeke back toward the counter, the owner realized what was going on.

"Turn out pockets!" he yelled at Zeke. "Turn out pockets."

Reluctantly Zeke obeyed and out came a whole bunch of coins.

"Dung-soaked boy." The dealer pushed a button on the counter. "You will not escape."

An alarm went off. Harsh and metallic, echoing around the shop.

"Run! Run! Run!" Jakey yelled.

The twins fled. Micah just stood frozen. Alim-Alim ducked under the counter as Micah stumbled back toward the door.

"Oh, no, you don't." The coin dealer grabbed Micah by the arm, his grip tight.

"I was helping you. I was the one who—oh, crap."

He pushed the little man, who staggered back. Coins rolled and cascaded into one another and against the glass case as it rocked precariously. Again, Micah headed for the door.

"Stop them! All of them!" Alim-Alim yelled in Arabic at a couple of curious neighbors.

"Get after them!" Micah also shouted, in English, pointing like mad into the alley.

Momentarily confused, the neighbors turned to look. Micah saw his chance and bolted.

He could hear his heart thumping. Moments later he heard yelling. He shot back a look. Out of nowhere, he saw a man on a bicycle careening down the center ramp on the stone steps. And catching up. Alim-Alim! He saw the coin dealer peddling away, hat gone, his bald pate furrowed in an angry grimace, strands of combed-over hair now sticking up like points on a compass. Micah managed to just stay ahead of him. And just as well. For coming behind the cycling coin dealer were two younger guys, running hard and yelling for blood. His.

# Chapter 9

Shireen rose from her prayers. Jamal was waiting for her.

Together they walked along the ridge toward the training camp. The village across the graveled hollow looked abandoned. But it was a ruse. Camouflaged tents flapped like giant butterflies, and hidden trenches were strung between bulldozed buildings. Shireen could see the place was filled with men, some in uniform, some not.

"This was once a thriving village, Shireen. Until the Jewish came. The village died. But, as you can see, the Rafah Martyr's Brigade has taken it back. From the air, the village is seen, but our activities are not. Seen but unseen. As you must be, my child."

They walked back to the villa.

Shireen opened the door of her room. Jamal followed her inside. Taking another key, he unlocked an adjoining door. It opened onto a room unlike any she had ever seen before.

Glittery stuff hung from lampshades, posters and photos were pasted on the walls. And clothes. Closets filled with clothes. Magazine clothes. Sequined blouses, tank tops, and sunglasses. Skin-tight capris. A quilted red jacket, shiny and soft. Scarves—Hermes!

"You will have to wear these Western things," Jamal said sadly. "Familiarize yourself with all the clothes, the degenerate music, magazines. Pretend to like it all."

"You want me to be Western? To speak English?"

"Or Hebrew. You must look and act the part."

After Jamal left, Shireen threw the magazines in the air. She grinned, thinking they would flutter down like in the movies, but they landed with leaden thumps. Casting aside her robes, she pulled on the new jeans. They bunched a bit at the bottom, but looked great. She squeezed on a silk fitted tee imprinted with an ad for a classic Hollywood movie.

"Wow! Me. In the clothes to die for." She spoke aloud and in English. Then she realized what she had said and hit her image in the mirror. What difference would it make? And what if God disapproved of what she wore? Would He know it was just a ruse? Shireen couldn't figure it out.

She returned to her room, plunked down on the bed. She wanted to see her family, her friends. And then she remembered Malvolio and his cross-gartered stockings. She smiled at his sadness. Shakespeare's characters still haunted her imagination. Ruthless princes strived for hollow crowns while flattering schemers ended their days in pools of blood. So many consciences buried so deep. Was she cast in that same company? How could she find out?

She took out the bag Suray had given her and slid out the book. Shakespeare. Sticking out from the pages was a piece of ribbon. She opened the book at the place marked. *Measure for Measure.* The ribbon was carefully stitched. Her sister had sewn *Peace* into it. Shireen sighed and smiled wistfully. Then began reading the play.

# Chapter 10

MICAH HAD NEVER RUN SO FAST in all his life. The back of his shirt was sopping with sweat, and he was gasping for air, but he did not dare stop. From somewhere, he harnessed a spurt of energy, sprinted forward, and cleared the narrow alley into a sluggish group of tourists. He almost fell forward as he shuddered to a stop. The crowd broke open and enveloped him. Then, at the edge of the tourist throng, Micah saw Alim-Alim and one younger man was gazing this way and that, furious at having lost his prey. With some relief, Micah watched them both take off back down the hill.

Slowly the tour group shuffled into an opening and Micah froze. Another angry man was looking right past him. Micah realized he was searching for a running kid, not a dawdling tourist. So Micah stayed within the group and followed them into a tiny chapel. When he came out, the man was gone.

Micah looked around to get a sense of his location. Beyond the front of the crowd was a colossal brown wall studded with brick and stone. Between the wall and the people was an empty space. The crowd seemed to be waiting, anticipating an event. Strutting into the empty space came a man with a monocle in one eye, a benign smile on his face, and a bejeweled turban on his head. Held between his hands was a metal birdcage with a bird perched inside. Very tall and very thin, the elderly man looked every inch an entertainer.

"Welcome to Jerusalem." He leaned forward, cupping a hand to his ear. "Is everybody here?"

He spoke an ornate kind of English with a slight Indian accent, although he did not look Asian at all. His complexion was cadaver-white, hair dyed as black as shoe polish. His mustache, also dyed black, was waxed and curled. The audience yelled back "Yes" in a variety of languages.

He seemed satisfied with the response, then turned his monocled eye toward the crowd as though trying to get a better look at them. People laughed, amused by his antics. The tall fellow pulled himself to attention.

This is going to be fun, thought Micah.

"Gentle ladies and gentle fellows.... You stand within the capital of mysteries. Your footfalls have trod the ancient ways and have led you to me, the Great Yimca."

The magician threw the cage into the air and clapped his hands together. Bird and cage were gone. Completely disappeared. Micah smiled. The crowd applauded.

Apart from the turban, the Great Yimca wore a silk cravat, an open shirt, a white linen dinner jacket, and black slacks. On his feet was a pair of sparkly velvet slippers that curled up like something from the Arabian Nights. He magically produced a parakeet, which fluttered a bit and walked around his hand. His assistant, a lady of a certain age dressed in an elegant sari, walked into the space carrying a box with a cage front. She placed it on a skinny, chrome-legged table. The magician showed the box empty and placed the parakeet inside and closed the lid.

Yimca now covered the cage front. He clapped his hands, and the sides of the box clattered to the floor. The bird was gone. And there, in its place, was a cat. A big black job that blinked chartreuse eyes and furiously began licking itself, quite indifferent to the applause his mysterious appearance had evoked.

The Great Yimca then passed one hand over the other, and the missing parakeet reappeared. The bird fluttered over to the lady in the sari, who took both bird and props away. The cat had long since vanished into the crowd.

Alone in the space, the magician asked to borrow some money. The usual assurances were given. One spectator offered him a twenty-pound note, signing it first so he would recognize it again. The magician folded the note and sealed it in one of three envelopes that he shuffled. He then numbered the envelopes.

As he replaced the pen, Micah thought he fumbled slightly. Was something wrong?

The volunteer was asked to select one of the envelopes. The other two were burned. Fire licked the air and bits of charred envelope quickly turned crinkly brown and changed to feathery, blackened embers. While everyone's attention was on the flames, Micah noticed a folded piece of paper had fallen from the back of the magician's jacket. Pretending to tie a shoelace, Micah picked up the paper. No one noticed.

The magician asked the spectator to open the remaining envelope and take out the signed twenty-pound note. Empty! The magician appeared aghast. The audience chuckled as the man's face turned into a blob of worry.

Micah knew the trick. The magician would reach into his inside pocket, take out a wallet, and from it, remove another sealed envelope. The signed twenty-pound note would be found inside. But not this time. Micah knew what he had in his hand—the tourist's money. Somehow it had not made it into the magician's wallet. But did the performer know?

"Fear not, good sir. You will be pleased to know I am carrying insurance—fire insurance, you know. In this wallet here—"

The magician reached for his inside jacket pocket. The smile dropped a fraction as he removed a wallet.

"In this.... As I said, I normally carry...fire insurance...well—"

The magician's voice wavered a bit. The audience laughed at Yimca's feigned concern. But his concern was genuine. Micah could see he knew the money was missing. Micah had to get a message to the performer, and let him know he could help.

"Mr. LePaul! I'll open the wallet, okay?" Micah shouted.

Paul le Paul. Hearing the name of the trick's inventor, the tall performer turned and looked at Micah, almost imperceptibly raising an eyebrow. Micah held his glance, as if to say "yes."

"And this boy here—does not trust me. He is taking it upon himself to open my wallet."

The audience cheered Micah on. The magician grinned and handed over the wallet.

"Well, well, well, so! Here, take it. Open the wallet; take out what you find inside."

Micah unzipped the wallet. He knew there would be an envelope inside; the money could be easily palmed. Not so easy to get the bill *inside* the envelope without being detected.

"An envelope! The boy has found an envelope in the wallet...ladies and gentlemen...my fire insurance. My fire insurance—did I not tell you?" The Great Yimca looked at Micah, adding, "Open the envelope and take out what you find."

Micah looked at the magician and wondered how he was going to get the bill into the envelope's secret slit without being seen by an audience that, by now, was watching him like a flock of falcons. Micah only hoped the magician understood the fix he was in.

"Just rip open the envelope and drop it." He then turned to the audience, adding, "Drop *all* of it. So all can see. I will be clear of it. No jiggery pokery."

Brilliant, thought Micah, perfect. No clever moves. Nothing.

Relieved, Micah tore the envelope in half and let the pieces flutter to the ground along with the twenty-pound note. Simple.

"And look what we have found." The Great Yimca pointed to the money and then to Micah. "Young man, can you hand me what was inside the envelope?"

By speaking so casually, the magician inferred the money had been in the envelope all the time. Smiling, Micah bent down and handed the signed bill to the Great Yimca, who handed it to the relieved spectator. Considerable applause ensued.

The lady in the sari reappeared, an ornate tray held on outstretched fingertips. The tray was elegantly swooped under the noses of the unsuspecting audience.

"Oh, come on, come on. Don't be shy, give generously for the Great Yimca. Give, give, give. *Donnez! S'il vous plait.* Don't hide your shekels under the bushels, ha-ha-ha. *Vite. Vite.*"

She moved through the crowd, coaxing, almost badgering them in an English mixed with bits of French. Two men were helping her, a hulking giant with a permanent grin, and a worried-looking man with a walrus mustache. The three of them collected what they could until the audience melted away. The Great Yimca beckoned. He asked Micah for his name.

"Micah, is it? Well, behold my troupe." Yimca waggled his hand with great enthusiasm. The walrus man and the giant were handing their collection bags to the elegant lady in the sari.

"Gentlemen, over here, if you please. Rianne."

The three ambled over and Yimca made the introductions. The walrus man was an escape artist called Colonel Jack Geddings, a retired army officer from the Royal Artillery and a Brit like Micah. He was an odd-looking man with a huge head, a lot of red hair tied off at the back like the tail of an old war horse. He had a large mouth and a big squashed nose veined with purple spiders, below which reposed an impressive copper-colored handlebar mustache. The very large black-haired chap, the Amazing Walloo, was a former circus strongman with arms like thighs and knuckles as big as walnuts. But he had a gentle face and an open smile, and Micah took to him right off the bat. Walloo had an accent Micah just couldn't place. It sounded deep as an echo and a bit rough at the edges, as if his English had been sifted through a vast Nordic forest.

"And my bride. From Portuguese India, the province of Goa. The Lady Rianne," said Yimca.

Lady Rianne held her hand to be kissed. Micah shook it. She laughed at that. She spoke both French and English in a lilting, almost musical accent. Micah was happily confused.

"The only one missing from our esteemed cast of characters is our Gypsy Goddess, the Contessa Eleni. Who is, no doubt, out and about telling fortunes."

"She's the best, she is. Never wrong." Walloo grabbed Micah's hand and began perusing it. "You ever had your creases read?"

"Unhand him, Walloo, you've only just met." Colonel Jack winked reassuringly at Micah.

"This boy, he possesses good creases. Deep. A long life-line."

"I'll take that," said Micah, as he took back his hand.

"Now I must be explaining," said Yimca to his pals. "I was in quite the pickle when this young man here steps up and helps Great Yimca from a most embarrassing situation, almost a disaster. Never to be repeated. How can I ever repay him?"

"I know." Micah piped up. "You could teach me some magic. Give me lessons?"

"He's *rapide*, this one. *N'est ce pas?*" Lady Rianne squeezed one of Micah's cheeks, which he didn't like, but he smiled anyway.

He sensed she was being friendly but had no clue about kids.

"I teach you cut and restored rope." The Great Yimca spoke as if it were a decree.

"I know that one." Micah was a little disappointed by this offer. "I do Slydini's."

"Special scissors, special rope…no, no, no. I will teach you Eddie Victor's. No fakes. You borrow rope, borrow scissors, if sharp. You know this routine? Come early, tomorrow, before we start show. And lessons will begin. But now, you stay? See our show? Yes?"

"Oh. No. I can't. I'm late. I'm horribly late," Micah blurted out, much like the White Rabbit. He had suddenly remembered the coin shop. The twins. Everything.

Yimca produced a small phone; no trick, but he made it look like one. Fortunately Gilly answered. The Great Yimca watched Micah squirm and wriggle as his aunt gave him an earful. Crestfallen, Micah handed the phone back.

Before Micah could say a word, Yimca had produced a handful of change. More magic. He poured coins into Micah's open palm, enough at least for cab fare home. Lady Rianne rolled her eyes into turquoise-painted lids, but couldn't resist an indulgent smile.

"Such a *jambon*. Make certain you have meter on taxi. No special-for-you price."

Micah thanked them both and took off. Outside the New Gate, he could not find a cab. So he got himself back to Damascus Gate station. Fortunately the clown-faced silvery train swept up to the stop after just a few minutes. As he got off at French Hill, Micah realized the twins would already be home with stories to spin. Or maybe they had been caught? He was about to find out.

# Chapter 11

Jamal was drinking espresso when Shireen appeared in tight jeans, sandals with heels, a shimmery top, and the quilted red jacket she had been told to wear. She looked completely different, a confident young teen with a wide smile.

They walked across to the village. Outside one of the tents, a skinny old man sat cross-legged on the dirt floor, sewing another red quilted coat, an exact duplicate of the jacket Shireen wore.

"Ah, the Shaheeda. Come close." The tailor beckoned. "You must try this. For size."

Shireen took off her jacket and put the other one on. They looked identical, but she almost sank under the weight.

"The jacket is heavy because it is filled with small steel ball bearings and carpenter nails." The tailor started peering at the jacket from every angle, marking it with a piece of flat chalk. "Feel in the right-hand pocket. The detonator. You must press the rounded end. For practice, do it now."

"I felt it click when I pressed."

"It clicks when you press. It's what you must feel, without looking. Then, remove your finger and let the pin inside spring up. This will activate the device and it will—"

"Explode?"

"And you will be rushed to Heaven on a wind perfumed with honeysuckle and jasmine," Jamal quickly added.

The tailor indicated a backpack beside the table. He asked Shireen to pick it up. When she did, she almost dropped it. Like the jacket, the bag was filled with ball bearings and nails. Awkwardly, she swung her arms through its loops and hoisted it up on her back.

"No, no, no, Shaheeda, no!" The tailor smiled and shook his head. "Do not carry it like that. Israeli students carry bags this way. Like a suitcase. You have much to learn."

"My name is Shireen, not Shaheeda."

The skinny old man cackled slightly, as if Shireen had said something funny.

"Anwar knows," Jamal said, then added, "To be called 'Shaheeda' is to be called a hero. A martyr. Someone who gives completely of herself in the destruction of the unbeliever."

"Shaheeda is a hero? And this is me?"

"Yes, it is you, my child." Anwar spoke with quiet certainty. "Shaheeda is a pretty name, no?"

As they walked back to the far ridge. Jamal spoke about Shireen's first test.

"To be seen but unseen?"

"And you must fit into their life, become part of their life—act like them."

"I like to act." Shireen smiled to herself.

"And you will, for tomorrow you take to the stage—in Jerusalem."

# Chapter 12

"AAAAH, THE WANDERER RETURNS." Uncle Bernard looked happy and relieved. He squeezed Micah's shoulder and chuckled. "Safe and sound, thank goodness."

Aunt Gilly gave Micah a big hug and tousled his hair. Micah thought she was going to mush up or something. Fortunately she didn't.

"Micah disappeared, like one of his little magic tricks," Zeke shrugged.

"We did look. But you know, the tourists..." Jakey's voice trailed away.

The twins were tripping over themselves to retell their story. Micah was presumably expected to go along. He knew this because both twins were speaking in English. Amazing, thought Micah, amazing. He looked at them, almost enjoying their squirmy, flop-sweating fear of discovery. Micah wondered what Uncle Bernard would do if he knew the truth. He wondered about Jakey. Was he just protecting his rotten brother? Micah didn't give a damn one way or the other about Zeke, but somehow, he thought that Jakey was becoming his friend.

"No harm done, no harm done." Uncle Bernard threw Micah a phone. "Easier to check in. We all have one. Who needs more anxiety than we've already got, ay?"

"That man. The one you met—" Aunt Gilly spoke with genuine concern. "Indian, you say?"

"Yes, from India or somewhere like that. Nepal maybe, I don't know, really."

"He tried to befriend you?" Gilly sounded a bit embarrassed.

Micah knew what she was thinking. They were probably all thinking the same thing.

"He's a good bloke. A magician. And totally above board. Married. Met his wife..."

"We have to ask, Micah. You cannot be too careful. People, some people, take advantage—"

"Bet he's a gypsy," Zeke sneered with obvious relish.

"Quiet, Zeke." Bernard sounded firm for once.

For a moment, Micah felt like blurting out the truth, but he held back.

"Well! Good! Food? Hungry? You hungry, Micah?" Gilly sounded relieved to be moving on.

Dinner was stuffed veal, baked spuds, and glazed carrots. Micah was glad he hadn't stormed off to his room. And besides, everyone was now speaking in both languages. Progress.

The next day turned out to be a school holiday. The Rothners had planned a hiking trip to Kinneret, on the Galilee shore. "Before the sea dries up," Uncle Bernard said, only half joking.

Micah begged off. A headache, he said. They did not push. Aunt Gilly gave him a set of keys, made sure he had the cell phone, and told him if he did go out, to be home by six. Then she bustled her sons and husband out the door.

The house was suddenly silent. Micah looked out the window. Blue sky, clean and clear. Unusually warm for winter. And the day was his.

Once Micah got to the Old City, he retraced his steps, following the hordes of tour groups strung out like sausage links. He weaved between them as they gingerly walked through the shadowed alleys. He found the wide steps. He stopped suddenly and looked around.

Apart from a few people hurrying back and forth, the neighborhood seemed oddly deserted.

"You are late. Come, come, dear boy. We have much to learn."

Micah turned and saw the Great Yimca waving his hand in a flamboyant gesture of greeting.

Yimca led him to a stone balustrade. He leaned against the wall and looked straight up to the sky. He seemed to draw in the sun, like a breath of air. Then he looked again at Micah, eyes full of excitement. Reaching into his pocket, he took out a small piece of rope.

Micah watched as Yimca cut the rope. The two coils of rope were unequal. This caused Yimca some consternation. He snapped the coils and they instantly became two equal pieces. Then both pieces became one. Again the rope was cut and again effortlessly restored. Finally Yimca grabbed the untied ends and snapped them tight. The knot sprang off the rope and flew into the air. He handed the rope back to Micah, completely restored.

"You see, no fake rope, no fake scissors. Good, no?"

"Good, yes."

"Now don't be expecting to learn in five minutes! Perhaps in five weeks—"

"Five weeks!" Micah rolled his eyes.

Nothing to it, he thought, as he held the rope, but even so, he fumbled the move.

"Bugger," he mumbled under his breath.

Then a blood-curdling roar followed by applause distracted Yimca from the magic lesson.

"Sounds like my Walloo."

Both turned to the sound of an imperious, husky voice. Yimca formally introduced his new student to the Countess Eleni, the fortune teller. True to her calling, Eleni had raven-black hair, large looping earrings, and a jingly necklace made of overlapping gold coins. Her neck was long, and she carried herself with the poise of an aging ballerina who still had a full dance card.

"Can you really tell fortunes? It's a trick, right?"

"Hand!"

Micah did as he was told. Eleni's grip was firm. She did not shake his hand in greeting, but examined it as if it were a specimen taken from a jar. Micah felt a bit unnerved.

"Shouldn't I cross your palm with silver or something?" He tried to be amusing.

"No." Her eyes flashed. "But you will cross the palms of strangers and make silver flow."

Micah took back his hand and stared at it, trying to see what she saw. He saw nothing.

"Now watch my Walloo," she said.

They all turned, Eleni's jewelry jangling merrily as she waved to the very big man at the center of an empty circle ringed with people.

Micah remembered meeting him before, but was quite unprepared for what happened next. The Amazing Walloo crouched, strained, and shuddered. His face was red and sweaty. His eyes were pinpricks staring hard at the three-inch-thick phone book in his hands. Imperceptibly, the book began to crack, to shudder apart. It was hypnotic to watch. Walloo groaned and growled like an old lion shaking its prey with his teeth. Then, he rose, tearing the book completely. He staggered forward, roaring with pleasure as two huge clumps of phone book came crashing down. The noise of the landing was drowned out by the applause.

Moments later, the Great Yimca, Colonel Jack, the Lady Rianne, and Eleni were circling the crowd with collection bags, weaving back and forth like sheepdogs penning the tourists, reeling them in for all the loose change they had. Afterwards, Lady Rianne tallied the meager takings.

"I don't understand, we are deluged with tourists, and they give next to nothing. *Rien!*"

"Cheapskates," Colonel Jack snarled, grumbling to himself about needing a cigar.

"This is our colonel, *chéri.* A little abrupt, but once you get to know him—"

"He's just the same," Walloo chuckled.

It was show time again. Walloo helped Colonel Jack into a canvas straightjacket. He slapped the colonel's arms across his chest and tied the ends of the corded sleeves behind his back. Straps were fastened. Then Walloo moved away, leaving Colonel Jack trussed up like an angry ostrich.

"Want to help?" asked Yimca, quietly.

Before Micah could reply, Yimca thrust a collection bag into his hand and started guiding him to the back of the crowd.

"We must hurry. Come, come."

Micah looked at Colonel Jack now running at the crowd like an enraged bull, grunting and straining, trying to get free.

"Shouldn't we wait until he gets out?"

"Colonel Jack rarely gets out. That is why we must be doing a lot of hurrying."

Yimca began smiling, shaking his collection bag at the curious onlookers. In the bottom, a few coins rattled, coins he'd previously put there.

"See the miracle," shouted Yimca, then he turned to Micah. "Work the Japanese group. Go on."

The Japanese tourists appeared hypnotized by Jack's antics. They weren't even taking pictures.

Suddenly Micah had an idea.

"Five," he said, not loudly but assertively. He held up his hand, fingers spread in front of the faces of the Japanese tourists. Blank looks started to fill in.

"Five," he said again, more emphatically. He held up the collection bag and shook it. Dutifully the tourists started reaching into their pockets. Five shekels. Five Euros. Five dollars. Some seemed confused but, amazingly, they all paid up.

"Five," Micah said again, moving deeper into the crowd, beyond the Japanese group. "Five!" More people coughed up five of some kind of currency. One American held out a ten-dollar bill, Micah plucked it from his hand and gave him five dollars in change. This made the American laugh like mad. Then two more handed over big bills, just to get change. And still more gave.

"Five!" yelled Micah.

"Five?"

Someone high-fived him. And quite hard. People nearby started chuckling. Micah looked up and was about to say that he was collecting monies not greetings, but then he stopped. Standing in front of him was the prettiest girl he had ever seen. Black hair framed her face in long waves, she had almond-shaped blue eyes, and her lips were softly curved into a kind of smile.

"I do not have—" She shrugged with her mouth but the smile stayed in her eyes.

"No problem." Micah grinned. "See you around."

Some fat guy, her father probably, grabbed her arm and pulled her away from the crowd. Just for an instant the girl glanced back and pulled a face, as if to say "oh, well" or "sorry," or something. Micah wasn't sure. Then she was gone.

Micah started working the audience again. *Five, five, five!*

Money poured in. After a bit, he felt his cheeks aching, and he realized he was still smiling.

Colonel Jack finally made his escape. With some panache, he flung the straightjacket into the air. Jack's face was red from exertion, like raspberry blancmange that hadn't set properly.

Lady Rianne came forward with Micah, who held up the stuffed collection bag.

"Quids in, ay?" Jack was amazed.

"Put him on the team," said Walloo wisely.

"On team? Darling, I put him on payroll, ha-ha-ha." Rianne smiled from one to another.

"A boy with good fortune. My Eleni is never wrong," said Walloo.

Eleni shrugged almost imperceptibly, refuting nothing.

"Return tomorrow. For a new lesson," Yimca happily proclaimed. "And new collectings."

"But I've got school tomorrow."

"After school?"

Micah's face lit up. He couldn't wait. And who knew? He might even see that girl again.

# CHAPTER 13

"I JUST CANNOT." Jakey was shocked.

"Yes you can, and if you don't I'll rat you out and that scum brother of yours about robbing the coin shop." Micah stared him out.

"You would do this?"

"I won't drop you in it, unless you drop me in it. We have a deal?"

The deal was struck. That's how Micah got out of school, which he hated. But it worked out. After the first time, he simply staggered his absences. Sometimes he'd take off just after first break, sometimes before lunch. Jakey always covered for him. The teachers didn't notice because Micah was there for part of the day. And at the end of school he was always back to catch the bus home. He told his new friends he was being homeschooled and his schedule was flexible.

Micah got into a routine of helping out with the troupe's show whenever he could. He helped with the collection. Sometimes he kept guard over the props. The most important prop was the cage box that housed Flinter Toes, the black cat in Yimca's act.

With Micah looking after things, Eleni was free to tell, or sell, more fortunes. The lunchtime crowd was a lucrative one. She sat behind her small portable table, somewhat statue-like, a crystal ball close to hand. And there she waited, like a benign spider, for future webs to weave. Fresh creases to read.

"Who's in my future, Eleni?" Micah asked one day.

"Ida."

"Ida?"

"I da-know!"

Eleni tried to suppress a smile. "But I know what's in mine." She held out her glass for a splash more of rosé wine.

Micah was sitting with his friends, enjoying a late lunch before returning to school. He loved the life they led almost as much as he enjoyed their somewhat eccentric company. They certainly looked the part, dressed to the nines in tropical cotton jackets, assorted robes and kerchiefs, saris, baggy pants, and straw trilby hats. Distinctive, theatrical, quite old but full of jokes and great stories about magicians they knew, and the history they shared. Micah was enthralled by it all.

When a happy quiet descended over the troupe, Micah saw his chance. He asked if he could show his card-flick trick. He tried to gauge their interest. There was none.

"No, I mean it, this is unique," he said. "Honest. It really is."

"Then do," Eleni commanded.

Micah asked Walloo to hold up a deck of cards. He didn't bother forcing a card. He just flicked one and it accurately sliced into the deck Walloo was holding. Everyone applauded politely. Micah turned to Yimca, who was gazing thoughtfully into the distance.

"I liked it. A clever stunt," Colonel Jack announced.

"That, my dear Micah, is the problem," Yimca said. "What you do is a stunt. It has no mystery, you know? You do it well, but it is not magic. And magic it must be."

"Can't I do it just once? Please?"

"I will think on it," said Yimca, with some finality.

"One day you come see our bus, our home on wheels. It big. Like me," said Walloo, changing up the chat. "And special entrance for Flinter Toes!"

"*Mais pas aujourd'hui!* Is in car park. Near the entrance to the Jewish Quarter."

"You cannot miss it," said Walloo. "I let you drive it. You would like that?"

"Yes!"

"No!" Eleni wagged a finger at her playful husband.

Micah laughed. He had wondered how they traveled from place to place. A converted bus, of course. Micah thought it must be great to just take off whenever, and to go wherever they wished.

"But *ici*, we live in a *petite pension.*"

"We live in digs. But hardly '*petite.*' It's a mansion in the Baka district," said Colonel Jack.

"And we deserve it," Rianne added.

Just before they took off, Micah asked again about his card stab. Again Yimca said he would think on it. Yimca could see how glum the boy looked and added, "I will come up with an idea for you to garner many fives."

Shireen was back in Jerusalem for onsite training. Although it was only a trial run, Shireen knew the bus ride was an important test. Much would depend on how she behaved, how she *acted*. She would have to blend in perfectly, seen but unseen, as the Oily One liked to say.

Shireen found a seat by the window on an empty row. She was overwhelmed by the noise. Children screamed. Kicked. Laughed. They paid no attention to her, but she paid attention to them. Boys mostly, all ages. Some wore glasses, some didn't. Some punched each other for reasons beyond Shireen's grasp.

She tried to close her eyes, tried to block out the noise. She took out her little Shakespeare volume and turned to her bookmarked page. Just then she felt herself bumped slightly. Someone had sat down next to her. Inwardly she groaned.

"Five!"

Shireen spun around. It was the boy from the Old City. And there he was grinning away, fingers of one hand spread out beside his face.

"It's you," she said, and high-fived him back. "Yes! Yes, it is."

"Isn't this brilliant? I mean this is beyond brilliant. I've never seen you on this bus; I would've remembered. Do you go to school near here? I do. I hate it but I haven't much choice. Mind you, I try and get out whenever I can—that's how you came to see me last week in the Old City and—"

"Slowly, please, slowly. My English is not too glad."

"Glad enough for me," said Micah, not bothering to correct her. She had a soft accent, mysterious almost. He pointed to the book on her lap. "What're you reading? Is that Shakespeare?"

"Yes. You know it?"

"Shakespeare? Of course. I'm English. Know all that stuff. Not by heart but—"

"You are from his land, you are from England?"

"Well, yeah. London actually. And London is where his plays were put on. Even now."

"They act the plays lots?"

"Lots. We have school trips to the theatre. It's so—" Micah just stopped himself from saying "boring" and went on with what he thought she wanted to hear. "Good, bloody good. Really. Well, it's classic, after all."

"Tell me one you like best?"

"The one with the witches. That was all right. And we just saw *The Tempest.*"

"Ah, Prospero! He is magical, he makes the sea—" She coiled and spun her hands.

"He's a magician. And the play's short. I mean, what I meant was—

Micah froze up. He didn't know what else to say about Shakespeare. The claw in his brain didn't hook onto anything, just snapped about in empty space.

"I am glad," Shireen said finally.

She raised her eyebrows slightly and smiled before turning back to her book. Micah could not believe he'd run out of chat.

The play with witches—oh, crap me. What was I thinking? I must have sounded like a complete— *"Macbeth!"* he blurted out.

Shireen nodded but didn't look up. *"How heavy do I journey on the way..."* She smiled as she read the sonnet. The quiet lilt of Shakespeare's poem was comforting. As she finished the page, she heard a soft sound, like leaves shaken together. The boy was handling a deck of playing cards in a most unusual way. The pasteboards seemed to melt into each other. He cut the deck in half and held the divided cards between the fingers of just one hand. Then the corners of the cards appeared to melt one within the other, and the two halves cascaded back into one. He had shuffled the deck with just one hand. Shireen was impressed.

"Take a card," he said.

Brilliant, Micah thought when she took one, pleased with himself, but then immediately berated himself for not thinking of it earlier. But at least he was back in his element. Shireen returned the card to the deck and Micah placed the deck in its case. He asked her the name of the card she'd picked. She shrugged, uncertain of her English.

"If you see it again, you'll remember it?"

She nodded. Micah liked the way she nodded.

Slowly, slowly, a card began to rise from the center of the deck in the case. Micah watched her face transform from surprise to astonishment. She waved her hand over the cards. No threads.

She grabbed the rising card and turned it. He noticed her mouth was open slightly, but she spoke no words. Her liked her mouth as well, a bit curly, pouty but not too pouty, he thought.

"Your card?" he asked, remembering what he was supposed to be doing.

She nodded happily, then looked at Micah with admiration. "You are sorcerer, you are Prospero Boy." She handed back the card with a smile.

"Prospero Boy, I like that. Want to see another?" he asked.

Her eyes and smile widened with anticipation.

"Micah, come on." Jakey shouted as he scooted past.

"Oh, crap me." Micah jumped up. "My stop. I'm always on this bus at this time. See ya."

He barreled down the aisle and made it just as the door was closing.

Shireen looked out the window. There was nothing she recognized, nothing! And all the students had gone. She checked the map and realized her error. The bus was moving again as she looked up. And there was the boy, waving. Shireen did not wave back. She was beside herself with worry. Shame-faced, she grabbed her things and hurtled toward the front of the bus, where she waited for what seemed the longest time for the bus to stop again.

She had forgotten to say her prayers, forgotten to press the fake detonator, forgotten to get off at the right stop. Forgotten everything. Caught up in the spell of Prospero Boy. Shireen scolded herself. Now what? *"Thus far the miles are measured from thy friend!"* And I'm still daydreaming Shakespeare! Shireen growled angrily then sighed loudly.

Zigzagging around incoming buses, she ran to the side of the terminal, desperately looking around for Jamal, but he was nowhere in sight. All she could see were people sprinting from one side of the road to the other, dodging the endless stream of cars that seemed intent on running them down. Across the road were large new buildings, not a part of the Jerusalem she knew. Lights changed. Halfway across the road, a car flashed its headlights. It was Jamal and he was livid.

"What happened?" he snapped at her. "Oh, never mind. Just get in. Get in. Quickly!"

Clutching her backpack, Shireen clambered in. Jamal accelerated fast, yet several infuriated drivers still managed to pull ahead of them, honking like demented geese.

"There is no pleasing these mad, mad people."

"I am sorry. I missed my stop."

"Think nothing of it, my child." He tried to appear serene, even winked his trademark eye scrunch. "Now tell me, did anyone speak to you? Ask questions of you?"

"There was one boy—"

"A boy? What do you mean? You met someone? " Jamal tried to contain his panic.

"The boy was a magician. He fooled me."

"A magician? Well, yes, the Jewish are tricky, that is for sure." Jamal stopped at a light. "But worry not. On your day of days you will trick them all—back to Hell."

Shireen secretly hoped she would never see that boy again. But what if she did? The boy meant no harm. And for a boy, she thought, he was almost nice and not even smelly.

"Jamal, the boy was from London. The boy with the magic." She sounded unsure, hesitant.

"And? And?" Jamal still sounded flustered. "What are you trying to say, little one?"

Shireen took a deep breath and thought of her day of days.

When she was rushed to Heaven, what of the others on the bus? Would they be rushed to Heaven, too?

"Jamal, the ones on the bus. I was thinking, if they are not the enemy—"

"All of them are 'the enemy,' Shireen," Jamal said quickly. "They are but offal to be left on the battlefield. That is the plan. That is what has been arranged."

"But this boy. He is from England, he is not Israeli—"

"Oh Shireen, Shireen, Shireen." Jamal honked at a car ahead of him, then pulled over. Yanking up the hand brake, he turned and smiled at her with infinite patience. "It does not matter about this boy. All those boys are the Jewish. The evil they do against us is in their seed. You understand?"

Shireen nodded. Now she understood. She remained silent for the rest of the trip.

# Chapter 14

On Friday Micah was back in the Old City. He had skipped out of school earlier than usual to avoid morning prayers and to spend more time with his new friends. As long as he got back before Shabbat began, all would be well.

"I have trick for you to perform in our show. Do it and you will be getting big applause!" Yimca produced a bunch of bananas. "Can you make your card stab a banana?"

"Don't see why not."

Yimca walked five paces away and held out a banana. Micah flicked the card. A split second later it was sticking in the fruit's yellow skin. Yimca walked another five paces and had him do it again. Same result.

"Good! How far you can do this?"

"Keep walking."

Yimca had walked thirty paces before Micah told him to stop. Again he hit the banana. Asked to repeat the trick, Micah missed. Yimca said not to take chances and walked back ten paces. At twenty paces, Micah could hit the banana every time.

Yimca slowly and deliberately peeled the untouched banana. The fruit had been neatly cut into three pieces. Micah's mouth opened, quite unable to say anything.

"How did you…?"

"With banana cutting you have big finish."

"But how did you do it?"

"Now go find the good Lady Rianne. She has needle and thread. She will be telling you how it's done. And then you do!" Yimca tossed the bananas to Micah and smiled enigmatically. "You go on after Colonel Jack."

Micah almost jumped off the ground. He looked at Yimca, choking on his thanks. Then he took off in a flash—before Yimca had a chance to change his mind.

Showtime came around all too soon. Micah's mouth was as dry as a camel's ear. Rianne gave him a bottle of water. He guzzled it all. Tasted none of it. Then it was time. Yimca made the introduction, gave Micah's shoulder an encouraging squeeze, and left him to it.

Micah said "*Shalom*, hello," and asked for an assistant from the audience. An off-duty Israeli soldier was pushed forward by a couple of his buddies. Micah took a banana from his pants pocket. That got a laugh. Micah had no idea why. But it made him feel better. When he asked the volunteer to hold the banana, the audience laughed some more. Micah followed Yimca's instructions, moving back five, then eight, and finally twenty steps from the soldier. The audience clapped each time his card pierced the banana skin, and when he peeled it…

The crowd's reaction improved each time he revealed the neatly cut banana. After the third show, the audience was applauding like performing seals.

Around lunchtime the visitors started to leave. It would soon be Shabbat and Jerusalem was about to become a ghost town. Right on cue, the performers packed up and headed for the bus. Micah helped out by carrying Eleni's table. He was feeling very much part of the troupe and he also tagged along because he really wanted to see their travel bus. Once they got there, Walloo showed him the secret cat flap and then Flinter Toes nimbly demonstrated how he got inside.

The old bus was filled with magic: production boxes, props and illusions in various sizes. There was hardly room to sit down! Micah didn't want to leave, he even found stacks of old magic magazines, tucked under one of the few bench seats. And when Yimca said he could take some, Micah lost no time picking out those he wanted. It was only when the gear was finally stowed that Micah noticed how late it was. The afternoon sun was setting over the Old City. Shabbat was about to begin; it would soon be way past sundown. Way past excuses for being late home.

Barely saying good-bye, he raced off down the hill to Ma'ale Ha-Shalom, the road that skirted the Old City, in search of a cab. No easy job. Micah ran across the near-empty highway and stared up at the Montefiore Windmill.

He looked around and could see nothing. The streets were almost deserted, no cabs, no people, no cars, no buses. No magazines! Micah suddenly realized he had forgotten them in his mad dash to get back.

"Hey! You want taxi?" someone shouted in English.

Micah looked over and spotted an off-white Mercedes that had seen better days. The car had green Palestinian plates. The driver was youngish, with teeth too big for his mouth. He looked like a happy squirrel.

"You a cab? Where's the meter?" Micah was skeptical.

"We don't need meter, we are brothers. Wanna see license?" He tapped a document on the inside of the windscreen, then beckoned. "Get in, my brother, get in. We figure price."

Micah clambered in. The cab was hot and the radio was blaring something that sounded like two cats fighting over a mouse. The cabby's head jogged to the music.

"Sounds painful," Micah pointed at the sound system.

"Turkish rap. All about the great Satan, the United States. But at least you can dance to it."

The car sped up, warm air flowed, gushing through the open

windows. No air conditioning. On the radio, the cats continued to fight over the mouse. The cab driver grooved along to it, dancing in place, bopping up and down as he drove, making the journey back in record time. Three blocks from the housing complex, he stopped and turned off the radio. He swung around.

"When I pull up, you get out. And run. So pay now, okay?"

"Why now?"

"It's your Sabbath. You should not be in cab. You'll see."

Confused, Micah paid up. The driver rolled up the windows and drove on, but with none of his reckless abandon. Now he toodled along like an old lady.

The first thud hit the car as it turned down the Rothners' street. Then a second. The windshield was hit with a white package. Brown stuff oozed.

"Crap," said the driver.

"What is it?"

"Crap. I told you. They're pelting us. Get out. Run!"

The cab jerked to a halt. Micah jumped out and the driver sped away. Micah ran into the building. From the shadows, he was pelted with more squelchy, wet packages. One hit him in the back. Another burst its muck in his path. People were yelling now. Teenagers.

Micah had never been so scared. He didn't stop running. Inside the complex, he stumbled up the steps. He was being followed. Another landing. He found the door and started pounding. Footsteps were right below him. The door opened, he slid inside.

"They threw crap at the car, at me. Diapers!"

"Hassidic kids. They patrol the area. Anyone breaking the Sabbath—" Gilly shrugged.

Bernard stared, anger and disappointment etched on his face.

"I'd better get changed," said Micah.

"Come on. Thank goodness you're safe," said Aunt Gilly.

Micah knew she felt bad for him. Even so, he noticed how sad she looked. He had let them down. He had missed Friday night services. Micah had been truant. And not just from school. From his family, his faith, his tradition.

Not surprisingly, he was grounded for a week. If he failed to comply, Bernard said he would call Paul in the States and tell him to make other arrangements. Micah knew that was the last thing his dad would want to hear.

After he cleaned up, Micah stayed in his room. And forced himself to sleep through the night. He stayed in his room for most of the weekend, brooding. There was overly polite conversation during meals, but not much else. It was a long weekend. For everyone.

Finally Monday morning came around. The boys got up, got ready for school. No one spoke. Uncle Bernard dropped them off at the bus stop, then drove off to work.

Micah jumped aboard the bus ahead of the twins. He saw the usual faces, but not the girl with the blue eyes and the Shakespeare book. And that smile of hers! He smiled at the memory. And he remembered her hair when it brushed against him. Like silk. Hard to forget. Not that he wanted to. He kept an eye out for her each day, but she didn't reappear. He thought about taking a later bus in hopes of catching her, but then he'd have to explain to his cousins and he was not about to do that. Not ever. Not that there was anything to explain. Not even to himself. It didn't matter. He just wanted to get through the week.

Micah fell back into the school routine, the work, the religious observance. He just got on with it. After school, he got on the bus and went home with the twins, but he missed his magic friends. And he really wanted to see that girl again. Not that they could be mates or anything. He just wanted to see her.

# Chapter 15

Days had passed and now it was time. Shireen stepped out of the tent with her weighted backpack. She noticed Jamal putting out a cigarette. It was Turkish; she recognized the smell. He hovered while Anwar, the old tailor, helped her put on the quilted jacket. He then stood back, looking very pleased with himself.

Shireen was ready. Her day of days had finally arrived.

Jamal and Shireen returned to the edge of Bethlehem a little after six thirty in the morning. The checkpoint had just opened, but the lines were already hundreds deep, mostly students and hotel and construction workers. The cars pulled slowly forward. The faces of the pedestrians looked resigned, bitter, or angry. This, thought Shireen, could take hours.

"Can we not go somewhere else?" asked Shireen.

"Better here. No dogs." He looked at her uncomprehending face. "Dogs could betray us. Bomb-sniffing dogs. Sniff. Sniff. Here there are no dogs."

One of the car lanes was jammed up. A car had been opened—doors, hood, and trunk. Outside the main pedestrian security area, they saw a hitchhiker being strip-searched.

"They do things like this. The Jewish. For no reason. No reason."

Jamal maneuvered the car into a newly opened lane. He even honked at someone who tried to cut ahead. They got to the barrier. Tire-destroying steel teeth gleamed ahead, flush with the road surface. Two soldiers approached. One cradled his rifle awkwardly as he checked their IDs. He asked Shireen to lean out to verify her likeness. His Arabic was quite good. Jamal started to get out of the car, but the other soldier shook his head. The back-up had gotten worse, and the soldiers were in a hurry to clear the checkpoint. Shireen noticed that Jamal did not have to be told twice.

They arrived just as the bus pulled up. Perfect. Opening the passenger door, he looked around, providing cover as Shireen hooked up the connectors to the backpack and the body circuit. She looked up and nodded. All done. She lifted the heavy backpack carefully, ensuring the wiring remained a little slack so it would not disconnect or become noticeable.

Jamal walked with her across the street to the bus stop. A boy hurried by. Shireen was relieved to see he was as weighted down as she was. The bus door opened with a swoosh. Shireen pulled herself up the steps and found an empty seat by a window. Jamal waved a quick farewell and scooted across the street.

The bus pulled up at the next stop. Kids piled in as they had the last time. Shireen was overwhelmed again by laughter and yells, and smells of gum and apples and bodies. She felt anxious so she took out her book, tried to read, tried to be still, focused and unconcerned by everything around her. But she kept reading the same part over and over.

The seat shook as someone bustled in beside her. It was him, Prospero Boy! She tried to make herself invisible. She wanted to see him, but she didn't want him here. Not then. Not ever. It couldn't be. Shireen tried to read. She leaned forward, hoping her hair would hide her face, hide everything.

"Hello, you," Micah said.

Why must he *sound* so nice? she thought. Slowly she looked around, and there he was.

"I've been looking out for you."

Shireen looked back down to her book without a word. Micah

thought she might be pleased to see him, but she wasn't. He didn't get it. What did I say? What did I do? His brain pretzeled into a bunch of knots and he gave up trying to untie them. Bloody hell, he thought, I don't get girls at all.

"I'm sorry," he said. It was all he could think to say. "I didn't mean to—"

He stared at her. Her mouth seemed drawn down. She looked sad. A moment later. she pulled back her long black hair and looked at him. Her fingers traced the outline of her neck, then gripped her shirt as if holding onto it for dear life.

"It is not you. It is me. I am sorry for this."

Sorry for what? he thought. He wanted to ask but—

"What about showing me a trick? Come on, English. Try and fool me, I'll give you a shekel if you can."

Micah looked around. The voice belonged to a boy with a pink, sweaty face that made him look like a cooked shrimp. He was leaning forward from the row behind, between Shireen and Micah.

"Bugger off," said Micah.

"I just want to practice my English." The Shrimp stared at Shireen, pointing at her book. "Hey, girlfriend, you read that? Say something in English! If you don't, I'll fart."

"You disgusting little wanker." Micah leaned over and smiled at Shireen. "Sorry—if he bothers you, just tell me and I'll hit him."

Shireen gave him a slight smile, then dove back into her book.

"Winker? What's it mean? Winker!" The Shrimp seemed oblivious to Micah's threat.

"It's not 'winker,' it's 'wanker,' you wanker." With that, Micah cupped the Shrimp's hot face in his hand and pushed him back into his seat.

"Hey! You cannot do that."

"I just did. Now stay put. And shut up or—" Micah leaned over, made a fist and almost swiped the Shrimp with it. The message was clear. The Shrimp stayed put.

Micah sat back down. The girl now seemed totally immersed in her book, and her raven-black hair curtained most of her face. She was wearing a bulky, quilted jacket and tight jeans that revealed long bean-pole legs and— Micah became aware that he was staring. He looked away before she realized it, too. Think, think, think, he told himself. He noticed that she was reading Shakespeare again. So why didn't I read up on the bloody Bard? Micah railed against himself, I'm such a berk! And why does she have to look so bleeding good? He thought about railing against her, too.

Almost mechanically, Micah started shuffling cards again. It somehow helped him think.

Shireen was trying *not* to think. But she couldn't stop herself. What of the others? What of *him?* Her mind was reeling. I must stop this, she told herself. To think, to think of—

Once again, she was beguiled by the sound of shuffling. She peeked across and saw the boy place a king of diamonds in the center of the deck. He didn't say anything to her, so she just watched. No harm in that. He tapped the deck and turned over the first card. The king was back on top. He replaced the card in the deck. Shireen watched him fan the deck. Every card was now blank except—the king of diamonds.

"I know how you did that."

The Shrimp had leaned forward and he made a grab for Micah's cards. The deck went flying onto the floor. Micah elbowed him and, with a yelp, he was gone.

"That was a bit rough. Sorry." Micah smiled at Shireen as he picked up the cards.

"Rough magic."

"Yeah, I suppose it was." He looked up. The corners of her mouth were curved in a slight smile. He liked that. And her eyes, those amazing blue eyes, were framed with long lashes. He remained crouched, picking up cards but not taking his eyes off her. She no longer seemed standoffish and was almost friendly, like the last time they'd met.

"Lord Prospero performed rough magic." She tapped the book on her lap. *"The Tempest."*

"Shakespeare. 'Full fathom five thy father lies…' Mum knew it as a song. When I was a kid." He began to sing quietly, "'Full fathom five thy father lies. Of his bones are coral made. Those are pearls that were his eyes…' Ding-dong, ding-dong bell, dell. Or something like that. Don't remember much else." He was happy to remember as much as he did.

"She sang that to you?" Her eyes widened, and so did her smile.

He nodded, embarrassed, then smiled back. Suddenly the blueness of her eyes froze over like black ice. But not out of anger. Micah knew it wasn't out of anger; she seemed sad but he didn't know why. Oh, crap me, he thought, why did I have to warble away like a bloody medieval wally.

His mother sang to him the words of Shakespeare! Even on her day of days, Shireen's thoughts of duty were tangled up with thoughts of Shakespeare. His songs, his words, his characters, imagining what might have been, wanting to have done things differently, unable to change the past. Just like now, she thought, just like now. And this Prospero boy whose mother sang—was it a song? She could not recall.

Shireen breathed deeply. She felt hot but tried to ignore it. She turned from the play to a sonnet.

*"Oh benefit of ill! Now I find true. That better is by evil still made better..."*

Yes, yes, evil! Better! She willed herself to be content but her mind reeled. Her throat felt fizzy. Her head was pounding. How could evil make this better? The boy beside me is not—

She felt as if her ribs had been laced and tightened. Something within her was writhing, moving. The sick feeling would not stop.

"Are you all right?"

Shireen stared at the boy with the rough magic, Prospero Boy. Beads of sweat broke across her forehead like strands of transparent pearls. And then she threw up on him.

"Oh, gross!" screamed the Shrimp, peeking between the seats.

"Sicker on the bus," someone shouted.

"Someone's sick?" asked a concerned adult.

"Sicker on the bus! Sicker on the bus!" It became a cruel chant.

All Shireen could hear was a raucous noise. Except for the boy's voice. Prospero Boy. His voice cut through the din. Ignoring the vomit on his clothes, he asked if she was all right. Gently he brushed sweat-stained hair from her pale, drawn face.

"You'll be okay. It's okay. Don't listen to them."

"Stop the bus." Shireen spoke quietly but forcefully.

"What? I can't do that."

"There is bomb on the bus. Stop the bus. There is time."

Micah lurched crab-like to the front of the bus and relayed to the driver what Shireen had told him, as calmly as he could. The brakes puffed and wheezed as the bus pulled over. Everyone groaned when the AC was switched off. The door opened. The driver, his face drawn, stood up and held the back of his seat as he addressed the passengers.

"There is a slight mechanical—failure. I want everyone out." He spoke louder than he meant to, adding, "Please leave the bus in a orderly way."

Everyone started whining or yelling at the driver.

"This bus is now out of service. Another will be along shortly. Everyone off. Now!" He looked at Micah, "Hey you, boy. You, too."

But Micah was pushing back through the throng of passengers. Jakey asked him what was up, but Micah just shook his head and shrugged. Jakey mumbled something, but it was lost as he was carried along by others surging toward the door. Everyone was making noise, laughing, shouting, enjoying the unexpected adventure and the prospect of being late for school.

Micah leaned over and crouched on the seat beside the girl, who looked surprised to see him again. And relieved, or did he imagine it? Micah wasn't sure.

"Is it in a bag, a case, or something? Did you see who did it?" He sighed when Shireen did not respond. "Well anyway, come on, you gotta get off."

"No! I cannot. You do not understand. I am—"

She pulled a small cylindrical object from her jacket pocket and pointed to the wires that disappeared up her sleeve. Micah looked confused as Shireen undid the button of her quilted jacket. He saw the bulging canvas waistcoat, more wires, and a battery pack. It was connected to the small plastic container, soft and black, draped across her stomach, a body bag for a dead rat.

# Chapter 16

Micah did not need to see more. He sprang up from his seat and smacked his head on the luggage rack. Micah saw stars, actual stars, like in cartoons. And the top of his head hurt something rotten. Shireen reached out to steady him. She grabbed his hand and helped him back into his seat. He sat for a moment squeezing her hand.

"You must go now."

"Oh, my head, oh, crap me."

The bash on the head had dazed him, but the moment of panic had passed. Micah looked at her, not really believing what he had seen.

"It's really you?"

Shireen nodded, then added, "You are safe. I will not harm. Please go now."

"Why?" he asked.

"It is arranged."

"But you can't. You're underage." Micah couldn't believe what he'd said, but then he couldn't believe he was still sitting there, talking to her, either.

"I am the one."

"Does your mum know what you're doing?"

"My family, my mother, they all know my path. They have already mourned my death. Now they are celebrating a new life. To be martyr is to sacrifice for something better—"

"How do you know it will be better if you're bloody dead?"

"I know because—" The boy's question had thrown her a bit, then she got to the nub of the issue. "They will have better life. All my family. I do for them."

"How could they have a better life without you?"

"It will be so! For me, there is nothing. Only what I give now."

"That's just…nuts. You're just being daft," Micah said.

"I am sorry. Now, please, you go, yes?"

Shireen anxiously watched him, willing him to go. But he wasn't moving. He was just staring straight ahead. Maybe he did not understand her English? Shireen was beginning to lose patience.

"Go. Please. I am Palestinian. You are the Jewish."

"Who cares?"

"You must go now." She spoke slowly and with quiet intensity.

"You're squeezing my hand," he said.

She looked down. It was true, she *was* squeezing his hand. She realized it must have happened when she had instinctively pulled him into the seat.

"And there is something in it," said Micah. "In my hand. And you're squeezing and—"

Shireen saw the wires trailing from her sleeve into their clasped hands. The detonator. It was between them now. She realized she must have been holding it when she reached up. She also realized she might have inadvertently pressed it. But she didn't know for sure. All she knew was that if they let go now, it might release the trigger.

"Do not move. Do not pull from me," she said.

"What is it? What are we holding? Oh, crap me. Oh, bloody—"

Micah squirmed in his seat. Shireen shot him a fearful, almost angry glance.

"Not move! Still, still." Shireen breathed out, then added, "It is safe. I think. We are here. Not in Heaven."

"No, we're not in heaven. So what happens now?"

"Nothing happens. That is good. But—"

"What's the *but* bit? Don't like the *but* bit."

"If I press down, it release. Like a top of pen? On spring. You understand?"

"Oh, I get it. You can't let go because, because it might release and then—heaven?"

"Yes. Heaven. But that unright."

"*Unright?* Yeah, I would say so. Too bloody unright. So we just sit here?"

"I think. Let me—"

"Sorry. You carry on, don't mind me." Micah felt cold sweat trickling down his back.

"Your little finger—" Shireen pointed with her head.

"That's my thumb you're pointing to."

Shireen moved her other hand over the two clasped hands.

"What are you doing? I thought you said not to move."

"You sweat. Bad for bomb. But good for me, I think. Do not try and help. Okay?"

Micah nodded. He could barely breathe. He wanted to turn away but couldn't.

Shireen worked the fingers of her free hand between the grasped hands until she felt the base of the detonator. The top was held in the fleshy part of Micah's thumb.

"Now, keep still, very still." She licked her thumb. "I will slide my thumbs in."

"It's *a* thumb, just *a* thumb. Not that it matters, but—"

Slowly the thumb then forefinger of her free hand slid upward until she felt the sharp indentation at the top of the tube-like trigger. She was pleased it was not moving, even though it hurt.

"Now slowly, slowly take hand away."

Micah's hand slipped out like a sweaty rag. He wiped it on himself as she clamped her hand over the fisted one.

"You are free," she said softly. "Go."

"What about you?"

"I will soon be free, too. I fulfill my destiny. Alone. No innocent suffer for me."

It didn't take a genius to figure out what she meant.

"Aren't you innocent?" he asked.

"No!"

"What did you do that was wrong, then?"

"This. All this."

"Then don't do it." Micah realized he was shouting and added, more quietly, "I'm sorry; I didn't mean to shout."

Shireen shook her head. Her hands appeared locked together in a violent prayer. She squeezed her eyes tightly shut. She looked so scared.

"Go. Please. Now," she implored.

"You held on. You didn't know it, but you did. You held onto me."

"I do not know—"

"Why were you sick?"

"I do not know."

"Don't you see? You wanted to hold on. You didn't want to let go. Of me. Of all this. Just stay put. They'll get it sorted out. Honest. You'll be all right."

"Please, understand. To be martyr, you must not stay."

"Then I'm staying."

Micah got up, looked out of the window. No one was nearby. In the near distance, he heard sirens wailing. Traffic was snarling to a halt. Not long now, he thought, not long now. He sat back down. He felt strangely achy. It was good to sit back down. Shireen did not ask him to leave. He hoped that was a good sign. He turned slightly.

Shireen's eyes filled with tears and her face was etched with lines that framed a silent cry for help. Micah wanted to tell her it would be all right, but he had no way of knowing. So he just sat with her. It was all he could think to do.

"I don't want you to die," he said.

Micah wished he'd said something clever. Something from Shakespeare. He really wanted to ask her name, but he didn't. He just babbled on.

"You know, when I saw you first in the street, I thought, if I ever see her again…well anyway, I did see you. Remember? On the bus last time? I've never been so pleased to see someone! Thing is, I'd been looking out for you. You see a lot of the same people on a bus route. So I was hoping I'd see you again. So anyway…here you are. And here I am, and—"

"Do not let me go," she said.

Micah saw something in her eyes: fear. A great fear. And he knew she wanted to live.

# CHAPTER 17

CAPTAIN ERON GILEAD GLANCED OVER the situation report. He looked around. The surrounding streets had been blocked off. Buildings were being cleared. Red police tape was being paid out, fluttering over small sidewalks and roadways like so many wounded kites.

Near the bus were abandoned cars, vans, an open grocery truck, motorbikes on their sides or upright on kickstands. No riders. It looked like a three-way traffic jam except for the eerie silence. And the lack of people. A still-life painting.

Gilead saw a lot of soldiers in uniform. But not like me, he smiled to himself. Truth be told, he did not look much like a soldier on the best of occasions, this day even less so. About thirty, lean and broad with black hair and striking gray eyes, he was wearing a bright Hawaiian shirt, khaki shorts, and hiking boots. Apart from a brace of dog tags and badges that gave him high-level access, he looked every bit like a tourist. But the look belied his abilities. He was a first-rate negotiator, often the point person in the tension-ridden no-man's land that separated the Israeli and Palestinian communities. Only today was different.

Today he was going into a minefield to disarm an unexploded bomb. And the bomb was a fourteen-year-old girl.

He sauntered into the mobile command post. An orderly waved him along while anxiously sifting through press passes. Classical music played in the background. Iced tea jingle-jangled in a pitcher. And there he was, beneath the canopied shade: Colonel Yossi Chazoom.

Gilead was mildly affronted when the man made no attempt to get up or salute. Chazoom's hands remained crossed over his ample tummy. He wore a long gold jacket, a crisp white shirt, Bermuda shorts, and blue Crocs. He looked even less like a soldier than Gilead. Even so, he was obviously pleased to see the younger man.

The feeling was not mutual. Chazoom was like a bad penny—always seemed to show up. A year earlier, at a bank robbery, he had put in an appearance. Until he realized the robbers were working for themselves and not for Hamas, Hezbollah, or another group on the terror-watch. Then he had lost interest and promptly disappeared. Now, he was attached to Israeli counter-intelligence, working as a Public Relations officer. Eron didn't buy a word of it. Chazoom was a lot more than a media hack but Eron never quite knew what he was. Eron detested the man's arrogance and eccentricities but had to admit, Chazoom was a problem-solver of great talent, a former analyst with the CIA whose language skills were beyond fluent. And right now, he would have to work with him.

"Eron! Well, well, how marvelous. Like a candy? Chocolate-covered dates. Surprisingly delicious. Almost healthy once you suck off the chocolate." Chazoom popped a date into his slightly mocking mouth.

"You in charge here?" Gilead waved away the proffered chocolates. He was impatient.

"Technically I share command with him, but..." Chazoom wagged a dismissive flipper toward a very young officer carrying too much body armor.

"'Im? You're joking." Occasionally Gilead dropped H's like a Cockney, even though the closest he had been to London's East End was East London in South Africa. "He doesn't like you."

"I know. I pulled rank to get you here. And he's a little…rankled?

He's eager to rush the bus, but before that PR nightmare happens I want you to go in. Apart from our suicide bomber, there's a boy, a tourist. English. Raised the alarm but stayed. Kept the girl calm. *Is* keeping her calm."

"Do we 'ave a name for the boy?"

"Micah Montsees. Currently living with relatives and…" As Chazoom talked, Gilead scanned the perimeter. He looked up. And then he saw it, a bright flash of light. The telltale glint came from a second-story window.

"The sharpshooters," he said angrily. "If I'm going in—"

"Did I say there were sharpshooters?" Chazoom appeared mortified.

"I want them to stand down."

"Done!"

# Chapter 18

The door of the bus was open but not much air was circulating. Micah sidled around the back of the seat to see what was going on outside. He saw a man in a gaudy Hawaiian shirt walking right to them, holding up water bottles.

"Tell him to keep away," Shireen said.

"I'm not doing that. He's got water and I feel like I swallowed a cactus." Micah swung back onto the seat. "And don't be scared. I told you, I'm staying—"

"I am not scared. I have shame. Is what I feel. That is what you see."

But all Micah could see was a beautiful girl, about his age, who liked Shakespeare and seemed to like him. And his magic tricks.

"It'll be all right. We'll be out of this soon. Honest." He almost believed it himself.

"I cannot leave this bus," she said.

"We'll leave it together."

"They will kill me. They hate me. I am the enemy." She suddenly sounded terrified.

"Don't be daft; they won't shoot you. They might shoot me, and if they did, there'd be an international incident."

Micah wasn't too sure about that but it sounded good.

Captain Gilead stood in front of the bus. The palms of his hands felt like furnaces. He hoped the water would still be cold when he reached the kids.

He was now within the kill zone. And he knew it. His past life didn't flash before him, but the past few minutes did. If only he hadn't taken that call. He would have been miles away by now.

Hiking. Free for two days, unencumbered and unconnected except to his backpack and a sleeping bag. Free to explore this timeless landscape. Gilead loved to hike. Barefoot. To touch the ground, to feel the energy that pulsed through his new home. He had walked the desert of the Negev. The Hills of Galilee, with the shrinking sea below. He had crossed the coastal regions toward Lebanon, the trade routes of the old Levant. Never happier than to be out of the office, in shorts and a tee-shirt, walking into a warm breeze on a deserted hillside.

He had grown up in Zimbabwe, which his parents of European, Jewish origins still called Rhodesia. They had been forced out and were now living in northernmost South Africa, where they kept a hopeless vigil for a beloved homeland. So when he graduated university, Gilead decided to move to Israel. He spoke Afrikaans, a kind of bastardized Dutch that had helped with Hebraic pronunciation. Despite a strong South African accent, he could speak English fluently and had learned to speak Arabic moderately well.

And now he was standing by the bus with one foot on the step.

"Micah, my name's Eron. Are you okay?" Gilead called out.

Micah was taken aback that the Hawaiian-shirt geezer knew his name.

"Yeah, I'm all right," said Micah, but his guts were in turmoil.

"And the girl? What's her name?"

"Dunno," Micah admitted.

Gilead was inside the bus. Slowly he made his way down the aisle. He could see them both now. Sitting together. The girl looked drawn and pale, eyes puffy. She looked at the end of her rope. He offered them the water. Micah reached for it. As Gilead handed Micah the water bottle, he indicated that Micah should go, but he shook his head.

"So what's going on?" Gilead asked casually.

"She's got the detonator in her hand, and she doesn't want it to go off, so she can't let go and—"

In fits and starts, Micah explained what had happened. When he finished, he gulped some water. Then, wiping the top of the bottle, he held it up to Shireen, who refused.

"What are you called?" Gilead spoke to Shireen in Arabic.

"She speaks English. Not English, English, but well, you know, good enough," said Micah.

Gilead counted to thirty in his head before the girl answered.

"Shireen? Is that an Arab name?" Gilead asked, reverting to English.

"Persian."

"Persian? Sweet," said Micah.

"That is what means." The girl smiled to herself. "Sweet."

"Your name suits you. Really," Gilead nodded.

Micah wished he had said that. Wished he had asked her name.

"You cannot stay here, Shireen, but we can help you get out of this."

"I cannot move," she shouted.

Suddenly Micah saw a wild anger in her eyes. The blue had turned ice-white. His mind reeled with a hundred replies blurring together. He held up the water again.

"You don't have to. We'll stay here. I'll stay. And this man here will help us."

Shireen was thirsty, but how could she drink? How could she betray her resolve? What of her family, the new house, the new beginning? Jagged thoughts raced through her mind.

"What of my destiny?" she said out loud, but not meaning to. "I have failed. I have failed everyone. And I know what I must suffer."

"Suffer not! A life without a pinch of failure is to liveth a life for naught! And to do-eth is to be depriveth a measure of success and honorable bounty," Micah declaimed inventively.

"Is Shakespeare?" she asked.

"Yes," he lied.

Shireen smiled a little and looked almost relieved. Micah smiled back. Gilead had no clue where that line had come from, but he didn't care. Somehow, it had done the trick and that was all that mattered. He signaled the bomb disposal unit. A technician entered the bus. As soon as he had sized up the situation, he took Gilead aside.

"If TATP is the explosive, that could be a problem. It's erratic stuff, prone to accidental detonation. We have to work fast. I suggest you and the boy leave."

"I'll stay," said Gilead. "And he won't go."

Micah watched as the specialist cut away the sleeve of her jacket, talking all the while. Micah thought he sounded like a dentist during a tooth-filling session, calm and encouraging. And it worked. Shireen remained calm as the explosive was carefully removed. Minutes later, a two-man disposal squad exited the bus with a reinforced concrete sarcophagus on wheels. Stowed safely within were the explosive materials the tailor had so carefully stitched together.

Micah remained with Shireen until she was taken into the ambulance, trailed by camera crews and photographers snapping the air like frenzied cicadas. She looked overwhelmed by all the attention, and just a little scared.

"I am so sorry," Shireen said.

"You did alright."

"Death was not in my heart."

"Glad of that," Micah said.

"I am glad of it, too." She reached out and squeezed his hand.

Surrounded by people like bees in a swarm, the ambulance slowly pulled away. More and more people poured through the police cordon. The media captured some great footage.

# CHAPTER 19

"WHAT HAVE THEY DONE TO SHIREEN? They will pay. They will suffer."

Farouz stood up and ran screaming toward the TV. Pushed from its pedestal, the set juddered and bounced off the rug that covered the concrete floor. Farouz turned away. Tears flowed from his eyes like acid, burning his face with rage. The younger ones started crying. Mrs. Obeid rebuked her son, not for his anger, but for attacking the TV. Suray said nothing. She thought of Shireen, secretly glad she had survived.

"The Zionist are a pestilence," Farouz ranted. "They must be eradicated."

"Yes, yes, eradicated," said Suray. "But why did you break the rabbit ears? Now the TV is little better than useless."

"Why have they spirited my child away like a demon? What will become of her?" Mrs. Obeid asked. "And what of us? What of our new home in Ramallah?"

"Our sister has been denied her destiny. And you talk about television and houses?"

Farouz stormed out. Suray looked at her mother as she comforted the younger children.

# Chapter 20

YOSSI CHAZOOM could not have been happier. He was enjoying the last few notes of Mozart's *Magic Flute*. After it ended, the music seemed to shimmer in place for several moments. He sighed to himself, then his mood changed along with the music. A strangely oriental fusion of funk and a rap-like chant pumped the walls of the apartment.

Chazoom did not hear the doorbell ring, but he did hear someone pounding the door. He stuffed a few nuts in his face and ambled over. Maybe it was a neighbor complaining about the music. Again! They seemed to take it in turns.

Sweet apologies dissolved on Chazoom's breath. He stood open-mouthed as Colonel Raphael Singer pushed past him into the apartment.

"Chazoom, where have you been?"

"Raphael, you could have at least waited for me to invite you in."

"Invite me in? I'm not a vampire, I do not need an invite. I'm a military officer with very little patience." Singer wanted to yell, but yelling always left him out of control. Instead, he breathed deeply. "Close the door. And your mouth, Chazoom. Thank you."

"I'll have you know, Raphael, that I, too, am a military man. Of sorts."

"Let's not go into those 'sorts,' Chazoom. And please turn down that noise. Like a bloody dancing parlor in here! Can't hear myself talk. Or think."

"Don't you like it? It's a mega-merge of hip-opera and klezmer."

"Turn it off. I'll say my piece and be gone. Then you can blast your eardrums for all I care."

Chazoom twirled over to his music center. He turned it off and smiled. Singer breathed in and out as if under great strain, trying to ignore the unprofessional character in front of him. All the more galling because they held the same rank, albeit in different agencies.

"Nuts." Chazoom took one as he held up the dish. "Macadamias. Like some?"

"No. Thank you. I am here because your people can't seem to do anything without your approval. My people tried to find you. But you were unavailable. On travel. In the field. In meetings. My staff got the runaround. And you know it."

"Guilty as charged."

"I don't have the time for your games. The girl. I need her."

Singer had always been a man of action. Many military types in Israel had become astute politicians able to work with legislators and bureaucrats. Singer was not one of them. His undiplomatic approach had excluded him from higher office, from greater power. He wanted to solve problems. Nothing more. And now he was taking action again.

Chazoom's eyes glittered with feigned happiness and betrayed not a hint of his inner panic. He cursed his own arrogance and shortsightedness. He had run roughshod over protocols. And now Singer was seething. Chazoom had to admit Colonel Singer was an impressive man. Despite his sixty years, he was still a fighter. And no fool. He had put himself through university. Studied languages and psychology and history. A cornerstone in the Directorate of Military Intelligence. And a bit of a legend. He tried a different tack.

"By the by, your Eron was exemplary. So brave. I'm tempted to poach him."

Singer, Gilead's commanding officer, did not take the bait.

"We must find out what the Obeid girl knows. And quickly. We need to know how many kids they're strapping bombs to. I will be in tomorrow. And I'm taking her in for questioning. No need to keep her in hospital anyway."

So that was it. It would be a turf war with Shireen in the middle. Singer was with the Israeli Security Agency, while Chazoom worked the Foreign Affairs Research Division or FARD, which dealt with security issues within the territories. Technically Shireen's case came under FARD jurisdiction, but Singer was not about to give her up to Chazoom.

"If I had my way," Singer was saying, "that girl would be in custody. Right now."

"Let the interrogations begin," Chazoom said with cold sarcasm.

An unspoken enmity existed between them, and Singer realized his bluntness was not helping. He coughed nervously, mumbled an apology, and handed Chazoom a business card.

"Call me. If you need to—I mean it, Chazoom. Let's not be enemies."

"Thank you, I'll keep this," said Chazoom.

Singer looked at Chazoom to see if he was playing him for a fool, but saw nothing untoward. Damn, he thought, the man is just too charming! He grunted good-bye, then turned and walked out.

Shireen felt cooped up and bored. She was being kept in the hospital for "observation," Mister Yossi had said. And she understood why. But at least she was allowed to walk around the hospital floor, with the guard in tow. He was in his twenties, a part-time soldier with freckles, red hair, and a pointed chin. His name was Davan. He didn't mind puppy-guarding this unusual girl. He liked the distraction.

Davan was the first Israeli soldier Shireen had ever spoken to. She had only seen soldiers on patrol or at checkpoints. And they just pointed and ordered and were filled with suspicion. Davan was a Russian émigré, and he seemed far more curious than suspicious. And, Shireen thought, he was far too friendly to be scary. So they talked. Practiced their English.

"Speak Amarrrrican?" He rolled his R's, his voice a soft stick on a railing.

"English."

"Inglish you. Amarrrrican me." He grinned. "Best thing in Israel, you know, is weather. Beautiful. Spring, blue sky. Autumn, blue sky. Winter, blue sky. Sun on face. Not in Moscow. God has a head cold in Moscow. Snot clouds. Always. Not here. God in good health here."

"How long you in Israel army?" asked Shireen.

"One month. I have served my two years. Now I go back one month every year. Very boring. But this month, much excitement. People. And you."

"Me?"

"You."

# CHAPTER 21

JAMAL WAITED IN AN ANNEX of the villa, just a few steps away from where Shireen had stayed during her orientation and training. He was on edge. But when he was called into the room, he saw a video cam and knew it would not be a face-to-face meeting. That, at least, was something.

He punched in a series of numbers. He waited for a prompt, then plugged in the code.

"Do you have me on speaker?" The voice was gravelly, more metallic than usual.

"Yes, All-knowing One." Jamal peered at the screen, but the image was blurred.

"I read your reports. It seems no one is to blame—"

Jamal breathed a sigh of relief.

"Except for the one who trained the girl." The mechanical voice was silent for a moment, then continued, "In future, cell phone detonators will be used in case a martyr loses his or her way."

"A wise decision, Leader. It will be a call to Heaven." Jamal laughed feebly.

"Yes, Jamal, indeed it shall be. One phone call, one signal would have solved this problem."

"Yes, Leader, but would she have answered?"

"She is a child." The voice was harsh, cold. "All children answer their phones."

"She will not betray us. I am certain Shireen—"

"Shireen!" The disembodied voice spat out the name. "She is a jigsaw puzzle of information. Our enemies need only to put her together. Pity she had free rein of the encampment."

"It was assumed, my leader, that what knowledge she garnered would travel with her on the flight to Heaven," Jamal said.

"But she did not fly to Heaven, Jamal. She flew to Jerusalem. But I want that flight to Heaven arranged as soon as possible. Is this understood?"

Jamal understood.

✦ ✦ ✦

Farouz walked around the antechamber of the small mosque on a light industrial street in the southernmost suburbs of East Jerusalem. Oil smells and sweat and brick dust permeated the air. But it was of no great concern. Where men gather…

Quietly, unnoticed, the imam glided onto the loading bay where Farouz was standing. Momentarily startled, Farouz just stared, expecting the imam to speak. But he did not. The old scholar took out a cigarette and lit up. Slowly he breathed out smoke in a long gray plume.

"Your name…Farouz…Persian?"

Farouz nodded.

Farouz forced himself to remain silent while the imam puffed away. The silence billowed. Suddenly Farouz lost patience. His face contorted like an angry child.

"Did you not see her with that boy? My own sister, she—"

"Let me stop you there." The imam smiled enigmatically, then went on. "I have prayed. Have you prayed?"

"Yes, yes, I have prayed, I have prayed to Allah to give me—"

The imam held up a rigid hand in front of Farouz's face.

"A fatwa will set in motion terrible events, hard to rescind. I have reviewed her case." The imam pulled on his cigarette. "There will be no fatwa."

"No…no fatwa? I am—" Farouz felt as if he had been punched with a fisted handkerchief.

"A fatwa can only be issued if Shireen has offended God. I have searched her words, the underlying subtext of what she says, what she implies, what she infers—" He drew in a long draft of smoke from his cigarette. "But no offense has been drawn. For all your sister's calumnies and lack of judgment, I see no blasphemy. It is simple. But your honor—it is your *honor* that has been besmirched, no?"

"Yes!" cried Farouz. "A thousand times, yes."

"Then you must strike hard to regain your…honor."

The imam turned and walked back inside. The meeting was over. Farouz considered the imam's words. *Strike hard.*

# CHAPTER 22

THE BLUE OF EARLY MORNING was harsh and brittle. The best parking spots had been taken, cordoned off with police tape. As Gilead circled the lot, he saw Chazoom pull into a handicap space.

"What the 'ell are you doing, parking there?" He shook his head.

"I'm psychologically crippled," Chazoom shrugged.

"I can well believe it."

They walked into the main entrance of the hospital, close to Emergency Admittance. Police and army units ringed the grounds. Inside, squads of army regulars were standing on either side of the security checkpoints. It looks just like an airport, Gilead thought. Only this was worse. At least at an airport you got to go somewhere.

"And here he is." Chazoom was ebullient. "Always punctual."

Chazoom approached a small regiment of special service officers in black suits, sunglasses, and earpieces. Gilead thought they looked like a contingent of deaf gangsters. Suddenly the suits broke ranks and a stately gray-haired man grasped Chazoom's hand.

"Prime Minister! Shall we go up?"

The meeting began very stiffly. It was all so set up. The PM was gracious but awkward. He smiled gruffly as a few pictures were taken. He gave Shireen his business card. That helped. She asked for his autograph. Everyone tittered nervously. Seconds passed like minutes. Then the Prime Minister said a few words on behalf of the people of Israel. The old man's glasses slipped and he could barely read the prepared speech.

Shireen felt a mix of emotions, smiling one minute, tears welling the next.

The elderly statesman was quiet for a moment, not quite knowing how to act around an emotional young girl. All he could see was a picture of fawn-like innocence, the lines of life barely traced upon her face. Besides, he didn't know what else to say. Somewhat assertively, Shireen tapped the side of her bed. The PM smiled and plunked himself down beside her. Shireen giggled. The PM chuckled. Then he threw his arms around Shireen. No more words. No more speeches.

Chazoom got one hell of a picture.

THANK YOU, SHIREEN!

The headline said it all. Within minutes the photo went viral. The world looked at the PM giving Shireen a bear hug. A hopeful picture that showed that two people who had shared nothing but distrust and hatred could share something more. Perhaps.

# Chapter 23

Shireen looked up from the speech she was supposed to memorize. Just one day after the PM's visit, her hospital room was being transformed into a makeshift studio and dressing room, with a film crew and assistants of all kinds.

From what Shireen could see, Colonel Chazoom, Mister Yossi as she called him, was very much in charge.

"Let's hear it. But not in Arabic. English. I'm thinking of the international audience."

"In English?"

"English. You can do it. The language of Shakespeare. And no reading! Yes?"

Shireen looked up, her eyes bright. She smiled knowingly, then put the paper down.

"I wanted to bomb and kill children. Students like me. For this act, I would have felt no remorse, harbored no doubt, or guilt, or pity. Because I, too, would have been dead. But I chose not to press the detonator. Because I was not feeling joy but pain and sickness. God had spoken to me through the words of the English poet. I discovered what is good, and what is bad, cannot be put aside and ignored. I was saved by these words and…and by the brave actions of a young stranger who would not let me die. And I knew Allah did not want him to die. He wanted us both to live." She swallowed, then looked into the camera. "To grow unafraid. In this land. And to be what Allah wants us to be."

It was over. The words bottled inside her had just poured out. Shireen could tell Mister Yossi was pleased.

"That's it," said Shireen, sighing with relief.

"That *is* it. Yes!" Chazoom was jubilant.

That night, Shireen's speech was broadcast across all media. Everywhere.

# CHAPTER 24

THE MAN IN THE PASSENGER SEAT of the rental car was barely twenty. He glanced across to Aziz in the driver's seat, who was gripping the steering wheel a little too tightly. Unlike Aziz, the man in the passenger seat was shaven. The beginnings of a beard had been scraped away earlier that morning. The Shaved One had bushy eyebrows set above dark, intense eyes. Two deep, distinguishing lines bored into his cheeks, setting his mouth in a permanent scowl. He wore sunglasses. He had a small backpack at his feet and a bunch of flowers on his lap. Red roses.

"Blessings be upon you. Do it well, my brother, do it well."

Aziz tapped his friend's shoulder and squeezed it. Then the Shaved One got out of the car. He walked toward the hospital, carrying the flowers and backpack. A neat, clean-shaven young man in slacks, a sports coat, and glasses. Aziz drove into the short-term lot and waited.

Security was still tight at the hospital. Visitors had to enter through a zigzag of tape. No one complained, but faces bore the customary looks of resigned frustration. Chazoom greeted his guests beyond the checkpoint. Uncle Bernard enthused about the limo ride, then changed tack.

"Was it like this when the PM was here?" he asked, eager for gossip.

"Worse, much worse," Chazoom assured him.

"Did you bring any of your magic tricks, Micah?" Uncle Bernard pointed to his nephew, miming *He's very good* for the colonel's benefit.

"Not really. Some cards, but not much else," Micah mumbled. The only trick he felt like doing was making himself disappear.

Chazoom walked with them to Shireen's room, where he glared at Davan to leave and resume his post. The young guard scurried out, mumbling apologies, almost colliding with Micah and Uncle Bernard by the doorway.

Shireen's face lit up when she saw Micah. For some unknown reason, Micah started to wave and immediately felt like a twerp.

He had thought to find her still in bed and sickly. But there she was, in a cool pair of capris with a black-and-white keffiyeh wound around her waist like a kind of belt, and a cotton shirt with sleeves flopping over her hands. She looked like the girl he had first met, a bit cheeky, like she could be up for stuff. He wanted to tell her that but he didn't.

Uncle Bernard made a big point of steaming across the room with his hand out. As Shireen shook it, she smiled nervously at Micah as if to say "Help!"

He tried to smile, but somehow his lips curled back and seemed to stick to his teeth like old chewing gum.

"I am so excited to meet you. And must, must say..." Uncle Bernard drew himself up. "On behalf of my dear wife, Gilly, and my sons—*our* sons, what was I thinking? Anyway, words can't express what I, my wife, and the others...I mean to say, the fact is, words fail me."

Alas, words did not fail him. Uncle Bernard continued to yuck it up, but Micah was not listening; he was looking at Shireen. Her black hair framed her face and veiled her cheeks perfectly, and how did she get those blue eyes? They're strange, he thought, but then he figured that, overall, she was definitely more pretty than strange, so that was all right.

Micah didn't realize he was gaping like an idiot until Shireen gave him a sly smile. He turned away, his face burning with embarrassment.

Uncle Bernard prattled on about his friendly Arab neighbors, and how he tried to get to the souk in the Old City whenever he could, and how much fresher their produce was. Shireen appeared interested.

Why isn't she squirming or yawning or sighing? thought Micah. She must be faking, he grumped to himself. Then again, she might not be. Then Bernard started fumbling with his wallet. He wanted to show baby pictures of the twins. Micah wanted to die.

"Wonderful. Now, Mister Rothner, would you like some coffee? Surprisingly, they make a good cappuccino here. And there's someone waiting for me downstairs. So, shall we?" Chazoom raised his eyebrows and tried not to smile.

"Oh, I love cappuccino. With skim milk, mind you. Have to watch the old waistline."

Chazoom guided the waistline-tapping uncle from the room. The door swooshed shut. Micah groaned in mock pain and covered his face with his hands.

"Oh, the shame, the shame. How he torments me—"

Shireen started smiling, enjoying the moment as well as Micah's antics. "He's Uncle Bernard."

"Uncle Ber-*nard*. Yes! But he means well, I suppose."

"Tuk, tuk, tuk."

Micah looked around. The room was quite large, with two beds, a bathroom, armchairs, a TV, bedside tables, and lots of flowers in lots of vases. He looked at her.

"You seem different. From when I last saw you. Better, I'll say that."

"Because of you— I can think of tomorrow, days for tomorrow. You understand?" She held out her hands to him.

"Oh, don't be daft." Micah crossed his arms tightly.

She shrugged with her hands and folded them in her lap. "What is *daft?*"

What's *daft,* thought Micah, daft is being like me and not holding her hand. He fumed at himself and wished he had a reset button. A great big one.

# Chapter 25

The Shaved One walked into the hospital's main reception area, within feet of where Gilead stood waiting for Chazoom. A security guard directed him to two entry points that fed into a single file. Everyone was asked to be patient by a young lady who smiled a lot. The Shaved One caught her eye and, smiling back, said he would be patient.

It took only a few minutes to get to the front of the line. He handed over the flowers and opened his backpack. Without looking, the security guard waved a stick inside and around the bag, then placed it on a small conveyor belt. The bag rattled through an X-ray machine without incident. The Shaved One was told to walk through the body scanner. He did.

The alarm went off.

The Shaved One stepped back. He took a metal eyeglass case from his jacket pocket. He handed the case to the guard, who opened it. He found a pair of glasses and examined them. Both case and glasses were placed on a plastic dish. These items were not scanned.

Again the Shaved One walked through the detector. Again the alarm went off. A look of realization spread over his face. He visibly relaxed as he removed another glass case from his inside pocket. He pointed to the sunglasses hanging on a cord around his neck.

"Prescription," he said. "Prescription sunglasses."

The guard did not open the second case, simply placed it on the tray with the other small items. The Shaved One walked through the scanner a third time. No alarm went off. The guard handed over the flowers and eyeglass cases.

# Chapter 26

"'What's gone and what's past help should be past grief.'"

"You and Shakespeare. You know loads more than me."

"This is not truth. You spoke his words, 'the measure of failure'—"

"Oh. That." Micah uncomfortably remembered his *faux* Shakespeare.

"What play did those words come?"

"Wonder what happened to my uncle?" He looked about Shireen's room, trying to think of something, anything to say that wasn't medieval.

"Or was it a sonnet? Perhaps, yes?" Shireen pressed.

"Perhaps. I don't exactly—" Micah shrugged.

"Tuk, tuk, tuk." She waggled a finger, but then smiled. "I am so good you are here."

"Yeah, well, that Chazoom bloke said I should visit and my uncle…so I thought, why not?"

Micah could see her eyes had become overcast. She looked hurt, or disappointed.

"I didn't mean I didn't want to see you. It's just—oh, crap me, I'm just the biggest idiot going."

She glanced at him and chuckled, but not meanly. Micah swore to himself never to criticize Uncle Bernard for talking too much ever, ever again. A moment passed.

"I met Israel Prime Minister; he smells of oranges. I took picture, my new scapbook," she said.

"Your what?"

"You keep scapbook?"

"It's *scrapbook.* And I don't. That's mostly, you know, girl stuff, and er…"

"And boy stuff?" She gave him a challenging glance.

"Well, I do magic and Scouts." He could tell she didn't understand. "Scouts, you know, we go on camping trips. Do badge work and stuff."

"With your friends?"

"They're not mates, just kids in my troop. But we go different places."

"I see different places and peoples in magazines. I put—" She hooked a thumb at herself, "in scrapbook, I put me. For pretend."

"That's nice. I was on the cover of the Loughton *Gazette* once. But that's about it."

"Mister Yossi thinks I will be on magazines in America. No pretend."

"Mr. Yossi? Oh, him, yeah. That's nice."

"Mister Yossi thinks I can be goodwill ambassador for my people."

"That's nice." Micah was not really listening but trying to think of something smart to say.

"That's nice, that's nice. All you say—'that's nice'!" she laughed.

"Gordon Bennet," Micah muttered.

"And who is Gordy Bennet?" Her bright blues sparkled with curiosity.

"He's… Oh, never mind."

"Never mind. Now. Magic trick? You promise. For me? Yes?" She looked at him with big, eager eyes. Black eyebrows rose up like two skinny cats having a stretch.

"Okay, all right," was all Micah could think to say. "Wait here. I have to prepare."

"No. Stay. Please. I will close eyes."

Micah looked away, then took out his deck and a pen and started counting cards. He looked up suddenly. Shireen's eyes closed more tightly than before.

"You were peeking! I'll be back. In a minute. And no peeking."

As Micah moved into the adjacent bathroom, he glanced back and saw Shireen's eyes were scrunched closed. He smiled as he shut the door. Right, he thought, I'm back in with a chance.

Hameeda had tried calling Colonel Chazoom but could not get through. So she decided to make the journey in person. At least she might get to see Shireen. But she had gotten jammed up at the checkpoint. No wave-throughs with just a cursory glance that day. The one-hour journey had taken most of the morning.

Hameeda entered the hospital and asked an orderly to take her to Colonel Chazoom.

The Shaved One got off on the fourth floor and went into an empty room. He threw the roses violently into the corner and pulled a doctor's coat out of the bag. He opened the unexamined glass case and took out a long knife handle. At the end of the handle was a metal tongue, which he depressed. A click heralded the appearance of a gleaming blade. The metal tongue was pressed once more, locking the razor-sharp blade into a fixed position.

He grabbed a clipboard from an unattended nurses' station. He walked on, pretending to read it. He looked down the corridor. At the far end, a nurse walked out of sight. A soldier was standing a third of the way down the hallway. It must be the room.

Davan saw the doctor approaching. "Check-up time?" he asked casually.

The doctor smiled as he peered over his clipboard. Suddenly

Davan felt something sharp—a radiating, needle pain that grew and grew in intensity. He tried to breathe. He felt sick. The doctor was so close. He was trying to pull something from his side, but it would not budge. And all the while, the pain was getting worse. As if someone had gotten inside him and was kicking and kicking. And the doctor, the doctor—

Uncle Bernard saw Chazoom talking to a young Arab girl, then beckoning to Captain Gilead and an older officer. He moved closer to the group, trying not to spill his coffee.

"He talks of honor for his sister but his heart is black with hate," the girl was saying. "Farouz said this would be the day. Today. You understand?"

Suddenly Gilead felt as if someone had just hit him with a brick.

"I'm taking the stairs. Quicker," he said, already moving.

"What's happening? Is it Micah?" asked Bernard anxiously.

Singer was at the elevator and beckoning Chazoom to hurry. The doors closed just as Uncle Bernard reached them, sloshing coffee over his hands.

Micah furrowed his brow in concentration. Cards, coins, empty glass. Tissues rolled up. Everything was lined up on the edge of the sink. He was all set.

"You have name, Prospero Boy? Sorry, I forget," Shireen called out.

"It's Micah." Micah smiled to himself. "Micah, the young magician."

Silence.

"Didn't forget yours," he said. "It's Shireen, right?"

Silence. Then Micah heard something. Thought it might be

Arabic, then a stifled cry. He flung open the bathroom door just in time to see a shadow, a figure looming over Shireen. A hand grabbed at her throat. There was a flash of a knife. Shireen's face was drawn of color as the Shaved One squeezed her neck.

"Ay, you!" Micah screamed.

The Shaved One turned in surprise and annoyance. Beneath his grasp, Shireen clawed the air as she stared up into the face of her attacker.

The first card flew from Micah's hand and nicked the man on the forehead. The second caught his cheek and bounced off, creating nothing more than insect stings. The third card was deflected. The fourth pinged the bridge of his nose. Another insect bite. But the man looked annoyed now.

One hand around Shireen's throat, he turned toward Micah. For a split second, Micah had a full-face target. The next card tore into the corner of the man's left eye. He screamed and clutched at his face, momentarily releasing Shireen from his murderous grasp. Angrily he lunged at Micah, the knife slicing wickedly through the air.

Shireen rolled off the bed, gasping for breath.

Micah jumped across the other bed and pushed hard against it. The attacker staggered and almost lost his balance as the sliding bed slammed against his legs. Then Micah saw a flash of silvery metal as Shireen swung a bedpan across the face of her attacker. The force of the blow made the guy topple backwards. Brilliant move, thought Micah. Shireen tried to hit him again as he fell, but she missed and the bedpan slid out of her hands and clanged onto the floor.

Scooting around the bed, Micah grabbed Shireen's hand and pulled her to the doorway. They saw Davan on the corridor floor, his stricken form outlined in red. Shireen screamed. The young soldier groaned. Miraculously still alive. Shireen reached down to him.

"Not now, come on." Micah pulled her away.

Pure panic drove him on, dragging Shireen with him. Then they heard a screaming, swearing oath in Arabic. The brute was after them! Micah and Shireen crashed through a set of doors at the end of the corridor. Alarms went off.

As the doors closed behind them, Micah and Shireen found themselves in a stairwell. They ran down the steps, almost tripping as their speed increased. Above them, they heard the door bang open. Footsteps closed in like clattering hooves, gaining speed, getting louder. Not daring to look back, Micah and Shireen kept running.

# Chapter 27

At the bottom of the stairwell, Micah slammed into the iron bar that held shut the emergency exit. He burst through with Shireen just behind him. They careened into a parking garage.

The air felt clammy and reeked of gas. Seeing a shaft of daylight through a gap in the concrete, Micah and Shireen ran toward it, down a level. They turned at the bottom, into another lower level.

"Where are we going?" asked Shireen.

"I don't know."

The light seemed to narrow as they ran to it. They were running to a gap in the concrete, not to a way out. Micah heard something, a squeaking sound. Footsteps. He grabbed Shireen and pulled her between cars. He put a finger to his mouth. Shireen nodded. They heard the sound again. Only closer.

He gestured something about the cars and pointed to the keffiyeh around her waist. She was confused, but she pulled the scarf free and gave it to him. Micah tied one end to the door handle of a Ford, then tied the diagonal end to the door handle of another car, creating a makeshift hammock. Micah helped Shireen climb onto it, then carefully clambered in, keeping them steady.

"Just don't let your feet touch the ground," Micah whispered hoarsely.

"Why?"

"Look for someone hiding in a car park. You look at the floor, right? Look for feet. Right?"

"How do you know he will look for feet?" asked Shireen.

"I saw it in a movie."

"What if he saw same movie?"

"Gordon Bennet!"

Suddenly Shireen's scarf, hammocked between the two cars, began to tear.

Micah grabbed the handle of the car nearest him and tried to pull himself up in a kind of reverse push-up. His legs swayed in the scarf, making Shireen lose her balance. Her mouth opened, but thankfully no sound came out. Just as Shireen was about to fall, Micah grabbed her foot. He heard running footsteps—how close, he couldn't tell. Then silence.

He's stopped running, thought Micah. He's looking to see if anyone is hiding, and if he sees us, he'll come for us, and when he does, he'll—

The attacker sprinted past them, drawn toward shouting. Seconds later, a car door slammed shut. A screeching echo merged into a metallic roar as the car took off. The sound began to fade. As Micah twisted around to see, he almost toppled them both, but Shireen's foot slammed onto the garage floor, holding them in place. Micah looked at her and almost smiled with relief.

The attacker had not seen the movie after all.

They ran from the car park into the daylight. Crouching low, they hugged pylons, hedgerows, anything to stay out of sight. They hid beneath some bushes and tried to block out the clatter and crunch of boots pounding pavement. And the shouting.

Micah looked through the evergreen patch. He saw armed men, some unshaven, some in tee shirts, some in fatigues, racing toward the hospital. Shireen looked terrified and Micah didn't know what to think. He couldn't tell if they were IDF soldiers or not. They certainly didn't look like any soldiers he had ever seen. He and Shireen had to get away. Away from the blood, the noise, the confusion. Away. Away to somewhere safe.

Micah and Shireen rolled out from the piney shrubs, landing hard on the sidewalk. Pulling themselves up, they stumbled across the street. Drivers honked, people shouted and swore, brakes screeched and howled with annoyance. But they kept running.

They stopped at a pedestrian-only street, the roadway filled in with paving stones. And people. Micah realized he had no idea where they were in this ancient-yet-modern cosmopolitan city. He looked at Shireen. She seemed just as lost.

They took off again. Shireen ran ahead like a skittish gazelle. Driven by fear and adrenaline, she went on and on. When she finally stopped, she looked around and saw Micah, a block away, bent over, arms on his knees. She trotted back to him. He was leaning against a wall. He looked sick. His mouth was open and sweat streaked down his face. Shireen stood beside him and gently stroked his back, staring down any funny looks that came their way.

"I will not run on more. We stay together. Okay?" Shireen was firm.

He looked up at her, finally caught his breath. "That geezer, the man who wanted to kill you? He knew you. You knew him. Who was he?"

"He is my brother, Farouz. I shamed him. He does for honor." Uncertainty clouded her face.

"Honor! What honor? What a bastard. Glad I'm an only child."

Shireen looked away, unable to speak. A moment later, she turned back with a dazzling smile.

"*Ping! Ping! Ping!* Magic cards. You rescue me, Prospero Boy—"

"You did good yourself. That bedpan. Too bad it was empty."

They went on, more slowly now. Stopping at a kiosk, Micah bought an expensive bottle of water. He insisted she drink first.

While she did, he dug for the phone in his pocket. The corner of a business card gently pricked his finger. Micah showed her the card.

"Mister Yossi. Yes." Shireen sounded sure.

Micah tried his phone. It was dead. He had forgotten to charge the thing. He swore as he jammed it back in his pocket.

"Better find one that works," said Shireen. "Then we call him."

# Chapter 28

Chazoom and Gilead walked across the outdoor hospital parking lot toward a postage-stamp patch of greenery with a weird bit of statuary and a couple of benches. A tranquility garden. Gilead was feeling anything but tranquil. He had gotten to Shireen's room moments too late. He had raced down the emergency stairwell, he had tracked the car to the above-ground car park, but it was all for nothing: the attackers had gotten away. He had fired repeatedly at the fleeing car. A window had smashed, but the car had not stopped. He hoped the bullet had found a mark, but he had no way of knowing. All for nothing. Gilead was mad as hell. And to make things worse, both kids were missing. He tried to focus on what Chazoom was saying.

"The girl, Eron. Her attackers didn't want her. Not alive, anyway. We have to find her. Well, I do. Keep her out of their clutches. And out of Singer's. If your boss finds her first, she will disappear. You know how this works." Chazoom stretched out on a bench, enjoying the winter sunshine.

"What do you mean by that?" Gilead was livid. "She may know where the training camp is and you'd delay us finding it? That's crazy."

"I will delay nothing. I just don't want her thugged about. Singer will have access to her—" He gave Gilead a sideways glance. "But under my supervision. Eron, listen to me, if things are handled correctly, we won't have any damaged goods. Shireen Obeid could be a real asset. I see her as a goodwill ambassador. She's a natural. She connects with people. I truly believe—"

Mozart chimed from Chazoom's pocket. He took out his phone.

"*Shalom.* 'Allo?" Chazoom stood up suddenly. He turned away and spoke quickly. "Are you safe? Both of you? Now, where are you…I can get to you, but I need your location. It's simple, just go to the end of the street, there are signs. And if you—"

Suddenly Gilead wrenched the phone away. "Now listen, this is Captain Eron Gilead. I want you to go to the nearest police—"

"It's not safe! Run! Run! Run!" screamed Chazoom into the phone.

He grabbed at the phone, which flew out of Gilead's hand onto the concrete pathway. Moments later, Chazoom was sitting on the grass verge, nursing a throbbing jaw.

"Those children trust me. I could have brought them in. I just didn't want the girl…hurt." It was not easy to speak.

Gilead ignored him. He kicked bits of Chazoom's broken phone as he walked away.

"You just going to leave me here? I could bring you up on charges, you know."

# Chapter 29

MICAH STARED AT THE PHONE he had borrowed, then handed it back to the sales clerk. They were in a convenience store. Shireen moved closer to him.

"You speak Mister Yossi?"

"Yeah. Then another bloke came on. That man from the bus, Captain Gilead. I didn't get it. Then someone shouted for us to run. Just run. Then the line went dead. Something's up, I suppose. Maybe it's your brother, I dunno."

"Where to run?" Shireen looked nervous.

"I don't know." Micah heard himself sounding as fearful as he felt. When they were fighting and running there was no time for fear. But now, that's all Micah could think about.

"I'm too young for all this."

"But we be okay. Okay?"

Micah looked into Shireen's eyes and somehow knew what she was trying to say. Beyond her skittishness, she seemed pretty solid. Good to have on his side. He hoped she felt the same.

Micah grabbed Shireen's hand and pulled her across the boulevard. He heard a screech of brakes and froze. Instinctively he looked to his side just as strange, pulsating music hit the back of his head. It sounded horribly familiar. Micah furrowed his brow and looked behind. An Arab guy was leaning out the passenger side of a beat-up white Mercedes, waving.

"Hey, Shabbos boy! Remember me, my brother?"

Micah grinned with relief as he recognized the toothy taxi driver from the previous Friday. He even turned off the ghastly music.

Shireen held back.

"He's okay, I know him. Come on."

"So, you get cleaned up, Shabbos boy? That was some ride, uh? Oh man, oh man! You must stink house bad." The cabbie waved a hand in front of his eagle beak and laughed, but not spitefully.

"Yeah, I was a bit of a mess."

"I don't forget you. I don't forget a good tip. Get in, my brother, get in. And your pretty friend. Two for one. Special friend rate."

They both clambered in. The cabbie looked at Shireen as she sat back in her seat, then the weird music kicked back in as he drove off at killer speed.

"Where you to be, eh, Shabbos boy? London? Ramallah? Huh?" he yelled above the din.

"Old City, the New Gate, er—"

*"Er? Er?* Mehmet." The cabbie laughed. "My name is Mehmet! You forget to remember."

Laughing, Mehmet gunned the car even faster. The discordant music still blared. "You know this song? You speak Farsi?" He glanced at Shireen.

"No." Shireen glared back coldly.

Micah thought the awful song summed up the day. And it wasn't over yet. He sighed and looked at Shireen, who kept staring out the window, into a world she was trying to avoid. Micah tapped her on the shoulder. It was easy to take her hand in the street and pull her along, but here, in the back of the cab, it felt awkward.

He wanted to be done with this, but he knew he had to help this girl. They were connected somehow. He didn't know what he was doing, but he knew he was doing the right thing. He tried to focus. Tried to recall what Chazoom had said on the phone. He wanted to meet up. Then it got fuzzy. Someone was shouting to run.

Something bad must have happened.

The music changed, blared loud again. Micah pulled a pained face.

"Turkish. You remember? The music. You like, uh? No like?" Mehmet was in his groove.

"I want to go home," Shireen blurted out suddenly.

"Where is home? Mehmet get you there."

"Just get us to the New Gate," Micah said firmly. He looked at Shireen and said with all the confidence he could muster, "You can't go home right now. It's not safe. Got to hold on. All right? We'll find my friends at the New Gate. They will help us. You will be safe."

"I make trouble for people I do not know. Why God make me this way?"

Micah fell silent, then put his hand on her shoulder. He wanted to give her a hug, and make her feel better, but he couldn't. So he punched her instead. Shireen let out a yelp and he saw wildness in her ice-blue eyes. She no longer looked like a scared rabbit. More like an angry raccoon.

"You hit me!"

"Sorry, sorry. It's just something, in England, that mates do, and we're mates, sort of. Okay?"

"Okay." Shireen mulled over what he said. "We mates?"

"We are. Us. You and me. Mates. Absolutely." Micah stared straight ahead.

"Mates," Shireen said this new word to herself, quietly smiling.

"What's funny? In case you've forgotten, we're in deep yogurt."

"I am with you. Is enough."

"Gordon Bennet."

"Who is this Gordy Bennet? You say about Gordy Bennet before. He is a mates?"

"No. *Gordon* Bennet. It's an oath, you know? Swearing. It's a nice way of saying 'gor blimey,' which is Cockney for 'God blind me.'"

"God blind me? But is shocking oath. Gordy Bennet!"

When they reached the New Gate, Micah offered his thanks and paid Mehmet, who waved to them as they ran across the highway, over the light-rail tracks, and through the gate into the Old City. They ran down a sloping alley into the ancient precincts, and when they stopped, Micah grabbed at Shireen's arm.

"Now stay here. I'll be right back."

He retraced his steps, hugging the wall at the awning of the gateway. He looked out. Mehmet was still there, making a phone call. Micah went back to where he'd left Shireen.

"That cabbie, he's still there. Making calls. Maybe he's tipping someone off about us, about where we're going. Maybe. Or maybe not. I dunno."

"But you say him is your friend? And now he betrays you, and—"

"I saw him looking at you funny-like. I don't know. But why take chances? Jaffa Gate. Come on."

"But your friends. They are here at New Gate. No?" Shireen's mouth set in a kind of frown, and he could tell her teeth were clenching because her cheek muscles bulged. Micah did that when he was annoyed and didn't want to show it.

"I just said that to throw the driver off the scent, you know? Just in case."

Shireen nodded as if she understood. Sort of.

They reached the Jaffa Gate within minutes. People were shouting in different languages. Babel. Tour operators waving pennants or holding up umbrellas were trying to herd their groups out through the gate.

No sign of Yimca and his troupe.

Micah and Shireen headed down David's Street, and then north toward the bazaars in the Muslim Quarter. Micah checked any open space in the hope of finding his friends. No luck. Just as he got to a tiny intersection, he realized he was on his own. Shireen wasn't there. He spun around, his eyes darting back and forth. He couldn't see her anywhere. His mouth dried and his heart pounded. He walked back, looking and looking and looking.

Somehow she had vanished. Just melted into the crowd.

# Chapter 30

"SHIREEN! SHIREEN!" Micah called her name again and again.

Had she been grabbed? The horrible thought bounced around his head. He retraced his steps as best he could, furtively glancing this way and that. He shouted for her again. People turned and stared. Micah ignored them. He didn't care what they thought. He had never been more scared. Then he saw her. Deep in the curve of a shadowy alleyway. Micah ran up to her and stared with ill-concealed anger. Shireen was gently placing a fluffy gold kitten on a stone ledge. The bewildered kitten turned on uncertain paws and meowed.

"Look, see?" She pointed as the tiny kitten scooted toward a larger, similarly colored cat stretching at the end of the ledge. "Must be mother. Little cat could not jump. I help him up."

"You did what?" Micah was really mad. "You went after a moggy? Are you mad? I thought you were gone. I thought to myself, she's been grabbed. Taken. You were gone. Gone. Get it?"

"Tuk, tuk, tuk!" Shireen grinned, unconcerned.

"This city is full of cats. Thousands. And you have to stop for this one. You got no bloody sense. Now come on!"

Micah grabbed her hand and yanked her forward. She pulled back and broke free.

"It was tiny kitten. It shake. In fright. Alone. Like you. Like me."

"Fine. Great. Stay here with the cats. *Shalom. Au revoir.* Bye, bloody bye," Micah yelled.

He stomped off, mumbling to himself. Then Shireen was suddenly in front of him, walking backwards, mimicking his scowl and his furious mumbles. That made him even madder. He tried to grab her. No use. As he ran forward, she uttered a shrieky laugh and ran ahead, out of range. Then she turned back again with a joke-angry face. Micah stopped and folded his arms as tightly as he could, still fuming. Shireen pretzeled her arms and fumed right back at him. Mirror perfect. She walked back to him, copying the same scowly mouth, the same scrunched brow. The same everything.

"Sorry, Mates. You mad me?" She pouted, but her eyes gleamed with humor.

"Yes, I'm bloody mad. Don't ever do that again."

He unknotted his arms and walked on. Shireen tagged along, just to his side and a little behind, like a scolded puppy. Micah stopped and indicated they should walk together.

"Owww!" Shireen had punched him hard in the upper arm.

"Mates!"

Micah shot her a look and saw she was grinning. It was hard to stay annoyed, even harder not to smile back.

Outside the Church of the Holy Sepulchre, Micah saw a few priests talking quietly in the forecourt. But no sign of his friends. He and Shireen sat together on the stone steps. And said nothing for the longest time. Finally, Micah stood. The magicians had not shown up. What could they do, anyway? he asked himself. They were kindly. But old, and not fighters, not soldiers. Maybe he and Shireen should find a cop. Micah didn't know. But he did know they couldn't hide out alone in an unfamiliar city. They had to find a phone, get help. They had no choice.

"Micah, thank goodness! Where are you?" Bernard beckoned frantically to Gilly.

Gilly beamed and clasped her hands together in a silent cheer. Bernard looked over to Colonel Raphael Singer.

"Can they get to the Jaffa Gate? We'll meet him there," Singer said, pointing hard to the phone. "Tell him we'll be there in twenty minutes."

He and Gilead had been at the Rothners' for over an hour, waiting for Micah to make contact. Chazoom had joined them just after they arrived. Singer had greeted the unconventional officer with gruff politeness. Gilead, still mad, gave him the cold shoulder. Chazoom had shrugged it off and made himself useful. He had casually interviewed each of the twins before heading back downstairs to sample Gilly's homemade donuts. Then Micah had called. The worst was over.

"Be there before you know it. You stay by the gate, Micah. See you soon. *Shalom!*" Bernard put down the phone. He looked exhausted.

"Right, Gilead. Let's go." Singer spoke directly to Bernard. "Mister Rothner?"

"I'll get my coat…"

"And I'll file a report. Need me for anything else, Raphael?" asked Chazoom, between bites.

"No." Singer was firm. "Stay and finish your donut."

# Chapter 31

THE CAFÉ WAS ON A SETBACK from a street parallel to the Mamilla pedestrian mall. Inside, the place was filled with the heady aromas of freshly ground coffee, Turkish tobacco, and sweat. Waiters shouted orders above the clatter of brass cups and saucers and steaming faucets spluttering hot water. Beyond an arched portico, a quiet, semiprivate area was curtained off from the main room. Just the way Jamal liked it. And there he sat with Shireen's perpetually angry brother, Farouz, and his friend, Aziz. The two who had failed. Jamal felt nothing but contempt for them both.

"Your eye still hurts you?" he asked with cloying insincerity.

"It is nothing." Farouz looked up, daring anyone to challenge his pain.

"You will be given another chance, Farouz."

"As it should be. I shall eliminate the seed of my father's shame." Farouz spoke haughtily.

"I did not make myself clear. That task is no longer yours to undertake, Farouz. You will be given a different opportunity. Inshallah—"

"But *this* is my opportunity, mine alone."

Jamal sighed. He smiled and quietly counted to ten.

"You will no longer be the instrument of your sister's punishment. The instrument will be joining us in the time it takes to drink my tea. Farouz, please? Coffee? Some mint tea, perhaps?"

"You talk of tea at a time like this?" Farouz scoffed.

Jamal closed his eyes and sipped his tea. He imagined being alone, far, far from this errant fool.

Farouz squirmed in his seat. He dipped a rag into ice water and bathed his eye. A wispy, amoeba-like cloud of blood curled in the water glass. Minutes passed. And then two men joined them.

The taller man had bulbous eyes and the complexion of aged beef. His companion was younger and skinnier. Jamal jumped up with surprising agility and embraced the taller man. Farouz was amazed by the effusive greeting. He watched as the taller man sat down opposite Jamal, smoothly, quietly, like a cat. Farouz noticed one of his hands was clawed, almost withered.

"This is Khalid. The instrument of whom I spoke."

Farouz knew of this man. By reputation. A respected hero of many reprisal actions against the Jews. He had also carried out three honor killings on behalf of grievously wronged Palestinian families who did not have the stomach, or the will, to undertake such a venture themselves. Loved ones were often overcome with grief or anger at the critical moment. Khalid took no payment, explaining that only the one who inflicted the stain of dishonor should pay.

"I am honored, honored," Farouz muttered.

Both he and Aziz attempted to bow, but Khalid would have none of it. He indicated with a wave of his withered hand that they should remain seated. He folded his fingers in the bend of a disjointed left arm. Khalid made no attempt to hide his infirmity. He introduced his friend as Mahmoud. A smile cracked within the younger man's mottled face.

And then Jamal got the call he had been waiting for.

"Time? Yes indeed, Leader, there is time. Time indeed." Jamal smiled to himself.

He turned off his phone and told the new arrivals that the intended target would soon be within minutes of their present location. Was it Providence? Was it somehow ordained? Jamal shrugged and aimed a glance heavenward.

"Our timing. Is fortuitous. Is it not, Mahmoud?" Khalid whispered in soft, measured tones. Thin red lips peeled back in a kind of smile revealing large teeth like a camel's.

Mahmoud nodded. "It is, God willing, a good omen."

Jamal gave Khalid a picture of Shireen. And a warning. "There are many police in this area. And Jewish troops."

"More challenging. For us. More humiliating. For them." Mahmoud grinned. "They will not even know it happened, until the life, it flows away—"

Farouz noticed that Mahmoud was much smaller than Khalid, but wiry and strong. The two had worked together on previous occasions. They would encircle their target, then close in. One in the front, one in back. Walking quickly, they would call out greetings to one another before striking. They would employ a small paring knife with a pointed tip and a thick rubber grip. Larger knives were all very well, especially the curved khanjar, but for close-in work, they much preferred a smaller blade. Two thrusts. One from the front, one from behind. No escape. And then the two would be gone, hardly breaking their stride, leaving their victim almost unaware that death cuts had been dealt with near surgical precision.

"Take him, too. The one who attacked me. A Yahuda." Farouz spat. He stood up so quickly he almost knocked over his chair. "I will go with them."

Suddenly his arm was in a grip as tight as a hangman's noose. Khalid released him just as quickly. Farouz slumped back into his chair.

"Farouz, Farouz, sometimes—" Jamal shook his head in disbelief.

"You keep me from my sacred task," Farouz fumed, nostrils flapping.

"Fool! You are as droppings from a dung tree," Jamal said in an intense whisper. "If your dead-to-you sister sees you, she will slither away faster than a reed snake. Do I make myself plain?"

Farouz looked dejected, but he nodded. Jamal turned to Khalid.

"Now go, my friend. Before time squeezes opportunity from our fingers."

The tall man stood up, waved his withered hand, and left without a word. Mahmoud followed him. Jamal sipped more tea. Soon it would be over, he thought. He cared nothing for the shame Farouz had suffered. But he did care about the girl. Sadly she knew too much. She had met others, many others. Seen so much. The villa, the secret village. A pity.

Jamal put down his cup, carefully dabbed his mouth, and smiled to himself as he recalled his short time with Shireen. A bundle of mischief if ever there was one. He sighed inwardly. He had said good-bye to her. A bittersweet parting for him. Hard to imagine Shireen was threatening the very destiny she was supposed to fulfill. Inshallah. He hoped her place in Heaven would still be assured, and prayed she would have a good death.

# Chapter 32

Getting back to the Jaffa Gate was easy. Shireen knew a shortcut, and Micah was happy to follow along. Suddenly Shireen stopped. She looked around, confused. But not for long. She pointed to a wide stone stairway and sprinted forward.

"Thanks for waiting. Gordon Bennet." Micah jogged faster to keep up.

He felt a wave of anxiety wash over him. He stared at every face he saw. He imagined Shireen's brother, or one of his crazed friends, leaping out at them. Shireen picked up on Micah's nervousness. She stayed close to him as they headed north.

They reached the rendezvous point, and there they waited by a wall, on the inside but with a view of the forecourt just beyond the Jaffa Gate. They watched locals milling around, taxi drivers looking for the odd tourist leaving the Old City.

Shireen noticed a very tall man walking toward them. Someone she knew? She dismissed the thought. He disappeared in the throng. Micah kept checking his watch and looking about for Uncle Bernard.

*"Him! It is him, the thief!"*

The torrent of words came out of nowhere.

Micah recalled the frenzied voice but couldn't place it. Jogging his memory, images flipped over like cards in a deck. Then he remembered. The curled snake ring. The smarmy voice. The cigarettes. The running. Oh, crap me, he thought. It was the coin dealer the twins had tried to rob!

Alim-Alim jabbed a waggling finger at Micah. He shouted

again, and two young men were by his side. Angry looks of recognition contorted their faces. Micah's stomach turned as he remembered them, too.

"Seize him, my sons," said the coin dealer.

One of the men, Nessim, pushed forward, a little ahead of the other. He lunged past Shireen, a fist aimed at Micah. Then a sharp, acid-like pain coursed through his shoulder. His other hand shot up as a thin ribbon of blood appeared. Unseen and unsuspected, Khalid withdrew his knife like a whiplash. Alim-Alim's son clamped a hand to the wound, wondering how it had happened. He looked for his attacker in the crowd.

Micah was already pulling Shireen away. He didn't understand what had just happened, but he had seen the knife and the two belligerent sons of the coin dealer.

"That boy." Khalid yelled, pointing a withered hand at Micah. "A knife. I saw it."

"I saw it, too." Mahmoud went along with Khalid's ploy, but inwardly he seethed, knowing this young fool had deflected the killing blow aimed at Shireen.

"He cut me." Nessim called to his younger brother, Ridwan.

"My son. My son—" Alim-Alim's hands fluttered uselessly, then fingers turned to fists, shaking with rage. "Find him, Ridwan. Avenge your brother."

In a thoughtless spurt, Ridwan took off in pursuit of Micah and Shireen. Unknowingly he ran right past Mahmoud, who had started to walk in the same direction.

Khalid watched them leave. A chance for Mahmoud to prove himself, he thought. Today had not gone exactly as planned, but the outcome would be the same. And if not today, tomorrow. Khalid was a patient man.

# Chapter 33

Where a small cobbled street divided, Micah and Shireen stopped for a moment. He asked if she had seen the man with the knife, and if she knew him. Shireen shook her head. She had seen no knife, just a red face, a look of surprise in large eyes, and then people pushing and shouting. Micah had pulled her clear and she had seen nothing more.

"Someone knew we were there. I don't get it. I just— Oh, God, that little man, the one yelling. I remember him. I'm sorry, I'm…it's all my fault."

She squeezed his shoulder and nodded, as if she understood. "We must run, yes?"

"Back down here, come on." Micah charged ahead, down the twisting alleyway. His voice echoed and bounced across the ancient stone. Moments later, he stopped against a curving wall. He didn't know where to run next. The street split into a stepped alley one way and a cobbled, curving path the other.

Micah headed into the alley but halted when Shireen shouted to him. She pointed to two signs propped up on the crumbling sidewalk. No exit. In three languages. The signs were self-standing, plinthed on wide wooden boxes that were propped with sandbags to keep them upright. Beyond the signs, Micah could see the alleyway narrowed to nothing, just construction scaffolding and a small cement machine. A dead end.

"Run, go on." He could barely speak. He leaned on a sign, exhausted, unable to go on.

"No," Shireen said.

"I can't. Run. Anymore. Don't you get it? You've got to keep moving. They'll kill you."

"No. You are Mates. I stay. I will spit my death in their face." She spat defiantly to show she meant business.

He looked at this strange girl who would not run from her killers if it meant running from his side. Micah sighed, tried to think. He walked into the dead-end alleyway, looking from one side to the other. When he trotted back, Shireen could not believe what she saw. A smile. Micah was smiling.

When they both heard the ominous clatter of footsteps on stone, just seconds away, Micah nodded to Shireen. And then the two of them completely disappeared.

# Chapter 34

ALIM-ALIM RAVED ON, playing to the gathering crowd until Eron Gilead grabbed his shoulder and his attention. He turned slightly and stared up at the man holding a picture of the runaways.

"It is him." As much for Gilead as for the mob, Alim-Alim recited Micah's crimes once more. "The Yahuda, he stole from me and cut my son. Police? Bah! Where are police when there is blood on the streets?"

"He did what?" Gilead was startled by the coin dealer's accusations.

"Look. Use your own eyes. The blood of my firstborn. How he bleeds!" Alim-Alim gestured toward Nessim.

"The girl, was she with him? Look, please look." Gilead now pushed the picture close to the injured man's face, forcing him to focus. Nessim squinted and nodded.

"Yes. She was with the boy. They ran back into the old quarter."

Gilead took off through the gate just as a medical team was arriving. Colonel Singer and his troops followed and began searching the immediate vicinity. His face grim, Singer told Uncle Bernard to wait by the car. Bernard didn't need to be told that something had gone horribly wrong.

Mahmoud stopped running. He leaned into a doorway. He listened. And heard nothing except his own raspy breath. The children were hiding, he knew it; he could almost smell their fear.

He could not see the vengeful youth who had run just ahead, but Mahmoud kept him within earshot. He had been following the sallow-skinned son of the coin dealer since the Jaffa Gate.

He knew he was out for blood, but for death? Mahmoud thought not. He peered around the doorway. Just yards away, he spotted Ridwan looking beyond some detour signs at the entrance of the alleyway. The young man stared at the demolished walkway and crept out of sight into the depth of the alley. Then he reappeared and kicked a sandbag.

Mahmoud watched as Ridwan took off down a well-trodden cobbled path, then he stepped into the light. He surveyed the small building site, the piled planks, the piles of sandbags. He stepped into the deserted alley. Halfway down the path, he stopped. He leaned into the wall and listened, as if the old stones might speak. He felt the knife in his pocket, held it tightly in his hand, seeking its fleshy scabbard, willing him on to the kill.

Gilead was still searching for the missing teens. Ever watchful as he jogged down the near-deserted streets and narrow thoroughfares of the Old City. No luck. A wrong turn led to the edge of the Muslim Quarter, still packed with locals going about their business. Gilead turned back toward the Jaffa Gate. He had been running in circles and he knew it.

# Chapter 35

A FILMY, GOLDEN NET began to descend over the city, softening the buildings, sharpening the shadows. It was almost dusk. A sudden pain seized Micah's leg. He cried out. He knew he shouldn't, but it was too late. His leg jutted forward and the sign that hid him toppled over.

He reeled over, gasping at the pain. Shireen emerged from the second sign and crouched beside him, pounding his leg with a flattened palm.

"Stop it. Bloody hurts," Micah rolled to his side.

"Is better for you soon. Perhaps, yes?" she asked hopefully. "I do more."

She flipped her hair over one shoulder so it wouldn't get in her way and got to work. Her fingers now worked slowly and firmly. She looked very serious, intent on what she was doing.

"Muscle jumble up. Not good, Mates."

"What did you do?" Micah propped himself up on an elbow. The hard knot in his thigh was starting to twist free.

"Magic." She smiled a sly smile.

"Very funny."

Micah stumbled as he tried to stand. With Shireen's help, he limped to the side wall.

"Got a cramp, stuck in that bloody thing." He pointed to the base of the wooden plinth.

"That bloody thing work good, Mates," she said.

Knowing they could not outrun their pursuers, Micah had outsmarted them. They had pulled the sandbags free from both plinths. Then they positioned the signs at a forty-five-degree angle so that someone walking down the center of the alley, between the plinths, would see nothing. If a pursuer walked by the wall, Micah and Shireen would be exposed. But no one would do that. At least Micah had hoped not. Once Shireen was out of sight in one plinth, Micah climbed inside the other. He could hardly breathe. He imagined Shireen curled up, as snug as a snail in her wooden shell. And there he was, like a stuffed pudding bursting at the seams of a baking tin. Uncomfortable though it was, he stayed put. Hidden away, almost in plain sight. Until he got that leg cramp.

"Is it safe now?" Shireen looked around.

"I don't know." Micah shook his head. "I saw two men, they both left. So I suppose we're all right for now."

Shireen stretched like a cat, then jumped up and shook her arms at the sky, breathing deeply. "I feel free, the sun on my head, feel good, Mates."

Very strange, Micah thought, she is definitely strange. He smiled and rolled his eyes.

"I saw them go down there," he said, pointing. "Come on."

They took off down the cobbled street, looking around cautiously. Micah saw no one. He looked up at a clear streak of sky that shimmered above them like dark-blue silk.

"The night tide. It comes in." Shireen was also looking skyward. "Drowns the sun."

"Is that what it does?" Micah smiled, without much humor. "One way of looking at it."

"Now we find your friends, yes?"

"That's the trouble—" He shook his head despondently. "I just don't know where they are."

"Maybe go home?"

"Go home?" Micah's face brightened. "Home, yes! That's where they'll be going. They won't be doing any more shows now. They would've called it a day ages ago."

"What they call day? I don't understand."

"Look, thing is, I don't know where they *are.* But I know where they will *be.* Eventually."

"Eventually?"

# Chapter 36

Bernard was in the car ahead, just him and a driver. "You can lead the way," Singer had suggested, but the truth was he didn't want to travel with Bernard Rothner. It would be awkward. Singer would not be able to talk shop. Or let off steam. He grunted.

"The coin dealer's son? The one who was stabbed, is he…?" he asked.

"He'll live." Gilead looked at his boss. "You think Micah did it?"

"The Montsees boy? Not a chance." Singer shook his head, took off his glasses, and dug his fingers into the sides of his forehead before adding, "But this knife business, it concerns me…"

Gilead rather liked his commanding officer; he was bluff and gruff, didn't shout but growled like an old bear. He even resembled one. And he could lead. His men, Gilead included, knew he would never ask them to do something he wouldn't do himself. And he could go beyond the moment and come up with conclusions that were often dead on. Although Gilead would never tell him for fear of incurring his wrath, the truth was, Raphael Singer would have made a good detective.

The two cars pulled up outside the Rothners' home. Singer went in first. Within minutes, the failed rescue was replayed for Gilly's benefit. She busied herself making coffee and putting out cookies, trying not to think the worst. Zeke seemed interested, but registered none of his brother's dismay.

Singer would not sit. He was trying to give the impression that everything possible was being done. His stiffness and natural awkwardness lent credence to this posture of confidence.

"There was a knife. Tell me, did—?" Eyebrows raised, Singer shot a look at Gilead.

"Micah, sir."

"Did Micah own a knife, to your knowledge?"

"No, no, he's not that kind of boy." Gilly was outraged and protective.

"Oh, Ima, you don't know him." Zeke was surly.

"Shut up, Zeke," said Jakey wearily.

"The coin dealer. He said the boy stole from him. From his shop. You know of this?"

"You went to the coin shop last week, all three of you." Bernard crossed his arms. "Well?"

"Micah stole nothing." Jakey spoke with conviction.

"Why're you protecting him?" asked Zeke, feigning shock. "Micah was shoplifting."

"I don't believe it." Gilly shook her head. "Not Micah. He's a good boy, and after what he did, he's a hero. He would never…steal."

"So why did the dealer accuse him?" Gilead asked.

Silence. Jakey squirmed lower and lower in his chair.

"Micah had friends? In the Old City?" Singer changed tack.

"Yes, magicians, you know, itinerants. Gypsies. Street performers. Never liked him going there but—" Bernard shook his head despairingly. "Most of the time, we had no idea where he was."

"You have reason to fear these people?"

"No. Micah adored them; they were teaching him magic." Again Gilly came to her nephew's defense. "It's Micah's hobby. He's a magician, he does tricks. Really very good."

"We never met them," Bernard shrugged.

"The man's name is Yimca."

"It's Hindu or something. Sanskrit. I don't know," Bernard

added, not too helpfully.

"Gypsy," said Zeke.

"Not at all." Gilly beamed. "Yimca took his name because of all the shows he used to do at the YMCA. Isn't that funny? Made me laugh when Micah told me."

"Does he have a last name, this Yimca?" asked Gilead.

Gilly shrugged apologetically.

Beyond the fact that they were an eccentric bunch of mixed nationalities, Gilead could glean nothing more.

"One thing—" Singer said, just as he and Gilead were leaving, "did any of you tell anyone about our rendezvous with the children this afternoon?"

Everyone shook their heads.

# Chapter 37

MICAH AND SHIREEN MADE THEIR WAY across the Old City through a jigsaw of ancient pathways, emerging into the narrowness of St. James Street. Moving quickly around the Zion Gate, they followed a sidewalk, passing several trinket shops and a cat catching the last of the afternoon sun.

Just before the entrance to the Cardo in the Jewish Quarter, Micah saw the open parking lot, right where he remembered. The lot was always full because the Quarter was only open to pedestrian traffic. A nearby falafel stand was not doing much business.

They skirted the lot's outside edge and approached the magicians' old city bus from behind so the vendor couldn't see them. Micah was not taking any chances.

"This is their bus. It's where they keep stuff. For shows. They're bound to turn up eventually. And I think I know how to get inside. Come on."

Reaching beneath the undercarriage of the bus, he released a small wooden ladder. Then he pointed to the flap cut into the side of the bus.

"It's where the cat gets in. You can, too, you're skinny enough."

"Me?"

"Yeah, I reckon. Just climb in, open the front door, and Bob's your uncle."

"Bob's your uncle?"

Shireen climbed up to the moveable flap and breathed in. She managed to squeeze halfway through. Then she clawed at air. She was stuck.

Micah heard a mumbled yell in Arabic. All he could see were legs kicking against the side of the bus. He grabbed Shireen's feet and pushed with all his might.

Shireen scrambled to get hold of something. Reaching across the floor of the bus, she grabbed hold of a strut and pulled herself forward, but not before a piece of metal snagged her thin cotton capris and the skin around her shin. She grabbed her leg and willed the pain away. She felt blood on her hand and tears in her eyes, but she clenched her teeth and didn't cry.

"You all right? You in?" Micah called up softly.

No answer. Shireen stood up and peered into the gloom. Many of the seats had been removed and replaced with large boxes and crates. On one seat she saw a stack of magazines that smelled musty and dry. Shireen groped her way to the front of the darkened bus and opened the door as fast as she could.

Micah bounded up the two steps inside the bus well. He pushed the door closed, then noticed blood on Shireen's hand and the jagged cut on her shin.

"How did you manage that?" He sounded more interested than sympathetic.

"Okay, it's okay. Water. Please. Yes?"

He gave her a bottle he found on a crate and helped her sit down. She drank some and sprinkled water over her scrape. It stung but then felt a bit better. Micah moved through the half-darkness to the back of the bus. He felt around for the flashlight he remembered seeing. He found an old metal tin and unbuckled its hasps. A first aid box.

Gently he pulled back the material of Shireen's pants, just above the cut. Within a minute, the nasty scrape on her leg was disinfected and expertly bandaged.

"Not too tight?" Micah looked up. He'd kept the flashlight on the floor, shining under the seat and not out the window, scared it might attract attention.

"You are good with this, Mates. Like doctor."

"Got a badge for it, you know, first aid. Scouts. Got a badge for most everything." He shrugged. "I just wanted to get as many as they got."

"Who is 'zaygot'? What is—?"

"Kids in my troop. Didn't help, though. They just thought I was too pushy, getting too clever."

"Tuk, tuk, tuk."

"Yeah, well, that just about describes it." He fished two wrapped candies from his pocket. "Have one. Go on. You've had a bit of a shock. Sugar's good for shock."

"'I chew the food of sweet and bitter fancy.'" Shireen stuck the lemon candy out on her tongue.

"Shireenspeare. That's you, innit? Gordon Bennet."

"Gordy Bennet." Shireen smiled back at him.

"So how do you know all this Shakespeare stuff then? I mean, you're really good at it. Better at Shakespeare lingo than ordinary chit-chat. Bit odd, really, but clever all the same."

"I learn from school. And books. Speaking books, yes?"

"Then you learned all that stuff by heart?"

Shireen thought for a moment before she replied. "Heart. Yes, by my heart. I learn. I like that."

Micah mumbled something about saving batteries, then he turned off the flashlight.

"The light, Mates, please! I don't like the dark."

"Okay, okay," Micah said quickly, and switched it back on.

Shireen breathed with relief. Micah flicked the light over a large lacquered cabinet painted like an old Chinese pagoda.

He gave Shireen the flashlight. She was grateful for that, but she noticed he was smiling and knew he was up to something. But what?

Micah opened the double doors on the front of the chest-like box, then directed Shireen to shine the light inside. It was empty. Closing the doors, he clapped his hands and twiddled his fingers as if casting a spell. Shireen giggled. Micah stopped his antics, and crossed his hands until she stopped. He reopened the cabinet. Something had appeared and almost tumbled out. It was a gorilla. Hairy and huge, with red glass eyes and tombstone teeth set into a great big smile like a TV host's.

Shireen almost dropped the flashlight. Micah pulled the overstuffed animal into full view, and both took a bow. Micah scratched under his arm, did *ooh-ooh* monkey noises, and made the hairy beast scratch himself, too. Shireen laughed and applauded and clicked her tongue until Micah had to shush her up. She was a good audience; he liked that.

Gingerly she walked around the box. Then she plunked down in a seat, totally flummoxed. She tapped the seat beside her. Flattered, Micah sat down. At school, girls would run a mile rather than sit next to a boy, especially him.

"Tell me your trick. How you do it, Mates?" She smiled her winning smile.

"Can't tell you that. Against the rules. And keep that light down."

# Chapter 38

The glittering light on the Old City walls had all but lost its luster, along with the golden sheen that had filled Mehmet's eyes. He had been looking for the kids for hours. This ruin of a city, he thought miserably, with so many ins and outs a man could lose his own shadow. Reluctantly he headed back to his cab. As he rounded a corner, he stopped in his tracks, and his breath caught in his throat. His guardian angel was still perched on his shoulder! For there was Shabbos Boy. And the Palestinian girl, the one on TV, not twenty feet away. Mehmet was so excited he almost called out to them. Wisely he did not.

He followed them as they turned into a parking lot nearby and disappeared. But where? Perhaps they had jumped into a parked car? He circled the lot like a prowling shark. It was now almost dark. There was some light in the Jewish Quarter, but soon all the shops would be closed. Things did not bode well. He could almost hear the wings of his guardian angel flap away in disgust. Then, just for an instant, he saw a thin ray of light inside an old bus. As the light shone upwards, Mehmet's hopes rose, also. He scurried around the side of the vehicle and heard muffled voices. It was Shabbos Boy and the bomber girl, *in that ancient bus!* But why?

Mehmet didn't care. He had things to do. First off, he had to get back to his cab, his phone, and his device.

To save time, he took a taxi. Paid the exact fare and gave no tip. On a side street by the New Gate, he found his illegally parked cab, pulled the ticket off the windshield, and tore it up. He never paid tickets. If he paid one, the Jewish would give him more.

Best not to pay any. A few minutes later, he was back in the lot by the Jewish Quarter. The bus was still there. So were the kids. Now it was time to get to work.

"More magic trick for me?" Shireen raised her finely shaped eyebrows into soft arches.

"More magic trick... You got a nerve," Micah scoffed gently.

He was getting tired. But he took out a coin and placed it on the small apron-table. His fingers turned in circular, mesmerizing movements over the coin. He lifted his fingers from the tiny tabletop. The coin had disappeared.

"That is—how did you?" Shireen was happily confounded.

Micah reached behind her neck and from a soft wave of hair pulled out the coin.

"Do again! But wait. I make it so I see best."

Shireen picked up the flashlight and focused the beam onto the miniature stage. Again Micah placed his fingers over the coin, which he once again rubbed clean away.

"Clever, Mates! Show me!"

"Not now. One day."

"One day?" Shireen turned down the light. Micah noticed she looked sad again.

"You hungry? I am."

Inside the brightly lit newsroom of *The Jerusalem News,* the night staff worked in near silence. Even the bank of TV screens on the far wall projected silent images. Sometimes they broadcast the same story and the screens would resemble a flattened Rubik's cube waiting for someone to twist them into one complete image. But no one ever did. In this sequestered environment, a land-line telephone rang at an empty desk. A woman got up and lifted the relic to her ear.

"*Jerusalem News.*" She spoke mechanically, wishing the message center had picked up. Two other reporters looked over as the woman suggested the caller contact the police.

"This exclusive, no one else knows. Only me." Mehmet was getting impatient. "A picture is worth a thousand dollars!"

"Words. A picture is worth a thousand words."

"What? You quibble at me?" Mehmet stared at his phone with a look of bewilderment.

"We do not pay for stories."

"You do not pay for stories? The paparazzi make thousands on this kind of picture."

"The tabloids. They pay." The reporter gave the caller the number of a news broker, wished him good luck, and re-cradled the phone.

Mehmet slammed his phone shut. Good luck? She wishes me good luck? He seethed, then started yelling at empty air about how cheap the Jewish were. After he calmed down, he called the number the journalist had given him.

"How much?" The news broker was direct.

"Two thousand," said Mehmet, not specifying a currency. A clever ploy, he thought.

Silence. Heavy breathing. Mehmet was about to say one thousand Israeli when the broker said he would be called back in the time it took to smoke three cigarettes.

"Be quick," he blustered. "I'm a fast smoker."

The voice laughed, unflustered. The laughter melted into dead air. Mehmet wished he'd asked for three thousand. Now he had to wait for three cigarettes to burn out the time. He wished he hadn't quit smoking.

# Chapter 39

Leaving Shireen with the flashlight, Micah took off in search of food. He did not have to go far. The rich, spicy aromas coming from the vendor across the lot drew him like water up a straw.

Back in the bus, the two stowaways ate in silence. Micah was glad he had ignored Shireen when she said she wasn't hungry. He had bought one shawarma, hot sliced turkey and crunchy salad bits in pita, and one falafel in case she was vegetarian. She was not, so they shared. Both sandwiches were inhaled in moments.

Micah handed Shireen a paper napkin.

"We should try and get some shut-eye. Sleep a bit."

Shireen dabbed her mouth, then her eyes. "Sorry—"

"What's up? Didn't you like the sandwich, then?"

"No, I mean yes. I am happy with our food."

But she looked sad, not happy at all. He was baffled. Girls, he thought, were like tricks that fooled him. If only he knew their secret. Especially the secret to this one. This one most of all.

"We are on a bus. Again," Shireen said finally.

"Don't think of that."

"I have to think. What I have done. Almost done. On bus. Not rehearsal. Not play. It all become real for me, you understand? I felt it. In me. I become death. I did not know before. You must believe, Mates, I did not know until then."

"Just all caught up with you, I suppose, but when it did, you knew it was wrong. Everything inside you said it was. And that was good. It was. It is. Now get some kip—sleep."

Micah folded a cloth and propped it on his shoulder. Shireen leaned into the makeshift pillow, cool on her cheek. Despite the dark, she felt secure enough to close her eyes.

"Thank you, Mates," she whispered.

# Chapter 40

Everything had taken longer than Mehmet had imagined. The phone calls back and forth. The waiting. Having to go and meet the buyer. But he felt good about the night's work. He looked around the small café. Hanging just below the high ceiling were sails of cigarette smoke billowing with expired breath. Mehmet sat across from a stocky man who seemed to sweat. A lot. He took out a wad of dollars. Dollars! Mehmet eyed the money greedily.

"For you, my brother." The man slid the money across the table.

Mehmet started counting it.

"Please," the fat man covered Mehmet's hand, "you insult me to my face."

"A thousand apologies, I did not mean—" Mehmet stuffed the bills into his pocket, no longer counting, not even looking at them. "I was not thinking. Some people, not you, but some—"

"I understand, my friend." The man held up a hand in a peaceful gesture. "Now, for me?"

"The girl's location. You can take pictures. Good, good pictures."

Suddenly the fat man was on his feet. "Where are these children?"

"They are on an old bus. In a parking lot."

"Then we go. You will take us to them."

Who was this *us?* Mehmet picked up on that. He glanced over his shoulder. His eyes widened. It was hard to hide his fear when he saw a tall, thin man with a withered hand standing there. And another man, wiry, smaller and sallow-faced. The men loomed over him like ominous shadows.

"You with the Brotherhood?" Mehmet gulped. "I called the

tabloids, I did not—"

"You spoke to someone who gathers and sells information. We offered the best price."

"I am not political."

"We all serve God, do we not?" The fat man stopped smiling. "Now we move."

Mehmet felt himself sweating. And not from the heat of the night. Walking out of the café, he had the distinct feeling he was under guard.

Darkness still clung to the early morning like the last guest at a party. Micah woke with a start. His flailing arms roused Shireen. She started spouting Arabic before Micah shushed her, whispering that people were outside. He pointed to the floor. She understood. Slowly they crouched down and slithered toward the back of the bus.

The front door opened.

Micah stared at Shireen, terrified. She shot her hand across the floor. Micah took it. Her grasp was firm and reassuring. He squeezed his eyes shut. His heart seemed to be pounding in his head. Then he heard the door of the bus slam shut. The bus began to shake. A sudden out-take of breathy air, like a hundred kids blowing out candles on the biggest birthday cake. A piercing metallic scream shot through the underbelly of the bus. Then a gurgling, ticking sound took over.

They were moving.

Followed by his new employers, Mehmet drove into the parking lot just as the first rays of sunlight made tentative stabs into the morning. He looked from left to right, right to left. No bus. Fool! Fool! Fool! Mehmet cursed himself. He had not thought to activate the tracking device in his car until now. The monitor in the dashboard blinked with mocking regularity. Too late!

As yet, the three following, the sweaty man and the two scary ones, didn't know the bus wasn't there. He could jackknife around and escape. They might give chase, but he knew the streets better than most, so he decided to chance it.

He started to accelerate into a turn, but the other car surged ahead. Both cars slammed on the brakes simultaneously. Mehmet tried to lock the doors. Too late. Instinctively he turned—and found himself staring at the point of a blade. A large knife held in a withered hand. The passenger door opened and Jamal swung into the cab. He smiled at Mehmet as he made himself comfortable. The other two stayed outside, keeping watch.

"You tried to leave without saying good-bye? Or were trying to deceive us? Either way—"

Jamal spoke at Mehmet but did not look at him. It was most unnerving.

"But they were here. Those children. On the bus. And the bus was here. An old Egged bus. I swear it. I don't know what happened. Keep your dollars. Here, take it."

Mehmet was very scared. He thrust the money towards Jamal, who casually brushed him aside.

"Can you not find them?"

"Oh yes, yes. It is not a problem. Look. See?" Mehmet pointed to his dashboard.

Jamal peered at the oblong green screen. A flashing red arrow was moving away from the city.

"A tracking device, I see. We shall have to borrow, yes?"

"No! I mean—it is embedded. To remove it from my cab will take hours."

"Then we shall take your cab," Jamal said smoothly, almost reasonably.

"But this is my living. I will need more money, you have not given enough."

The back door opened. Khalid slipped into the car. His head was bowed slightly.

"First you want to give the money back. And now..." Jamal glanced at Khalid. "And now, our brother's greed competes with his stupidity."

"Should I finish with him?" Khalid whispered.

Mehmet whimpered like a frightened animal. He pushed the car keys onto Jamal as he scrambled out with his life and his dollars. Jamal hardly noticed him going. The slow-moving arrow on the map had him mesmerized.

# Chapter 41

Gingerly Micah pulled himself up and peered around the pagoda-like cabinet, then plunked back down beside Shireen.

"It's my friend Walloo! He's driving," he whispered.

"Is okay?" Shireen looked anxious.

"Well, it will be—I mean, I'm pretty sure it will be. Once I explain everything."

But he knew that "explaining everything" might take a bit of time. In fact, it might take a lot of explaining. He wanted to come clean because he didn't want to get Walloo in trouble. But right then, getting out of Jerusalem without being chased, knifed, or beaten up didn't seem like a bad idea. Micah pressed his face to the corner of the window and tried to think. Then he closed his eyes and thought of nothing. Micah had no idea how long he slept, but when he woke up the bus was hardly moving.

"He saw me, he saw me," Shireen was repeating. "The Oily One. The Oily One is up there!"

"What are you—? Calm down," Micah whispered as forcefully as he could. "Whoever it is, he can't see you. The glass is tinted. You can't see in from outside. Who's this 'oily one' anyway?"

Micah looked out and up. All he could see was a stalled cab on the overpass ahead. Two men were looking into the engine. A third, a tubby man in sunglasses, was staring down at the jammed highway.

She told him about Jamal, getting more scared with the telling. Then the bus stopped. Without another word, Shireen dove to the floor and clawed her way towards the cat flap at the back of the bus.

Micah crawled after her and grabbed one of her ankles. "You can't, not now. We're sticking this out together, okay. Okay?"

Shireen stopped struggling. When she turned back around, Micah saw all the fear she felt. But the madness had subsided and he released her.

"Don't give up," he said, and held out his hand.

She took it and scootched over to him. The bus still wasn't moving.

"Why we are not going?" asked Shireen.

Micah looked out and realized why. Soldiers were moving between the lines of cars, searching each one methodically. When Shireen saw the troops, she was almost too terrified to speak.

"Why're you so scared of the Israelis? They're not after you."

"They are. They hate me." Her eyes flashed with tears frozen with terror. "The Jewish are the enemy of my soul. I hate them."

"And Mister Yossi, and Eron? And what about me? I'm also 'the Jewish.' You hate me, too?"

Before she had a chance to answer, the old crate of a bus started up and rolled forward slowly, like a tumbrel. A patrol was approaching and, on the bridge, the man who wanted Shireen dead was still watching.

"Mates," Shireen gulped, "what we do?"

"We disappear," Micah whispered.

"Again?"

"Again."

# CHAPTER 42

MICAH CRAWLED ACROSS THE FLOOR to the lacquered pagoda cabinet and clambered in, waving at Shireen to follow. Once inside, they scrunched up as small as possible. The interior was painted with large white and red stripes like shiny hard candy.

Micah unhitched two small catches. The box shuddered and two flaps the height of the box started to move and swing inward to the center of the box.

"There's a mirror surface on the outside of both flaps. They come together. At an angle, it looks like the box is empty. The shiny stripes help the illusion. Better than if it was black inside."

"Yes?"

"Remember the gorilla? You know, *ooh, ooh, ooh?*" Micah arched his arms and scratched his pits. Shireen smiled and nodded.

"Same thing. With this box, you can vanish stuff as well as produce something. Just don't talk. Sit well back. Relax. You'll see, but no one else will."

Shireen squeezed herself into the back wall of the box, folded her legs, and held her arms around them as tightly as she could. Micah followed in after her, then he drew the mirrored side panels of the box together, like the prow of a ship. Micah knew that from the front, the box would look completely empty.

As he pulled the mirrored flap panels together, the secreted part of the cabinet was plunged into complete blackness. And that's when it happened.

Shireen felt the sides of the flaps touch her face. Suddenly, she couldn't see or think, and all she could hear was a loud screeching, howling sound filling her ears. And it was her.

Micah couldn't see anything, either, but he knew what was happening. Shireen was clawing at the sides of the box, screaming in loud, sobbing bursts. Micah reached up, flipped open the catch, and released the mirrored panels. A shallow shaft of light flooded back in to reveal Shireen's fingers and hands wildly flaying about. Strangely her eyes were wide open but she could neither see nor hear Micah. Blind panic had seized her. Micah tried to restrain her arms, her hands, her fingers. He felt a searing pain along his chin as a nail swept by.

More light entered the box. A cat cried out in a harsh whine. A flash of fur, the whisk of a fat tail, and it was gone. Micah looked up. Walloo was staring down at them.

"You scared Flinter Toes." Walloo was calm.

Micah could not read his friend's mood at all.

"Hello, Walloo, fancy seeing you here—look, we're in a spot of bother. Well, more than a spot; more like a bloody great puddle, if you take my meaning. The bad guys, they're after us. Well, her, actually. Please don't give us up."

Walloo patted Micah's shoulder reassuringly, then peered into the box. Shireen was still crouching, staring. Reacting to nothing, to no one.

"You're all safe now. Come, young lady. Let me help." Walloo beckoned to her good-naturedly.

Shireen looked into the big man's gentle face and slowly reached for his outstretched hand. A moment later she was out of the box and hugging Walloo as though he were a long-lost friend. When she saw the scratch on Micah's face, she gasped, frightened by what she had done.

"Don't worry about it," Micah said. "Just don't do it again."

The cars behind started to honk. Walloo looked up and saw the traffic had moved a little. Two car spaces had opened up ahead of the stationary bus.

"Both need to hide. In second split, okay? And no screaming ab-dabs."

"We'll be as quiet as sand in an egg timer."

"As quiet as—I like that. Clever." Walloo nodded sagely. "Now, my lady, back in box."

"No!" Shireen started shaking her head and hands uncontrollably.

"She can't, she'll freak out again," Micah said.

"She can, I know how." Walloo leaned down and gently held her thin shoulders with his big hands. "You trust Walloo. Yes?"

Walloo was focused completely on Shireen, seemingly unaware of what was happening outside. Micah was not. The honking was getting louder. Someone was trying to pass the bus. The soldiers were getting closer. And the taxi that had scared Shireen so badly was still parked on the overpass.

Unconcerned, Walloo produced a thick scarf.

"Close eyes," he said quietly. "It is all right to do."

Shireen obeyed. With infinite care, Walloo blindfolded her.

"What do you see?"

"I see nothing."

"Nothing is good. Now lean back in box. And relax. There." He winked at Micah. "Now all good. Tickety-boo, like the way Colonel Jack say it. Now you, Micah, inside. Snuggle up."

Micah did as he was told. Walloo closed the box on them. Then he brought the inside panels together. Micah felt the darkness. It was close and oppressive. He shut his eyes and wished he too had a blindfold. He grabbed Shireen's hand.

The bus moved a few yards, stopped again, and the door was

opened. Clomping noises. Voices. Soldiers. Thudding noises. Shuffling footsteps. The bus was being searched. Laughter. Micah could recognize Walloo's voice.

Unexpectedly Micah heard tapping noises against the side panel of the box. Startled, he squeezed Shireen's hand more tightly.

The front of the box was being opened. Suddenly a loud, screaming growl filled the box. There were rapid scratching and hissing sounds. Then surprised gasps tumbled over incomprehensible swearing and nervous laughter. Flinter Toes! Micah realized Walloo had put the cat in the *front* half of the pagoda box, to provide the needed misdirection. And it worked. The soldiers searched no further. Chuckles and shuffling footsteps faded to nothing. Then the engine started up and the bus was on the move. And Micah knew they were safe.

"It's all right. I think it's okay. The soldiers. They've gone. Hang on." Micah leaned up and fumbled around the roof of the box, looking for the release clip. He opened the panel a crack, then yanked off Shireen's blindfold. She blinked and sighed, grateful for a glimmer of light. She leaned up on her elbows and returned Micah's smile. She gently touched the scratch on his face, then landed a tap on his shoulder with a soft fist.

"Call that a punch?" Micah said with relief.

# Chapter 43

Colonel Singer looked across at the magicians' vehicles just as they moved back onto the highway. The convoy consisted of a minivan with a roof that opened into a small trailer and an old Egged bus that looked like a small Greyhound cruiser. Gilead vaulted up the slight embankment to where his boss was standing, watching.

"The kids aren't on board, sir."

Gilead had sent a couple of soldiers to the old bus while he supervised the search of the minivan. Nothing was found. Except on the Egged bus. Gilead told his boss about it.

"A cat? Was it a black one? Magicians have black cats, I believe. So what did Mister Yimca and his elusive troupe have to say for themselves?"

"Hadn't heard from Micah in days. Had no idea what had happened."

"They don't watch TV? No computers? Phones? Luddites?" Singer asked.

"They heard about the girl, but didn't know Micah was involved. When I told them he was missing, they were upset—not faking. I told them to call if Micah got in touch."

"Where are they heading?"

"A place in the Negev. A farm. They gave me their location, contact numbers, and—"

Out of nowhere, opera music started blaring nearby. Singer rolled his eyes. Yossi Chazoom had deigned to put in an appearance.

He was in a little hybrid clown car, windows wide open so everyone got earfuls of Puccini, whether they liked it or not. The music finally ended and Chazoom ambled over, cradling a rolled-up golf umbrella like a rifle. Singer bristled. Chazoom was blithely uncaring. He flipped Singer and Gilead a salute of sorts, then opened the golf umbrella and spun it around, casting a large pool of shadow around himself.

"*Turandot,* 'Nessun Dorma!' Yes? No? Oh. Well, never mind. So, I heard the children were spooked. Got away." Chazoom zeroed in on the current problem. "And now we're searching highways and byways for them, yes?"

Singer mumbled something inaudibly insulting before heading back to the command car. It was going to be a long day. Ignoring Chazoom, Gilead watched the street performers drive away. He almost wished he could join them as they headed southwest, bound for the Negev, instead of being stuck at a checkpoint searching cars.

✦ ✦ ✦

Jamal pulled over on a spur heading back to the city. He wanted to be off the overpass, in a less conspicuous place, before calling his section leader.

"I saw the police showing pictures. They searched every vehicle, including the bus we had originally tagged. No one was found on board."

"I know."

"You know? How did you—?" Jamal was flustered.

"That is irrelevant, Jamal. The fact remains the girl disembarked somewhere without your knowledge. Is this not correct?"

"Ah, Leader, your grasp of the situation is perfect." Jamal could think of nothing else to say.

"Enough, you dung-eating dog! Mobilize our brethren. These errant children must be found. Then kill the girl. And the boy. If he interferes, deal with him also."

"Both children, Leader?"

"If the boy is in the way—must I repeat myself, Jamal?"

"No, my leader." Jamal swallowed hard as he put away his phone.

Nobody spoke on the journey back. Jamal reflected on what had transpired. How had he been deluded? And how did his boss know the children were not on the bus? And where was Shireen? Jamal stared at the electronic marker on the dashboard. It seemed to be winking at him, mocking him. Jamal turned it off.

# Chapter 44

At the imperceptible edge of the Negev Desert, the magicians' convoy pulled up at a truck stop. Farm produce and food stands were nearby. And camels. Saddled up in gaudy cloth and adorned with gold tassels like old-fashioned lampshades. Ten shekels bought a trip around the parking bays and gas pumps. There were no takers. Not then. So the camels sat on their haunches and chewed the air with languid disdain while they waited for a tour bus.

Walloo insisted the kids come clean. He said it would be for the best. They knew, deep down, he was probably right. Micah marched up to the van, Shireen and Walloo in his wake. Yimca saw Micah wave a tentative greeting but he remained aloof. He tried not to show how happy he was to see his young apprentice. Yimca folded his long arms like coils of rope. His eyebrows arched into question marks, and his eyes looked for answers.

"*Voila!* You were *ici.* All the time?" Lady Rianne gave Micah a hug.

"Not now, Rianne." Yimca spoke sternly. "Micah…if you had been discovered, all of us would have been upstream in a canoe paddling with a chapatti. You understand me?"

Micah explained what had happened, and why they had stowed away on the bus.

"Walloo?" Eleni looked at him sternly. "You should tell your Eleni before arranging rescues."

"They made their own arrangements, my darling. I was innocent." Walloo almost smiled.

"The police may see it differently. Technically we've kidnapped them," Colonel Jack scowled.

"Of course not," said Micah. "We were waiting for you lot, but we fell asleep and then Shireen saw that slob, the oily one, on the overpass. The one who wants her dead. Well, that did it for her."

"And how do you know this 'oily one' didn't follow you here?" Colonel Jack asked.

"We weren't found at the checkpoint, were we? And he was right there. Looking. Why would he follow an empty bus? So don't worry. We haven't dropped you in it."

"Got it all worked out." Colonel Jack raised his voice. "You took it on yourself to involve us in this—escapade? And you think we're not dropped in it?"

"I didn't know what else to do. I'm only fourteen," Micah yelled.

"There's that, I suppose." Jack calmed down, added, "Well, what's done is done."

"And *I* have done this. Do not blame Mates." Shireen grasped his arm protectively.

"Your loyalty is very touching, my dear, but it doesn't change a thing." Colonel Jack was gruff.

"A lot of people are looking for you." Yimca looked at Micah as if deciding his fate. Then he spoke again. "You will be making call. And you will be explaining all that has transpired. If your uncle and auntie are agreeable, you and Shireen may spend the night with us. But *they* will be making decision. Not us, not you. Them. You understanding? Now go and do."

"But my phone's dead."

Yimca reached up and grabbed at something. One by one, he opened his fingers, and there was a phone. He handed it over with a slight but solemn smile. Micah knew it was Yimca's way of saying he was no longer mad. Micah plugged in the number.

Uncle Bernard came on the line. After assuring him they were safe, Micah squirmed out the rest of the story. Then he handed the phone to Yimca, saying his uncle wanted directions. He would come first thing in the morning.

Colonel Jack shook his head in weary resignation. Without a word, he clambered into the van. The two women got on board. Micah and Shireen just stood there, not quite knowing what to do. Then Walloo honked the bus horn and beckoned them both back on board.

"We can go with Walloo?" Micah asked.

"He would be upset if you didn't," said Yimca with a chuckle.

Micah and Shireen raced each other to the bus. Shireen won, but waited for him at the door. Micah grumbled something about not being ready, Shireen just laughed and ran inside.

Soon the bus was speeding along and Walloo was telling his now legitimate passengers about the troupe's farm, Golden Terraces.

"We are going home," he told them, "to the desert once roamed by Abraham, Moses, and the children of Israel."

"It is holy place." Shireen stood up in her seat. "For all peoples."

Amazing, thought Micah. He wondered what it would be like.

The desert soon enveloped the landscape. The highway seemed like an intrusion. Huge sand dunes, gray with age, came into view. They appeared to be carved with straight sides and flattened tops piled in layers one upon the other, diminishing in size like stretched-out pyramids. The bus jolted and Shireen grabbed hold of Micah's shoulder for balance. She remained standing, looking out, unafraid, her hand on his shoulder. He wanted to touch her hand, but didn't want to be thought daft. So he just sat still, hoping her hand would remain where it was.

And it did.

# CHAPTER 45

THE LITTLE CONVOY TURNED OFF THE HIGHWAY and headed deeper and deeper into the Negev. The winding road became narrower, coarser. Micah and Shireen looked out on the barren landscape, where nothing seemed to flourish except scrub and turquoise bushes that grew out of rocks like bonsai rejects. They turned onto a track made of packed sand that looked like baked flour.

"Look," said Micah, grinning and pointing.

Shireen gasped with delight and strained to look out. A herd of gray-brown single-humped camels had suddenly appeared between the dunes moving in single file parallel to the road. They ignored the bus and just followed one another, trotting at some speed and with great purpose. A wild caravan. Nothing like the camels tricked up for tourists at the gas station. Micah and Shireen watched them until another dune rose up and they disappeared from view.

Shortly afterwards, Walloo pulled off the road and stopped. He wanted to show them something. They walked across the small road to the edge of a ridge. The view was breathtaking. The earth swooped down into a vast arid chasm. The escarpment was gashed and crumbling, like a huge cake broken into halves. A hundred feet below, on the flat valley floor, was a dry riverbed.

Micah stared down at the phantom watercourse, twisting along like a huge snake frozen by time. The farthest side of the ridge looked hazy and distant and strangely inviting.

The others honked and sped past. Golden Terraces was just minutes away. Walloo shooed his passengers back onto the bus.

They parked a short distance from the farmhouse, just beyond the expansive yard. Walloo clambered down from the bus with

Flinter Toes under one arm. As he handed him off to Colonel Jack, the cat wriggled free and ran into the shade to scratch out a hole in the earth.

"For him, the desert is one big litter box," Walloo said.

Colonel Jack harrumphed but left the cat to his business. He headed for a stone wall at the edge of the ridge beyond. Yimca walked toward Micah and Shireen who were looking toward the colonel, hesitant to follow him.

"What is this place, this is ancient wall, yes?" Shireen asked.

"Indeed yes," said Yimca.

"It looks like it was connected to a castle."

"It is connected to history, Micah. From the time of the Nabateans, when the ancient tribes of Israel roamed these parts," said the old magician, grandly. "Built, we think, to help collect rainwater. That wall has been stacked and re-stacked for thousands of years. Imagine."

Jack stood in the lee of the old wall, as if he belonged to it. He turned away from the breeze to light a cigar. Puffs of smoke plumed and blew away in gusts.

"I didn't mean to upset him," Micah said suddenly.

"Jack upsets himself. Set in ways. Some ways good. Some ways bad."

They walked back across the farmyard toward the house, the ladies following at a leisurely pace, enjoying the warm gold of the afternoon. The farmhouse was a one-story structure of whitewashed stone and cement blocks. Beside it stood a barn and a large storage facility. Between the two outbuildings were a couple of lean-to sheds and a few animal pens. In the terraced fields beyond, the stowaways spotted green and yellow blobs of tiny young peaches. Black irrigation piping connected every planting on the farm like veins bringing the body of earth to life.

With a clatter, the door of the farmhouse burst open and a rag-tag group appeared. A girl of about six was *plink-plunking* on an odd-shaped mandolin, and a boy a year or two older was feverishly crashing cymbals together. From the doorway, a man strolled forward playing a darabukka, a goblet-shaped drum. The noise the threesome made was not melodious but it was exuberant. Behind them, a young woman stood in the doorway, smiling and clapping to the music, welcoming the travelers home.

"*C'est formidable, non?*" Rianne laughed happily and started clapping along.

Everyone joined in. The joyful noise ended to laughter and applause. Walloo took a child in each arm, playing helicopter to their squealy delight. Amid the revelry, the woman grabbed Micah and Shireen and pulled them inside. There were rugs strewn across the paneled floors, plants blossomed in alcoves, and paintings hung from the white stucco walls. Shireen smiled at Micah and he smiled back. He felt as she did: the house was as cozy as a favorite blanket.

Introductions were made. Denesh and Aisha and their children, Manoush and Layla. Shireen was surprised to learn they were Muslim.

"And you are here," said Shireen, slightly puzzled.

"Yes, we are here. Like you." Aisha smiled enigmatically.

"You from India, like Yimca?" asked Micah.

"No, no, we are from Pakistan," Denesh chuckled. He was a short, wiry man with the complexion of Assam tea. He went on, "I am Ahmadi, a minority within Islam, one not met with much approval. Which means we pray with one eye always open. If you get my meaning."

"In Pakistan you must worship Allah all in the same way. We wanted to worship without worry," explained Aisha.

"In Israel? Why here?" Micah was confused.

"Why not? We have religious freedom in Israel. Our friends here are all different religions. Yimca and the Lady Rianne are Jewish, Eleni is Christian Copt from Egypt, and Walloo is Catholic from Hungary. And Colonel Jack—

"No one knows of him," Aisha shrugged. "But we all share the same God, do we not?'

Shireen nodded thoughtfully.

"And sometimes we pray—together," Denesh whispered conspiratorially. "In English."

"And not Arabic?" Shireen was shocked.

"Why not?" Aisha's smile was rueful. "Were you not taught that Allah knows all things?"

Shireen had never met such an unconventional Muslim woman. Even Miss Jehar would have been shocked by her attitude, her way of being. And her clothes!

"I do not wear the hijab," said Aisha, as if reading Shireen's mind. "I am devout. But…"

Shireen could see herself in Aisha, and it wasn't just the billowy silk top and skinny jeans she wore, and the hijab she did not wear. Shireen had found a kindred spirit.

"I believed in the rights, the freedoms I read within the Quran. The freedoms for women. But many of my kin believe I dishonored them. You understand?"

Shireen nodded. She understood only too well.

"How did you meet this lot?" Micah indicated his motley crew of friends.

"In Jerusalem. They gave us work. Portering and such. Then here—" Denesh held out his hand expansively. "They gave us a home. And a share of the land and its harvest."

"It is a place for our children to grow up without fear of—oh, look, poor man." Aisha hurried over and pried her rambunctious offspring from Walloo's tottering frame.

"The children get bigger or I get older." Walloo caught his breath.

"Both," said Eleni succinctly.

"Come, come..." Denesh beckoned to the group. "Aisha has surpassed herself."

"It is good to be home." Yimca breathed in on a smile and rubbed his long hands together in anticipation. "And home never smelled so good, I'm telling you."

Woodsy smells of cinnamon and saffron and roasted meat filled Micah's nostrils and made his mouth water so much it was almost painful. He followed the delicious aromas and peered into the fiery wood-burning oven. The embers glowed like bits of a broken sun. Pots were stacked in the oven's opening, trapping the heat and keeping food warm.

Soon the instruments were stowed away, and the children, Manoush and Layla, laid out plates around a large table. The great room in which they all gathered was big and airy, a combination kitchen, living, and dining area.

Micah suddenly realized everyone was speaking English. Except Rianne, of course.

"Micah, *chéri*—" Once she had their attention, she announced that Golden Terraces was in the "*Jardin* of Eden."

Micah smiled politely but didn't believe a word of it.

"It's true. Sometimes it comes back." Eleni leaned forward as if revealing a secret. "When it rains."

"We harvest rainfall as others harvest a prize crop." Aisha spoke almost reverentially.

"But less rain concentrates flavor." Denesh explained the benefits of run-off desert agriculture. "Too much water makes fruit big but little flavor. Our peaches burst with sweetness."

"And we grow flowers." Aisha pointed to the bouquet on the table. "Tulips, roses. We take them to the cooperative and they are sent all over the world."

"My mum loves roses," Micah suddenly remembered. He swallowed with difficulty. The young couple reminded Micah of his own folks.

Shireen punched his arm. Hard. She had noticed his sullenness. Not anymore. He turned to get her back but she was gone, slipping like an eel under the table. She popped up at the far end and made a face at him.

"*Mon dieu,* they act like children."

"We *are* children." Shireen laughed.

"Then do better." Eleni tried not to smile. "And where is dinner?"

"The lamb is resting," Denesh said nervously.

"It has rested enough. Bring!" Eleni was a woman of few words.

Denesh shrugged, then began to carve as Walloo thumped the table, knife and fork clutched in ham-like fists. Steam rose and the agreeable aromas of fire-roasted meat wafted across the room. Everyone started making *ooh* and *aah* noises.

While Rianne blessed the bread, Micah glanced around at this happy band and smiled. Other words were muttered. Different words by different people in different languages.

Vegetables and custard-colored rice were passed around, and Denesh served the lamb, which was savory and sweet and smelled of apricots and roses. It was, Yimca announced, the most delicious meal ever. Everyone agreed. After the feast, the table was moved back—it was time for dancing.

Shireen looked a little nervous at first, but, as the music played, she found herself drawn to it. Micah watched as she raised her arms and spun around, playing imaginary castanets, gliding, swaying to the beautiful yet plaintive music.

"She can samba," said Yimca admiringly.

"She's amazing." Micah was grinning.

"What is this music?" Shireen shouted.

"Portuguese." Yimca shouted back as he maneuvered Rianne around the floor.

"I do not understand this Portuguese."

*"Au contraire, chérie,* I think you do." Rianne laughed her tinkling laugh.

The mood of the music changed. Slow dance. Shireen moved toward her friend.

"Oh, no. Oh no. Get out of it." Micah shook his head, feet glued to the floor.

"Come on, Mates."

"Clear off!"

Ignoring him, Shireen grabbed his hand and pulled.

Micah stumbled forward. Without letting go of his hand, Shireen spun around and locked him up close. Micah breathed in fearfully. Fortunately she spun out again.

"The music, I never heard or felt. To dance. To do all this! I feel so alive." She looked happy.

He didn't know what she was talking about, but it didn't matter. He felt just as she did.

# Chapter 46

"Good dinner?" Jack was still standing by the wall that went nowhere, half a cigar clamped between his teeth.

"Fantastic. The best," Micah said.

Jack smiled to himself. A smoke ring billowed like the wings of a tiny bird, and then it was gone. The smell lingered like wet leather, and Micah tried to get upwind of it.

"Lots of food left. If you want any."

"Heard the singing. The music. Made me smile." Jack looked at the wide horizon. "You should go back in. Probably having dessert. Shouldn't miss that." Jack rolled the cigar between his fingers and scanned the roadway.

"You're standing guard, aren't you?"

"Pah. I just wanted a smoke," Jack snorted. He puffed on his cigar and let the smoke roil away. The breeze was picking up slightly. "They call me an old worry-guts, you know."

"I don't."

"Look over there—can you see it?"

Beyond the farmhouse, the arid landscape began to change. Jack cast a hand across the rocky terrain, pointing out a strange, unworldly patina of glittering darkness.

"Doesn't look real. Never seen anything like it."

"The land holds secrets. Prophets have rolled out of this desert for thousands of years. Filled with fervor. Some good. Some bad. But if you're inclined to believe in God… Mind you, if you don't feel it here, you won't feel it anywhere. Close your eyes. Go on."

Micah squeezed his eyes shut.

“Feels like you don’t exist. But you do. You are. We’re all part of something more than all this. Now open your eyes…look to the horizon. You see?”

Micah opened his eyes, the night sky had made landfall.

“Part of something. Like you said.”

“Yes, yes, that covers it.” Jack puffed on his cigar. He changed tack. “Tell the others I’ll be along. The weather’s blowing up.”

Colonel Jack was right. A sudden burst of unusually warm air sparked the end of his cigar like a firework. As he walked back, Micah felt the strange warmth, too. A new wind was coming in from the south, gusting heat in its wake. When he got to the farmhouse, Eleni was leaning against the door, looking up at the sky, watching silent explosions of yellow lightning appear and disappear.

“Is it going to rain?”

“Something will come down. But not rain.” Eleni’s eyes glinted cryptically. “And soon.”

Micah looked up, heard a distant echo. He looked at Eleni. Her eyes were closed, she sniffed and tasted the air. Something was brewing in the atmospheric cauldron.

# Chapter 47

JAMAL HAD SPENT MOST OF THE NIGHT assembling his team in the secret village. Despite arriving in the foulest of weather, they all seemed eager to serve, to fight. Turning from nature's mayhem, he turned to face the mayhem he had brought together in the desert villa. His gaze drifted from Khalid, the withered one with the killing knife, to the sallow-faced Mahmoud. Both seemed calm and confident. In contrast to Farouz, who paced up and down, shadow-boxing, throwing nervous jabs to the air, cheered on by his friend Aziz.

"I am keeping you from something more important, Farouz?" Jamal was smooth.

"I must keep myself strong."

"Of course." Jamal's sarcasm was lost on Farouz. "For the fight ahead?"

"It is Allah's will."

"And that is all to the good, my young friend. Now, I have news. Your sister has—"

"I have no sister."

"Your *sister*," Jamal insisted, "and her young companion have been located. God be praised."

"God is great," Khalid said, his eyes closed as if in prayer.

Soon we shall finish what we started. All will be well." Jamal spread his hands in an arc. "And all here will be safe."

Farouz punched the air with a fist. Jamal groaned inwardly. What a clown this one is, he thought. Aloud, he explained that Shireen had been on the bus after all.

"But the bus was searched." Mahmoud was puzzled.

"Not well enough. Stupid Israelis!" Jamal sounded testy.

"The tracking device. It is still in place?" Khalid asked quietly.

"It blinks with perfect regularity. Come."

Jamal rolled out a detailed map across a table.

"Make a note of the coordinates. Memorize the location, do not write it down."

He pointed to a spot on Route 60. "Here. A fueling station. Here we shall rendezvous. Find our weapons, and, God willing, we shall complete our work. Farouz and Aziz will travel in one vehicle, Khalid and Mahmoud in another. I will travel alone. Less suspicious if we go separate ways."

"When do we begin?" asked Khalid.

"As soon as the storm has passed. At least the storm disables our enemy as it stops us."

"The wind would not stop me! I will find her. I will deal with her." Farouz boasted.

"Patience, Farouz, patience. You are the grand witness of this honorable action. Khalid and Mahmoud are the ones chosen for this action."

"My instruments." Farouz smiled.

"Indeed. Your instruments." Jamal smiled back.

"Can we not go across the mountains?" asked Mahmoud.

Jamal shook his head. "Too dangerous. The border is electrified. And why risk being caught in the desert by a roving patrol? Like everyone else, we go through a checkpoint."

"So! We go into their cages." Farouz smiled broadly, referring to the fenced walkways that funneled pedestrians from the West Bank into Israel. "But we shall emerge as lions!"

# CHAPTER 48

THE WIND WAS AT FULL FORCE NOW. Micah had never experienced anything quite like it. Tiny sand pyramids seemed to rise up on the farmhouse floor like bread in a hot oven. The door flew open. Colonel Jack stood there, his hair was blown upwards like so many toothpicks.

Shireen helped Rianne break out candles and flashlights in case they lost power. The children stowed away everything from the kitchen table. Aisha closed up the oven. Eleni glided to the door, threw back the bolt, and waited. Walloo appeared, carrying a pile of shutter slats under a big arm as if they were newspapers. He was ready. Denesh threw Micah a coat and goggles.

"Keep him close." Yimca pointed to Micah.

Walloo nodded and tapped Micah on the shoulder. Jack was back out first, followed by Yimca and Denesh. Then Walloo filled the threshold, Micah close behind. Eleni and Aisha pushed against the wind and closed the door behind them.

Micah followed in Walloo's big footprints like the boy who followed King Wenceslas, but the wooden slats caught the gusting wind and slowed their progress. Micah could barely see the others as they headed across the yard to secure the animals. Readjusting his goggles, Micah clomped after his big friend to the back of the farmhouse.

The wind was howling, stronger than before. They worked quickly. A shutter was swung inward, lined up, and a wooden slat was dropped in and the shutter locked into place. Then another, moving methodically around the house. As Micah pulled the last shutter in place, he stuck his head into the window's slight indent. He spat out grit and tipped clumping sand from his goggles. He was about to move away when a light inside attracted his attention. Shireen. He was about to tap on the window to surprise her but then he saw her making a call, huddled over, as if she didn't want to be seen.

Then Micah realized Walloo was tugging at his coat. He dropped the last slat into place and followed his friend, using him as a windbreak. Arrow-like grains of sand still managed to sting his cheek and get into his mouth. But he didn't care.

He stumbled and Walloo scooped him up like a twig and carried him, walking sideways to shield him from the brunt of the storm. Slowly Walloo felt his way to the front of the building, where he put Micah down and opened the door. The others were already safely inside.

"How that fur ball got out, I'll never know," Colonel Jack was saying as Flinter Toes jumped out of his coat and onto the couch, where he started licking himself.

Everyone watched for a second or two, taking some comfort in the cat's obvious indifference to the tempest raging outside. Even Jack smiled beneath sand-filled whiskers.

Rianne made tea. Jack reached for something a little stronger, which he shared with Yimca. They clinked glasses, toasting the solidly built house, a breakwater in a sea of howling sand.

The wind blew through the remains of the night. It blew sideways, downward, and every which way. The phones were out. Denesh alternately tried the land line and cell phones, plugging in various numerical combinations as if playing the lottery. But no winning number came up. They remained cut off. It was very unsettling.

Micah looked around. Eleni and Rianne were playing cards, dealing seconds, shuffling aces, happily cheating one another.

Colonel Jack was pacing, a new cigar clenched in his teeth, unlit. Walloo and Yimca were playing with the TV. And Shireen was reading.

Probably bloody Shakespeare, Micah thought, riled up. He had to know.

"When I was outside, I saw you on the phone. Who were you calling?"

"I was—Hameeda, my friend. I phone to her. I speak to her."

"Did you tell her where we were?"

"No!"

# Chapter 49

JAMAL PULLED UP TO A LINE of early morning traffic and slowly edged along to the checkpoint in East Jerusalem. He left his car and keys with a bored IDF soldier, who handed over a numbered chit without a word. Another soldier herded him into a stream of people moving toward a large, hangar-like building. Through a turnstile, he entered a wire-framed corridor.

The gamy nearness of those around him made Jamal want to hold his breath. Day workers, shopkeepers, schoolchildren and older students, families visiting relatives all shuffled along the cage-like tunnel. An amplified voice yelled to keep moving, moving, moving.

Jamal finally came to an enclosed walkway that allowed one person through at a time. After a cursory search, he was told to walk on. Emerging into a large hall, Jamal followed painted arrows on the floor. At the exit, a sign read, “Welcome to Israel. Enjoy your stay.” The words were spelled out in four different languages, but their meaning was conveyed long before Jamal reached the sign: Don’t stay long. Jamal had no intention of staying longer than he had to.

Jamal was surprised to find that he was the first to arrive at the austere-looking gas station. He bought a can of soda at a convenience store close by and waited in the small parking lot. When the others arrived, they would all travel together. A convoy would look conspicuous.

Soon, soon, he thought. Soon.

Khalid and Mahmoud pulled up fifteen minutes later. Mahmoud pumped gas. Where were Farouz and Aziz? Jamal started getting concerned, they should have been the first to arrive. He waited another half an hour. No sign of his young blowhards. Suddenly Jamal had a sinking feeling in his gut. He waited no longer. Inside the men's room, he went directly to the hand dryer nearest the window. A "Not in Service" sign in three languages was taped across the metal box. This was it. He noticed a small pile of white dust on the floor. Not a good sign. Working quickly, he unscrewed one side of the machine. He would have to cut a small hole in the thin drywall behind it to retrieve the nine-millimeter Luger semiautomatics. But the hole had already been cut. As he swung the dryer clear, he smelled the gun oil, heavy, cloyingly sweet. He knew. He knew, even before he reached inside what he would find. Nothing!

The weapons were gone.

Jamal refastened the blower to the wall. It took a moment because his hands were trembling with rage. He threw cold water on his face and looked at himself in the cracked, moldy mirror. The easy smile would not appear. He walked back out and told the others. Farouz and Aziz had gone rogue. And there was no one to blame but himself. Jamal recalled, with mounting anger and embarrassment, their last conversation at the training camp.

"The Jewish are clever at finding weapons," Farouz had said with a modicum of respect.

"The weapons are well hidden. In the bathroom. Behind the hand dryer," Jamal had announced triumphantly.

"We shall have no blood on our hands," Farouz had said, grinning. "They shall be clean."

Jamal had acknowledged the remark with a smile. A smile!

# Chapter 50

At Golden Terraces, everyone was up early. Manoush and Layla shepherded the young guests to the kitchen table, then took off to play. Micah heard their gleeful voices echoing across the farmyard, which had been turned overnight into a sandbox of sorts.

He pushed cornflakes around a plate, but wasn't hungry. Shireen wasn't eating either. They sat at opposite sides of the table, trying to ignore one another.

Yimca ambled in, greeting them as he poured himself some coffee. Micah mumbled a "good morning," but nothing more. Shireen kept her head bowed. Yimca raised a quizzical eyebrow.

"Have you seen what it's like outside?" he asked.

Micah just shrugged.

"Oh, Micah, as you no doubt realize, your dear uncle will not be joining us for breakfast, or even lunch. The sandstorm, you know—"

"You don't think he tried to get through, do you?"

"No, no, I'm sure he did not. The authorities would keep people away from the area. But they clear roads quickly, especially the highways. I'm sure the roads will be open by this evening. We will even have phones by then. Shireen, will you be traveling back with Micah?"

"I do not know." She shook her head.

"Well, we have time to make good decisions. But right now, I think we all need some air, yes?" He beckoned them both toward the door. "Come, come, we shall walk where no one has walked before."

With some reluctance, they followed the old magician. Micah squinted in the bright sunlight. The roughness of the desert pavement had been completely smoothed out. The freshly blown sand had filled crevices and cracks in the land like caramel. Yimca walked to a small dune, then turned and smiled.

"The storm was not as bad as we imagined. We all survived in one piece, did we not? The farm still stands, *we* are still standing. Things settle down. And we get on with it. Do we not?"

Micah knew Yimca was telling them to get over themselves, but he was still angry about Shireen's phone call. And Shireen? Right then he didn't care what she was thinking, or feeling, or anything. Even so, she looked pretty sullen.

"Anyone seen Flinter Toes?" Jack bellowed as he marched up to them, kicking sand in his wake. "He missed breakfast, must have gotten out. Can't see any paw prints. Bloody tiresome creature. Seen him? Anyone?"

"Perhaps he hide in bus with special door?" Shireen pointed to the sand-locked vehicles.

"The cat flap? Yes, of course!" Jack tipped a couple of fingers against his forehead in a kind of salute, then trudged off toward the parking area to find his errant feline companion. He stopped for a second, adding, "Oh, almost forgot. Walloo wants you two in the barn."

"Well? Go! Both of you." Yimca shooed them away.

Not walking together, they skirted the edge of the farmhouse and made for the barn. Micah went in first and called out. Walloo appeared holding scuba masks, scarves, and gloves. He plunked everything down on a nearby workbench.

"Cleaning up?" asked Micah.

"No, no, you'll see. Now, where did I put—?" Walloo muttered to himself and began looking from shelf to shelf.

Micah realized this must be the magicians' workroom. He spied half-built illusions, long mirrors, planks of wood. Spray paint. A lathe. Bolts of black velvet. The barn smelled of paint and grease, metal filings, and mystery. Well, Micah thought so. Shireen couldn't wait to get back into the light. She hung back by the door.

"Knew they were here somewhere." Walloo held up what appeared to be three huge platters. As he got closer Micah saw they were short, flat sleds with ropes and handles.

"We made adaptations. Now come on, you two. This is to be big fun."

"Where we going?" asked Micah.

"Where we going?" Walloo was grinning. "We are going surfing."

Farouz maintained a safe and steady speed for most of the journey. He could not risk being pulled over. Not after coming so far. The fate of his sister was entwined with his besmirched honor. This was something *he* had to do. Only Aziz understood. Farouz stole a look at his friend.

Aziz was pushing cartridges into the magazine. It was harder than it seemed, and the more bullets he loaded, the harder it became to load as the spring inside compressed even more. Finally he slammed the filled chamber back into the gun. He weighed the loaded pistol in his hand with some degree of satisfaction. Then picked up the next one, just to get the feel of it.

"Two each, one for each hand," Farouz laughed.

"Like cowboys in old movies," Aziz laughed back. "Avenging cowboys."

That was it, thought Farouz. People like Jamal, or even Khalid, could never understand. None of them could. But it no longer mattered. *Avenging cowboys*—Aziz was right. That's just how Farouz felt. The day belonged to him. His honor was about to be reclaimed, and with his loyal and trusted friend by his side, Farouz had never felt better. Never more certain of his destiny.

# Chapter 51

"Surfing? What is surfing?" asked Shireen.

"It's supposed to be fun. At the seaside."

"I never been seaside."

Micah didn't reply. They both watched Walloo as he strode on ahead, toward the dry river gorge. Not looking at one another.

"You still mad, Mates?" asked Shireen at last. "I know. It was foolish to make call. But it is done thing."

Micah could see she felt bad, but he didn't feel like letting her off the hook.

Walloo ran back to them. He puffed up sand with every giant step. He chided them for dawdling, but did it with a big grin. Dutifully they proceeded to the edge of the ridge. Walloo waved his hand over the gorge as if he had just produced it. Micah said, "Wow"—and really meant it. Shireen just stared.

Sand had cascaded into the valley, filling up the crevices and cracks as if the entire valley had been covered in smooth, molten gold. Walloo handed out water bottles, then the diving masks and scarves and gloves.

"You must be joking. You see how steep that is?"

"It is like to ski," Walloo explained. "Don't go straight down. Go on angle."

"Really?" Micah sounded doubtful.

"Look at the waves of sand," Walloo pointed to the curly, soft corrugations in the sand. "See how sand comes to soft peaks and drifts down? That's what you ride."

"Why?" asked Shireen, not unreasonably.

“I’m with her. And I don’t like heights,” said Micah.

Walloo brushed aside their concerns. And then he was gone. With the board held close to his chest and belly, he launched himself over the ridge. Sliding sideways, he shot down a sand hill below the ridge. It was an amazing sight. Walloo was a very big man, but he sand-surfed with style. Lying on the board, legs curled up behind him, he carved the hill with apparent ease. Zigzagging down from the ridge, his board parted the sand like a warm spoon drawn across honey-colored ice cream.

Micah and Shireen exchanged reluctant smiles. It did look like fun.

“More like sledding, only different. Think I might give it a go myself.”

“Wait!” Shireen grabbed his arm. Her mouth was set hard.

“What’s up?”

“I never want you angry with me, Mates. Ever. It hurt. Here.” She moved her hand to her stomach. “Knots made of stones.”

“Don’t want to feel bad about you, either.”

“Can you forgive me? I do not mean for phone call. I mean, for what I almost did.”

“I know what you’re on about—I know, I know, okay!” Micah snapped, then reeled himself in. “You were promised stuff. Made to feel you were doing good. You were led on.”

“But I followed.”

She pushed tears away. Micah could tell she hated them being there. She didn’t blubber, and she wasn’t looking for sympathy. But she was looking at him for something.

“So you followed. Most people do. You should see the kids in my school. Follow their own shadow if they could. But you stopped. Being led. You went your own way. Did what was right.”

“Yes, yes, I did. I try to do that.” She sounded relieved.

For once, Micah felt he had said the right thing. He had meant it, too.

"Come on, you two!" Walloo's voice echoed up, reverberating from the wadi floor far below.

"Hold your horses!" Micah yelled back.

A sudden gust of wind blew up and smacked the board against his chest, almost knocking him over. He forced the board down on the fulcrum of the ridge and gingerly went for it. But he slammed his feet down into the sand and came to a stop just a few yards down the hillside. He looked around. Now that he was on the slope, the sandy cliff no longer looked quite so daunting.

Micah took off again, angling sideways. He picked up speed. The sand flying past his ears sounded like a faucet turned full on. Walloo was waving in the distance, but Micah could see nothing but sand. Leaning into the board, he hit another sand peak. Now he was really going fast. He had to bite his scarf to keep it in place. He bounced and smacked atop another sand peak, which altered his course and sent him plummeting straight down. No angles. The sand spray picked up and plumed out like a wave. And Micah was riding it faster and faster.

The ride turned from exhilarating to frightening in a matter of seconds. He could barely see. The sand roared in his ears, sounding like a million glass particles rushing past. He hung onto the board handles, and leaned to one side. The board angled slightly, and slowed his descent. Micah was back in control and he felt himself smiling. Suddenly all was quiet. He looked up. Walloo was anxiously looking down at him.

"*Beseder*? You okay?"

Walloo pulled him to his feet. Micah shook himself like a dog.

"Fun, you had fun? Yes?" Walloo was nodding, all grins again.

"Gordon Bennet! Yeah! Yeah, that was fun!"

Micah jammed his board into the sand, wiped his eyes, and looked up. Shireen was just taking off down the ridge.

She glided at first. Slowly. Then she turned and began picking up speed like Micah had. She plunged forward, bouncing over the sand like a stone skimming a pond. Walloo was yelling, cheering her on. She landed in a soft bank on the riverbed. As she stood up and waved, golden streams poured off her. Micah and Walloo clapped. Their applause echoed like damp thunder.

They hiked back up the hillside, and when they reached the top of the ridge, Walloo pointed out the trail lines the boards had made. They could almost trace their fast and frazzling journeys to the wadi below. Walloo looked expectantly from one to another.

"I feel sandy, in all…everything! And…" Shireen looked away demurely.

"Bet she needs to go to the loo." Micah was not exactly discreet.

"Of course." Walloo smiled. "Okay, you two, back to house. Clean up, yes?"

"Not me; I'm going again." Micah launched himself over the ridge.

Shireen and Walloo heard muffled yelps of "Geronimo!" as he zigzagged down.

"He is doing not bad; that's it, that's better." Walloo watched with a critical eye.

"Go, Mates!" Shireen cheered.

"You say 'mates'?" asked Walloo.

"Yes, it mean *friend.*"

"I know that," Walloo said. "But *mates* is two. Micah is one."

Shireen thought about it, then her face brightened. "Micah is better than one. He is *Mates.*"

# Chapter 52

Yimca and Colonel Jack stood in front of the farmhouse, talking in hushed tones. When they saw Shireen and Walloo, they stopped talking.

"We made it back. And in one piece, almost." Walloo announced happily. "Micah is still surfing."

Yimca smiled, asked about the surfing, but to Shireen, his light banter seemed brittle and awkward. She sensed something was wrong. Colonel Jack said nothing, but his face was grim with worry.

Once they were inside, Yimca locked the door. Shireen sat down on the carpet and started playing with the children, grateful for the distraction. She piled up toy bricks, but in her mind unimaginable fears were piling up even higher. She was too scared to ask questions, but not too scared to listen in.

"I could be terribly wrong about all this," Jack was saying. "Worrying for nothing."

"You know better than most, Jack, there is no curry without heat," Yimca said.

"We must think what to do." Jack puffed air from his nostrils like a riled bull. Flinter Toes wiggled and jumped clear, then fled into a bedroom. "We have no weapons."

"We have guile." Yimca tried to sound reassuring.

"Guile does not trump guns, my friend. And that's all there is to it."

Shireen watched as the old comrades sat down at the table. Rianne and Eleni joined them. Rianne tried to smile but Eleni was subdued; perhaps she, too, sensed that something was wrong.

"Do we have any choice, old fellow?" Yimca asked.

"I suppose not," Jack sighed.

"What is happening?" Shireen stood up. "Please tell me."

"Let's get Micah back here now," Colonel Jack said, ignoring Shireen.

"You read my mind," Walloo smiled at Shireen as he made for the door. "For safe side, yes?"

"What is it you fear? It is the Oily One? Jamal?"

Shireen stared furiously at Jack but it was Yimca who answered her.

"We are not certain," Yimca said evasively. "Jack?"

"I found this." He showed Shireen the remains of a small black box about the size of a cell phone. Tiny entrails of chrome and green wire stuck out of the broken casing. "It's a tracking device. Quite powerful. Found it beneath the bus. Actually I didn't find it. Flinter Toes did. Tried to jump it, silly little bugger. I'm glad he did, though. I smashed it as soon as I pulled it free."

"Who did this?" Shireen looked scared.

"We don't know. It's a worry. It is that. And you, you have…this is our home." Jack breathed in, then spoke more calmly. "Oh, what's the use. You are not to blame."

"I am to blame. You are angered with me, and should be," Shireen said, deeply ashamed.

"Oh, yes, I am angry. I am very angry. But not specifically with you. There is a difference."

"I am sorry. Shireen, I am sorry. I will leave. The danger is mine, not yours."

"I will go. Now." Shireen was firm.

"No, *chérie*. We will not let you," said Rianne protectively.

Yimca changed the topic. "Any luck with the phones, Denesh?"

"We have been trying," Denesh shrugged.

"*Non.*" Rianne waggled her phone like a dead fish. "The atmosphere, *n'est ce pas?*"

"Strange atmospherics." Eleni sniffed. "Can you smell it? I can smell it. Rain has come."

Rain has come? Yimca shot a puzzled look at Jack, who shook his head. Part seer, part perceptive ad-libber, sometimes Eleni got it right. And sometimes she did not. Either way, they all knew enough not to ask for an explanation.

Shireen walked to the window and stared out, willing Micah to appear. But there was no sign of him. For that matter, there was no sign of Walloo. Nothing. Only a grackle bird high above, weaving circles of silence. Shireen was consumed with remorse. She darted for the door.

"You will wait here." Colonel Jack intercepted her.

"I will not wait. I will find them." Shireen's eyes gleamed with cold blue anger. "I will not wait while you do nothing."

"We shall *all* wait. And while we wait, we shall think, and we shall plan, and we shall keep our heads." Colonel Jack spoke like the commander he had been.

Shireen shook her head. "You do not know them. None of you."

"They do not know *us.*" Eleni smiled with certainty.

Micah reached the top of the ridge. He stabbed the board into the sand and took a long drink of water. He looked down again. Yes, I can do this again, he thought. It was fun, it was—

The sky moved too quickly. Everything became a blur as he tumbled backwards. The water bottle went flying. A sharp pain coursed down his side. For an instant, he felt sick to the pit of his stomach. He fell back and hit the crusted, hard sand.

The smell of sweat and onion was close. A gun was even closer. The sick feeling came back as he stared up at Farouz Obeid, Shireen's brother.

"We shall give her up." Jack looked up, his face bright, eyes gleaming. "We shall give her up."

Yimca looked shocked until Jack whispered in his ear. The old performer's face lit up and his mouth half-mooned into a wide smile. Then they both started laughing, frightening the cat away. Shireen looked at them, perplexed and a little scared.

"'My masters, are you mad?'" She hadn't meant to quote Shakespeare, but she could think of nothing else to say.

The farmhouse was suddenly powered with unseen energy. Once the stunt was explained, everyone knew what to do without being asked. Except Shireen. She watched Rianne and Eleni cut black cloth. Denesh sawed wooden planks while Yimca unscrewed part of the door's threshold. Even the children were helping, hanging black cloth from the windows on the back wall of the great room.

Jack opened a musty old case. Shireen watched him sort items. Cotton wads. Cigarette lighters. Cloth wicks. Tiny gelatinous vials filled with fluid. Yimca held one up and squinted, asked Jack if it would work. They were planning something, but Shireen could not figure it out.

"Aren't you glad I still smoke?" asked Jack with a smile.

"Sadly glad," Yimca conceded, with some regret.

Shireen watched, not knowing how to help. Yimca must have heard her unspoken plea, for mere seconds later, he was standing before her, tape measure in hand. He magically flipped a knot in the tape before handing it to Rianne.

"Now, Shireen, stand straight and still, *s'il te plait,*" said Rianne.

"What are you measuring? And the door, why they doing this?"

"You will see, you will see." Rianne sounded oddly mysterious.

Shireen watched what was going on. The magicians seemed to be rehearsing for something but she wasn't sure what. Yimca was practicing a trick with a Zippo lighter. Jack and Denesh were cutting away part of the door frame. They appeared to be building a false front, an opening where the door closed. Shireen looked on, quite bewildered.

"Now, please, keep still." Rianne measured Shireen's height and the depth of her body profile.

"I do not need clothes. I need to help."

*"Je sais,"* Rianne said patiently. "And you *will* help. You will be the star!"

Although Rianne was being flippant, Shireen realized they were all preparing for trouble. After the door frame was re-jigged, Aisha and Denesh started to pack emergency supplies. Denesh wanted to stay, but Yimca would brook no discussion.

"And Shireen?" asked Aisha.

"She has to stay. She has to play her part in all this." Jack looked at Shireen, who smiled encouragingly at Aisha.

"'All's well that ends well,'" she said.

Jack nodded, as if to acknowledge Shireen's resolve. The young family headed out the back door, and an uneasy stillness settled over the house.

"You could not have made me go." Rianne was definite. "I would have put my feets down."

"I will be here when my Walloo returns." Eleni also made her decision clear.

"Of course, my dear ladies," Jack smiled, not a bit surprised.

# Chapter 53

SHIREEN LOOKED AROUND. The windows in the great room had been shuttered, natural light all but extinguished. The doorway had been narrowed, black cloth pinned across the floor just beyond the threshold. It was like being backstage in a theater, but they were really inside a giant illusion. Now they would wait. Now Shireen understood what she would have to do, but she was not sure how it could possibly work. They had walked her through the plan, but only once. Then Yimca had said that these elaborate preparations might never be used.

"But if it comes to it, we'll be ready." Jack looked at Shireen. "You ready?"

"Yes," Shireen lied, then looked up fiercely. "I am not feared."

"Never thought you were. Now come on, chin up."

Chin up? Shireen was confused. Perhaps it was part of the plan, she thought, so she lifted up her chin. Colonel Jack, trying not to smile, gave her a gentle pat on the shoulder, then walked over to the back door. He peered out, looking worried again. Shireen was worried, too. Neither Micah nor Walloo had returned. It had been too long. Something was wrong. She felt it. They all felt it.

"What is it, old friend?" Yimca was by Jack's side, looking out beyond the silence.

"It's not what's out there." The old soldier punched his chest. "It's what's in here…and the waiting. Always the bloody waiting."

"If only we knew what we were waiting for."

Farouz pulled Micah to his feet and pushed him forward, gesturing with the gun. Micah fought back the impulse to run. He had to think, think of something he could do. He dropped to his knees and braced himself for what would come. The kick from the other one sent Micah sprawling. He scrambled sideways, no closer to the farmhouse.

"Get up! You will be a part of my plan. If not, it ends for you here," Farouz growled.

"They won't give her up."

"They will. She is not of their blood. You walk now, or die? Choose."

Micah slowly got to his feet before collapsing again. He was faking, but he had to delay. It was all he could do, but at least it was something. The next kick came harder than he could have imagined. A vicious peg leg to his thigh. Micah cried out and rolled over, not faking this time. Laughter pounded his ears. Two arms grabbed him from behind, raised him up, then threw him down like a bag of trash.

Once again, Farouz used the weapon to point the way forward. Micah staggered up and hobbled along but very slowly, veering slightly away from the house. He glanced back for an instant. Farouz looked so confident, so sure of himself, and Micah knew why. They would use him as a shield, hide behind him, and when they got close enough— And the worst of it was, Micah could do nothing about it. Except delay.

Jack maintained his vigil, staring out into the desert. A match was struck and something crackled. Smelled sulfurous. One of his old-fashioned wooden matches. Jack slowly turned around. Shireen had taken one of his cigars from the wooden box, snipped it, and was now expertly preparing it. She gently warmed the foot of the cigar, rolling it between the tips of her long fingers and the ball of her thumb.

Jack watched her, mesmerized. She struck another match and lit the center of the cigar's tapered end with the warm side of the flame, carefully, so as not to burn the wrapping. She drew in a draft until a small gray curl of smoke appeared, then looked at the cigar approvingly.

"I did this for my father. I do this for you."

She removed the label and handed Jack the cigar. He bowed graciously.

"'I talk of dreams, which are the children of an idle brain, begot of nothing but vain fantasy…' Or something like that." Jack puffed gently on the cigar. "You know it?"

"I did not." Shireen waggled the Romeo Y Julieta cigar label. "Now, I think I know."

Jack smiled. He had thought that a cigar that day might have tasted like grate ash. But he was wrong, it had never tasted so good.

Walloo retraced his steps to the ancient wall the Nabateans had built. Shielding his eyes, he looked down but could see nothing. No Micah. Walloo didn't know what to do next.

He decided to walk a bit farther along the ridge. To his right was the parking area. He thought he heard voices. Cautiously, he ran along the sandstorm embankment, and the dune gradually leveled out. Now he heard voices more clearly. Flattening himself to the ground, the big man crawled forward. He saw a Jeep parked near the edge of the rising, hidden from the farmhouse. He saw two men. One wearing sunglasses, young and anxious. The other looked sallow but was muscular, bigger. He pulled up what looked like a rag sack.

It was Micah.

Walloo wanted to rush them, but he knew it would be futile. They had guns. Two a piece. Walloo did not. He forced himself to remain patient. For now.

He watched as Micah got to his feet and stumbled forward, prodded on by the men with the guns. When they were clear of the vehicles, Walloo slithered backwards the way he had come. Using the embankment as cover, he lowered himself over a parapet along the wall and waited.

As Micah and his captors made their way toward the farmhouse, Walloo circled behind. Scrambling back up the parapet, he took cover behind the dune hiding the Jeep. He didn't know what the gunmen were planning, but he felt Micah was not in immediate danger. Even so, he had to be careful. Whatever happened, they would not leave the way they came. He approached the Jeep. The hood was locked. Using his enormous strength, Walloo started peeling back the hood almost as easily as if it were a lid on a can of sardines. There was soon enough room to get a hand inside the engine, then an arm. Fingers flitted like a spider over the car's innards. Any wire he touched was disconnected. Moments later, he found an ignition coil. He yanked and slowly withdrew it from the car. Walloo smiled to himself. The Jeep was dead.

The farmhouse was little more than a hundred yards away. Looking back for a split second, Micah saw a smile at the corner of Farouz's mouth. With a gun in each hand, he and his friend now strode along like gunslingers in an old Hollywood western.

Micah started to cough, then he gripped his stomach and keeled over as convincingly as he could.

"Can't move," he said in a cracked voice, hoping they would believe him.

Aziz stuck one gun in his belt then dragged Micah to his feet, pushing him on. Again Micah fell over. Farouz kicked him forward.

"Up! Up! Or you die."

Using his hands, Micah pushed himself up very slowly.

"My friends, in the house—" He turned to his captors and pleaded with them. "They are old—leave them alone, please."

"I want only the one who was my blood," Farouz shouted.

He fired into the air.

The noise was deafening. Micah gasped.

"You Jewish in the house. Your boy is scared. Look!" Farouz enjoyed humiliating Micah, but it also served a purpose. "He knows what I say is the truth. Come out! Bring me the dishonored one of my blood. Or the boy dies. Now." Farouz sounded very matter-of-fact. He put one gun in his belt and passed the remaining gun from one hand to another, trying to act cool.

"Be ready, my friend," Aziz said, pointing.

The door opened slowly to reveal a gaping, shadowy blackness. Yimca came out first. He had his hands up, palms facing out. He looked very, very old. Rianne followed, her eyes fixed on Micah. Then Eleni, imperious as ever, staring with contempt at the gunmen. Colonel Jack came next. His hands were over his head in a kind of arch, fingers cupped, trembling. He was looking down as though ashamed, humiliated. He shuffled forward slowly.

Micah felt angry and embarrassed. It wasn't fair. They were too old and he was too young and—

Shireen appeared in the doorway.

"No!" Micah screamed.

"Farouz, I beg you, please, please, not this—" Shireen implored.

Farouz flung Micah aside. He looked at his sister as she begged for mercy, but to him she looked guilty. Was guilty. The sentence was just.

Micah looked on helplessly. Farouz raised his weapon, took aim. And fired.

Once.

Twice.

Hot bullet casings spun in a shallow arc and landed in the dirt. But the bullets had found their mark. Taking no chances, Farouz fired a third time.

# Chapter 54

But Shireen did not fall. She cracked open and shattered into hundreds of diamonds before collapsing in a cascade of mirrored glass. Farouz fired again into the empty blackness of the doorway.

Micah couldn't believe what he had seen. Then, within the deafening, explosive gunfire, he heard a terrifying roar. Walloo! He must have followed them to the farmhouse.

Walloo tackled Farouz like a linebacker. As they hit the ground, he tried to wrench the weapon from the gunman. The other pistol, stuffed in Farouz's belt, became dislodged and clattered harmlessly out of reach just as another shot was fired. Micah heard a bear-like roar and saw Walloo—as if in slow motion—arch up and fall back, a bullet wound in his thigh. Farouz scrambled free.

Not knowing if he should grab for the gun on the ground or help his wounded friend, Micah froze.

"Micah! The gun!" Walloo yelled at he stuffed a fist to the bleeding wound.

Micah snapped out of it and did as he was told. Then the screaming started.

Micah looked up and saw Jack's hands squeezed into fists. And from between his fingers, tiny, deadly jets of flame were shooting out at Farouz's friend with frightening precision. Aziz's hair, his face erupted into flame.

When Yimca and Jack had shuffled pathetically forward, arms held up in surrender, their hands had appeared empty. But they were not. Aziz had stood with the weighty confidence only two loaded Lugers could provide, enjoying his power over the old men who whimpered and bowed in abject submission.

In seconds, the Zippos were between Yimca's fingers. He had flipped the lighter caps, spun the flint wheels, and thrown the lighters at the steady streams of lighter fluid Colonel Jack had squeezed from the capsules he had expertly palmed.

The burning man wheeled blindly around, screeching and firing, screeching and firing. Yimca tried to wrench the guns from him, but the inferno held him back. The burning man would not go down and would not stop firing. In a running crouch, Jack rugby-tackled him head-on. The attacker stumbled—but not before the next-to-last bullet in the clip had found its mark. Jack twisted around and fell to the ground.

"Jack!" Yimca yelled. His hand was almost fisted by the ferocity of the fire as he tried, despite the pain, to grapple the gun away from the burning man.

And then another shot was fired.

Aziz froze where he stood surrounded by fire. Yimca pushed himself clear and the gunman collapsed.

"Now what?" Micah still had the gun trained on the target.

"Put the weapon down. Carefully."

Micah did as Yimca told him.

The two stared at the smoldering corpse. The stench of the man's burns, the smell of his death, hung in the stillness of the air like a man on a gibbet.

# Chapter 55

Shireen helped Colonel Jack push himself to a sitting position. Micah was soon by their side.

"He's been shot, but there's no blood." Micah looked perplexed.

"He bleeds inside. I know this," said Shireen forcefully.

"Water." Jack mumbled, almost to himself.

Micah handed him a water bottle, but Shireen snatched it away.

"No! He wants. But no. Bad inside for him," Shireen wiped his lips and the inside of his mouth with water. "This better."

"She's right," Jack said softly.

"I was trained in many things." She looked at Micah. "If he drinks deep, not good."

Jack knew if he drank deeply, he would choke. It had all happened before. Years before. Somewhere in South America. Only then he had been younger. Stronger.

"Walloo. Needs some help," said Jack, barely audible.

"On my way."

Micah gave the old colonel a little smile, then he looked at Shireen.

"I stay," she said.

Micah nodded then headed over to Walloo. Eleni was already beside him, using her shawl as shade from the sun. She had his head propped up, but the rest of him was sprawled out, seeping blood onto the sand. He had a fist in the wound, not that it was doing much good. Micah sprinted into the farmhouse and quickly returned with a large spoon and a strip of bandage. Eleni watched closely as he prepared a tourniquet. He sensed her unease.

"Scouts, don't worry," he said.

"Scouts?" Eleni weighed the word carefully.

"First Aid. I got a badge for it." He was matter of fact. "It's his femoral artery, it's all torn. But I know what to do."

"Do!" Eleni proclaimed.

"This might hurt." Micah tied the rope-like cloth high above the wound. Blood still pumped out. He tied the end of the bandage to the spoon and started winding it.

"Hey, Micah, my friend, this cannot hurt more than—oooooow! Woooow!"

"Stop whining. Heroes do not whine."

"Yes, Eleni."

Micah twisted the bandage until the blood slowed to a trickle and appeared to stop. "Hold this." Micah put one of Eleni's hands on the big spoon. "Don't let go."

As Micah stood up, a friendly face came into sight. Denesh was running toward them brandishing a phone.

"The bird is up! We got through. Made contact, and—"

He stopped short when he saw the carnage. He took everything in, then called emergency services. The road, he said with some relief, had been cleared.

Micah heard crunching sounds underfoot as he and Rianne helped Yimca into the house. On the floor were the glittering remains of the mirror that had hung on the door to create the illusion. To fool Farouz.

"This was brilliant," Micah said, fascinated by the false panel on the side of the door.

They gently guided Yimca onto a couch. Micah could now see how bad the injury was. Yimca's arm hung by his side, burnt red, framed by blackened bits of cloth.

"An ambulance is coming," Micah said. "It'll be all right. Don't you worry; it'll be—"

"Go look, Micah, the door." Yimca winced with pain but tried to smile. "You notice the angle? There is a doorstop nailed in the floor. Kept the mirror 'door' at a forty-five-degree angle."

"So Shireen stood here—" Distracted, Micah aligned himself in the hollow of the rebuilt doorjamb. "And her image was reflected outside."

He jumped to the front of the threshold. The door panel seemed invisible. Micah could make out his reflection in the shattered door frame. He could also see the flaw.

"But how could she just *appear* there?"

"She was always there. Covered in a black cloth from head to toe," said Rianne.

"Black cloth on the floor, the door panel, the wall behind; no one could see—"

*"Noir sur noir!"* Rianne repeated for effect.

"It gave us…the misdirection…we needed." Yimca's face was a smiling mask that hid the growing pain. "A classic illusion, Micah, a classic. The doorway, everything was covered in black, including Shireen. When she let go of the cloth, she appeared to be facing front, but in fact she was *behind* the secret door panel. Staring at her own reflection. Clever, no?"

"And that's what her brother saw? Shireen's reflection."

"She played her part well. A good student," said Yimca.

"So where is she?" Micah looked around. "She still with Colonel Jack?"

"She came into the *maison* just moments ago," said Rianne.

Micah called her name a couple of times. No answer. The house was eerily still. Empty.

# Chapter 56

THE WORD *ESCAPE* SHRIVELED in Farouz's mouth and turned sour. He stared at the Jeep. He tried to close the hood with his one good arm—the other had been useless since the giant tackled him. He cursed with frustration as he struggled with the twisted metal. But the gaping wound in the vehicle would not close. And then he heard a noise away and above in the distance. The *thuck-thuck-thuck* of helicopter rotor blades churning heavy air. He knew what that meant.

It had all gone so wrong. Farouz had been deceived by those old fools at the farm. And now this! As he staggered clear of the eviscerated car, he heard something else. A familiar voice. Calling his name. It was her. No mirage. Perhaps, he thought, perhaps now.

"Stringy."

Shireen had left the farmhouse through the back door. In the aftermath of the firefight, she had seen where her brother was going. Using the orchard as cover, she followed him to the parking area. In the confusion, and with wounded to tend, she knew her friends would not notice.

"You are hurt," she said nervously.

"You come to gloat, Stringy?"

"I do not. I come to plead. For the sake of our mother. She has lost enough."

"She has another daughter."

"I do not speak for myself, you haughty fool. I speak for you, Farouz. Your war. It is over."

"My war is just beginning."

He began to stalk her like prey, approaching her in diminishing circles. He was unarmed and wounded, but she backed away all the same.

"In memory of our father, Farouz, I beg you—" The words did not come easily.

A growling yell started deep within him, rising up like a crazed fever. He rushed her, his good hand tightening and clenching with anticipation, like a hammer. In that instant, Shireen knew the hammer would always come down. And she jumped clear of it. For a split second, she saw nothing but space. Blue space.

The terrifying moment was held, frozen in time. Then she fell.

Farouz's fist pounded and swiped dead air. His victim was gone. His balance was gone. He stumbled. Seconds later, the sloping sands enveloped his scream.

# Chapter 57

MICAH RAN FROM ROOM TO ROOM yelling Shireen's name. She was not there. Where had she gone? And why? I've got to find her, he thought. He knew Yimca would not want him to go alone, would want him to wait, but his anxiety over Shireen overrode everything else. He went back outside and shouted to no one in particular to say he'd be right back. Jack tried to call after him, but the pain silenced him.

Making his way to the parking area, Micah saw a Caterpillar plow making short work of the sand barrier on the approach road. Behind it was the impatient red blur of ambulance lights. Above, the noise of a helicopter blotted out all other sounds as it swept across the plateau toward the farmhouse.

Good, he thought, his friends would be safe. All his friends—except one. He ran.

Atop a new sand dune, he stopped and scanned the surrounding area. When he spotted a Jeep with part of its hood ripped up, he jumped down and went to investigate. The car had been vandalized. A muddle of footprints led to the edge of the ridge.

Shireen fell on the sand-covered hillside, spinning downward as though in a vast drum. Suddenly in the whirling tumult came a second of clarity. Sand-surfing! Shireen remembered. She jackknifed out of the fall, landing to the side of the ridge. It took a moment to realize she had stopped. Stretching out, she turned and body-surfed down the steep incline.

She came to a stop just above the stony valley floor. She looked about. No sign of Farouz. She stood up, a bit wobbly at first, then ran down the last few feet onto level ground. She was elated. And then her foot plunged into a sinkhole and she fell forward.

Micah cupped his eyes and forced himself to look along the contours of the dry riverbed. He saw Shireen. At the same time, a swirl of dust came pouring down the hillside like a sand-filled wraith. Micah strained to see. The dust settled and he was sure. Micah watched Farouz shake sand from his clothes. He stood less than twenty yards from where his sister lay. He reached down for something.

A hurtling rock caught Shireen in the stomach and she keeled over. Micah realized what was happening. Farouz was going to stone her. Micah screamed out to her. Shireen heard her name bounce around the valley. So did Farouz. He looked up for a moment and smiled. Then he turned back to his grisly task with renewed force. The rock hit Shireen in the leg. She cried out and her piteous wail cut through Micah like a blunt and jagged knife. Then he saw the sand sled. No more, he thought, no more.

Grabbing the board, he tightened his grip on the toggles and went over the ridge. The sled smacked the sand and Micah went forward. And down. Sand hurtled past, scuffing his knees and hitting his face like tiny glass pellets. He ducked as best he could, but there was no escaping. He hit the top of a small dune and was in the air for a split second before heading straight down. He didn't care. Rage had overwhelmed his fear.

Finally the board skimmed a rock that protruded from the hillside like an iceberg from the sea, bigger than it first appeared. Micah tipped up and rolled over and over. Sand clogged his mouth, stung his eyes. He came to a stop. The board had cracked in two, but he was in one piece, just yards from Shireen.

"Look out!" he screamed. Too late.

A jagged rock smashed into her upper arm, which was raised up to protect her face. Excruciating pain left her almost breathless and she felt as if her arm was being torn apart. Another stone pummeled into her shoulder blade and she screamed in agony.

Micah ran to Shireen and used his broken board as a shield to fend off a killing blow aimed at her head. The stone hit the board, then fell to the ground. Micah picked it up and threw it the way he threw cards.

The stone cut through the air and caught Farouz in the knee. Micah threw another. Farouz cowered. Micah scrambled forward, throwing one rock after another. Micah tasted salty sweat—it stung his eyes, but he dared not blink, dared not look away. Farouz started throwing again. But Micah wasn't stopping. And his aim was getting better. A jagged flint grazed Farouz in the jaw. He yelped and stumbled back, momentarily shying from the fight.

Micah glanced at Shireen. He saw a gash on her ear, and her arms were badly scraped and cut. Her neck looked inflamed and raw. The beautiful outfit borrowed from Aisha was torn, and blood was seeping through. He was overwhelmed by her injuries. And dangerously distracted.

"Mates!"

Micah raised the board over his face, but the rock came in low. A sharp pain burst onto his shin, then another rock smashed into his knee and brought him down. The board fell out of his grasp. He was momentarily defenseless.

"For punishment, the ancient ways are best." Farouz sounded jubilant as he turned back to Shireen. "Allahu Akbar!" he screamed.

"You do this for God? Liar!" Shireen spoke from the heart with all her remaining strength.

Farouz dug his fingers into a sharp-edged rock. "Do you not see

His will Shireen? Do you not see the divine purpose in your death?"

"I see only you. This is not God's purpose."

"Blasphemer. Allah is my avenger. There is no God but God."

Micah grabbed up the board and staggered over with it to shield Shireen. As Farouz threw, Micah leaned over slightly, trying to protect his friend. The jagged missile caught him in the arm as it spun off the board. It hit him like a hammer blow. He wavered, pain surged through his upper arm, but he would not be stopped. He rose up again, determined to keep the board between Shireen and her crazed brother. He would not go down again. Not without a fight.

Farouz saw all this as a final act of bravado. He had them both at his mercy. Casually he fingered another stone. He felt its sharpness. His face tightened with cruel resolve. The game was over. He would finish with the boy. And then his sister.

Twisting his upper body to gain greater velocity, he prepared for the final killing throw. Then Farouz froze. A breeze blew against his face. And a chill cascaded down his spine and puckered the skin on his arms.

# Chapter 58

OUT OF NOWHERE, A WIND HAD PICKED UP along the dry riverbed. Micah and Shireen couldn't see anything, but they were both aware of something changing. Micah smelled a strange odor. It smelled like rain but it wasn't rain. And it was getting stronger, more intense.

They heard a roar like a loud, unceasing chant that just grew and grew. And then they saw it.

A toppling wall of water was hurtling, skidding forward, tilting from one bank to the other, surging closer. Dozens of tiny waves jumped one another, trying to get ahead. Micah and Shireen could barely comprehend what they were witnessing.

Created by the rains in the north, this was like the runoff water collected during the time of the Nabateans. The ancient ways of farming and irrigation had fallen into disuse, but the rainwater still flowed as it had for millennia. And now it was flowing toward them with frightening speed and unstoppable force.

The floodwater reared up the steep sides of the wadi at over six feet. Closer to Farouz, in the center, the water ebbed much lower. As Micah and Shireen scrambled, painfully and slowly to the wadi's edge, they could see him standing there, tossing a stone from hand to hand, looking at them, sneering, almost smiling, obviously enjoying their distress. He seemed unconcerned.

The water wall was still less than two feet high. Tiny white horse waves gurgled along, almost playfully, neither threatening nor very dramatic. The water might reach just above his knee, Farouz figured, just cresting—

He was totally unprepared for the full force of the flood.

He was thrown off balance as if a rug had been pulled from under his feet. Farouz fell backwards into a seething mass of muscle-thick water and completely disappeared. Seconds later, his stunned and frightened features broke the surface. His hands flailed around, trying to gain purchase. But there was nothing to grab. Farouz could not get above the narrow band of floodwater for more than a second or two.

Micah and Shireen could only stare wordlessly. They clung to the side of the wadi, helpless witnesses to their would-be killer's struggle less than a stone's throw away.

They could not see that beneath the water's turbulent surface other forces were at work. Small rocks were being dislodged from the wadi floor, pushed along with the powerful force of the unstoppable current. Stone fish. Hungry fish.

With all his might, Farouz lurched up once more but crashed back down, carried on the narrow, relentless tide. And the stone fish swam against him, pummeling and pummeling.

Then the incoming river tide reached Micah and Shireen.

The full force of the flood appeared to surge up, as if out of thin air. Micah felt the spray moments before the deluge engulfed them. His arm was hampered by the broken board, but it was too late to dislodge it.

He spun around for Shireen, cried out to her, but a mouthful of brackish water doused his words. All he could hear was the noise of the surging water as he was carried off with the board. He broke the surface and glanced wildly about. He saw a hand through the water, fingers splayed like the points of a stricken star. He grabbed it as the board rose up on a wave of water. He pulled hard.

Shireen kicked with her feet and reached out. Grabbing Micah's shirt, she hauled herself forward.

Finally she was beside him, one hand around the farthest rim of the board. The life-saving sand sled buoyed them along on the cusp of the flood. Micah was past caring where the waters took them. The maniac brother was gone. They were together. That was all that mattered.

# Chapter 59

Khalid and Mahmoud sat in the car, keeping council with their thoughts. Jamal was also quiet. Shireen's death had been sanctioned. But the loud-mouthed Farouz and the groveling Aziz had jeopardized the mission by going it alone.

Mahmoud drove in silence. Khalid sat in the back. He wants to say something, thought Jamal, but chooses to remain quiet. Good. He was in no mood for small talk.

They were overtaken at great speed by several military vehicles. Above them, Jamal heard the familiar, metallic *thuck-thuck* sound.

"The Jewish are busy. What is going on?" asked Mahmoud, breaking the silence.

"Stop the car," Jamal said. "Turn around."

"We turn back?" Mahmoud sounded surprised. "What of the girl? I thought—"

"You thought?" Jamal snarled disdainfully. "The mission is postponed. Farouz and Aziz have obviously failed. Failed us. Failed everything."

"What?" Mahmoud was bewildered. "Where did you find this knowledge?"

"Look around you. Look above you." Jamal jabbed Mahmoud in the shoulder. "Do you not see IDF helicopters and armored cars heading in the same direction as we are?"

"We do not know that for sure," said Mahmoud.

"You think that fool and his creature succeeded? Turn about. Take me back to my car."

"There will be other opportunities, my brothers. We must be

patient," Khalid smiled knowingly.

Mahmoud slowed down, then jumped the median strip and headed back to the gas station to pick up Jamal's car. Jamal tried to relax. He thought of the missing weapons. He knew their cost. A Luger cost a thousand dollars. Bullets almost two dollars each. Always dollars. American dollars. Black market dollars. It was all so unjust.

Then he thought of that impetuous, arrogant fool, Farouz. He hoped he was dead. But what of the girl? Shireen could identify him. And others. What of the secret facility? Would she give them away? So many questions.

Jamal had no answers.

# Chapter 60

Eron Gilead and the rescue team drove as fast as they could along the curve of the ridge to get ahead of the rushing waters in the hope of finding the missing teens.

The rescuers worked quickly. Steel pitons were hammered into the rock face on either side of the wadi gorge. A safety line with tagged loops was hung and secured. Moments later, climbers were rappelling down to the dry floor below just as the flood waters appeared.

One waded out and grabbed a body as it floated by. Gilead traversed down for a closer look. A young man. Skin and lips ripped, revealing teeth in a deathly leer. The mouth oozed silt. The face was so badly beaten it was hard to make an identification. Thankfully he could see it was not Micah who had drowned. Gilead guessed it was Farouz.

A strong current ripped across the surface of the water, carrying Micah and Shireen with it. Pushed into a slight curve in the twisting embankment, they were bounced against a rocky promontory that looked like a rusty iron girder. The board they had clung to crumpled on impact but somehow cushioned the blow and their watery landfall. It seemed like hours, but their ordeal had lasted no more than a couple of minutes.

Choking and spluttering, they looked up. For the moment, they were safe. No longer moving in a horizontal avalanche of water and stone. But they could feel the current trying to drag them back into the maelstrom even as they hung on to the rocky wall. They looked longingly at a flat ledge just a few feet above them, but wisely they stayed put.

They clung as best they could to the rock face. Although Micah's feet were almost touching the silty bottom, it was still hard to keep from going under.

"Hurts," Shireen said suddenly, and sank into Micah.

Her lips were cracked. Half her face was a livid purple bruise, and a gash had buried itself behind one ear, which was swollen and red. He could see the edge of another bruise along her neck. The cold water helped stem the bleeding, but she could barely move.

"You'll be all right, don't worry," he said with lame English optimism.

"I am so cold."

"Yeah, I know, it's freezing."

"I am sorry, Mates. Farouz—"

"Why'd you bother with him? Why?"

"I tried— I wanted to make him not hurt you. No more. My death would be for good. You understand?"

Finally, some sort of explanation.

"I thought you went after another moggy," Micah said. "A cat. Wish you would've done."

He smiled, tried to make light of it, but he could see Shireen was fading fast. Micah wished he could do something, anything.

He looked around, saw another ledge across the watery hollow. Ten feet above them a jagged slit of blue. The rock face parted to form a kind of chimney. He thought about pulling himself up, pushing against the opposite wall, ascending imaginary rungs of a ladder. That's what they did in the movies, but he figured he'd get halfway up before he'd come crashing back down.

He decided on a less dramatic approach.

*"Hatzilu!"* He cleverly remembered that was *Help!* in Hebrew.

He also shouted in English. He yelled till his throat died, then he sluiced his mouth out with the floodwater. It tasted like something left for months in the back of the fridge, only worse. He shouted again, beyond the large cracks in the rock, straight into the blue above. When he stopped, he noticed Shireen was sinking. Lower and lower she slipped down the rock face. Her eyes were closed. Micah tightened his grip and hoisted her back up. Her eyes opened in great fear. Or pain. He couldn't tell. He just knew he couldn't let her slip away. Not now. Not ever.

"I heard you! Look up."

Micah looked up. It was Eron Gilead. And he was looking down at them, grinning. Shireen did not open her eyes.

"'Bout bloody time," said Micah, his voice hoarse and surly.

Gilead laughed. Straddling the fissure in the rock, he swung over to a smaller ledge. Micah was a bit jealous of his agility though he was relieved to see him. Sort of.

"Just stay there," Gilead said cheerfully. Then he was gone.

"Stay there? Where's he think we're going?" Micah coughed up more water. "What a wally. Don't know what you see in 'im, I really don't. Gordon Bennet."

"Gordy Bennet."

Micah thought he saw a glimmer of a smile, but he wasn't sure.

# Chapter 61

"THERE HE IS!" Uncle Bernard flapped his arms around his rounded chest like an excited penguin.

Embarrassed by the attention, Micah squirmed in the wheelchair.

Jakey and Aunt Gilly applauded as he came closer. One arm was covered in large adhesive bandages. Yellow stuff had been daubed on his face and one arm. Under his sweatpants, his knee and leg were bandaged up. He was still a bit of a mess, but he felt fine, better than he'd felt in days. He appealed to the nurse pushing his chair.

"Can I get out of this? I can, you know."

"Hospital rules." Her uncompromising smile ended that conversation.

The nurse turned to Bernard and Gilly. "Here's a prescription for the pain. He needs to rest. There's nothing that won't heal."

As the nurse took off, Micah looked up at his aunt.

"Can we go to the third floor? I won't be long. Promise."

Bernard wheeled Micah, quite unnoticed, to where Rianne and Eleni were sitting. They sat side by side, bolt upright, staring straight ahead like a pair of sentinels. Micah knew they were waiting for news of their loved ones.

"Five! Five! Five!"

Rianne looked up like a startled bird, then flopped back down.

"Oh, *mon brave!*" she said, in full fluster.

Micah leaned forward and got a tapping hug and a bit of a squeeze. Eleni peered across at him, acknowledging his war wounds with cool approval.

"How's Walloo doing?" asked Micah.

"Bullet passed through his thick thigh without touching bone. I tell him, 'Walloo,' for nurture. 'Be strong,' for encourage. Then, 'move on!'" Eleni said with some degree of pride. "But not before he gets an arterial graft. I don't even know what that is. " Eleni swallowed hard. "Tissue. Just one. Playing at soldiers. At their age."

Rianne handed her the box. Eleni blew her long Roman nose until it almost echoed. She clutched her tissue. Quite unexpectedly, Rianne burst into tears. Eleni pushed the tissues back into her friend's lap and gripped one of her hands. Paper hankies streamed out like silk scarves from a magic box. Helplessly Micah looked up at his uncle, then at Gilly, who came over and gave Rianne a hug.

"*Je suis desolée.* I do not know, I am so—" Rianne gulped down her sobs. "Yimca is in burn unit. Colonel Jack went under the *couteau*—the knife, you know—and *pauvre* Walloo..."

"All my fault. None of this should have happened." Micah stood up. He felt like a fraud sitting in a wheelchair.

"*Non, chéri.*" Rianne regained her composure. "It is fault of bad men. Who kill for religion. Kill for unknown offense. Kill for 'honor.' Kill for nothing!"

Much to Micah's relief, Rianne now seemed more like her old, feisty self. Then a voice boomed across the hallway. Micah heard the rich fruitcake voice and smiled. Jack had wheeled himself into the waiting room. The old soldier looked wild and disheveled with a manic gleam in his eye. Micah didn't know whether to salute or hug him.

"Good morning, my lad. And you too, my princess." Jack bowed his head with feigned deference toward Eleni, who eyed him with justifiable suspicion.

"You look drunk," she said disdainfully.

"Gave me some wonderful whiz pills. Size of machine-gun

bullets. Suppositories, they said. I took them the normal way. Straight down the gullet, not up the… Well, nothing French for me, I can tell you."

"Colonel Jacques! *Tu es très* naughty."

"Wanted to see you ladies before I wrestle Morpheus to the ground."

Eleni and Rianne rolled their eyes and berated him for being out of bed, for not following the rules, and for taking his medicine the wrong way. Jack just smiled, loving every minute.

"Glad to see you're up and about, Colonel Jack. They said you had bits removed."

He wheeled himself about to face Micah. "Bullet hit the spleen. So they took it out. Apparently it's an organ we can live without. Eleni always said I had too much spleen, eh, Eleni?" Jack was on form.

"Pity they didn't take out your gall while they were in there." Eleni smiled.

"But you like my gall." He tried for a grin but winced instead. "Be right as rain in a week. Seen your friend, Micah? Doing all right, is she?"

"Yeah, I saw her. She's doing good. Loving the attention."

"I've seen her, too. Here, take a peek."

Slowly Jack pulled a newspaper from the side of his chair. And there was Shireen, with a RESCUED! headline. More inside, it said. But Micah was drawn to a story below the fold about the resumption of talks between the Israelis and Palestinians. He scanned the page.

"Apparently," said Jack, "they're agreed in principle. You know, the Side-by-Side Accord. Mind you, they couldn't agree on a signing date until the president of the United States agreed to take part in the ceremony."

"A ceremony means nothing," pronounced Eleni.

"Well, maybe, but the Side-by-Side concept is a good one, my dear. It's pragmatic. If they can at least do that—"

"If they do that, I will eat my *chapeau,*" said Rianne.

"Well, if nothing else, it gives them all a chance to chew the fat. As Churchill said, jaw-jaw is better than war-war," Jack said. He looked at Micah and raised an eyebrow. "Something on your mind, lad?"

Micah folded up the paper. "I'll keep this for Shireen, she'll want it for her scrapbook."

He said nothing else, but Jack pointed a warning finger and said to stay out of trouble. Then Bernard said it was time to leave. As Micah said good-bye, Eleni grabbed his hand and held on tight.

"A bright shadow brings death."

"What?" Micah was taken aback. "Shadows aren't bright. And what death?"

"Your friend, Shireen!" said Eleni impatiently. "Death follows a bright shadow. Same difference."

"Yeah, but what does it mean? Is she going to die?"

"No idea. Things come into my head. I speak out. Finish." Eleni's eyebrows arched. "I utter words of portent. Not all the time…but when the mood strikes. You should know by now."

"Like a riddle?" Micah asked carefully.

"Not *like* a riddle. Portent *is* a riddle, silly boy."

"And what do I do?" Micah asked.

"You remember to remember. Then you will know what to do."

"Love a good riddle," Bernard blustered over the unexpectedly tense moment. "They're such fun, don't you think?"

On the drive back, Eleni's odd portent nagged at Micah in the worst way, like an itch he couldn't get to. Death would follow a bright shadow? A bright shadow would bring death? He had no idea what that meant. But Eleni thought Shireen was still in danger and Micah felt that, too.

He tried to think it through. How did the guy with the knife know about the meet-up at the Jaffa Gate? Was there more than one? Were they friends of Farouz? Doubt it, he thought, or Farouz would have been there, too, taking the first stab. And what about the coin dealer? Was that really a coincidence? And who put that tracking device on the bus? Micah closed his eyes and tried to clear his head. He stared out the window. So many questions. And no answers. He yawned. He knew his eyes were red-rimmed with exhaustion, and he felt he could sleep for a week. At least Shireen was safe, for now, at least.

"Just has to get better," he mumbled to himself. Even if she's odd, and goes off after moggies and spouts Shakespeare, and even if she's made for trouble, she's…

"You'll see her again," said Gilly perceptively. "But first, home. Get you all comfy."

But Micah never heard her. He was long gone, dead asleep.

# Chapter 62

Shireen looked around. Her hospital room was small and functional and hummed with bubbly noise. The Soroka Medical Center was a large hospital in Beersheba, in the Negev. Shireen put her hands on the window to steady herself, then looked down. She saw young people on steps. Students? A university? She was uncertain.

A bored nurse gave her breakfast, a fruity granola concoction that tasted better than it looked. At least to her. Shireen smiled. Her pain, like her fear, was beginning to slip into memory. She remembered seeing Micah. And then nothing except lots of sleep.

"You have a visitor," the nurse announced.

"Hameeda!"

Shireen's best friend rushed over for a hug, almost tipping the breakfast tray. She stopped short when she saw Shireen's bruises and bandages.

"Oh, sorry, sorry."

Shireen brushed it off, eager for gossip not sympathy. The two held hands and smiled. Then Hameeda's smile drooped. Shireen could tell she had something to say but didn't know how to begin.

"Ha-mee-da?" Shireen stretched out the name.

"I went to your brother's funeral. Masked men showed up. They fired guns in the air and then left as quickly as they had come. It was all very odd. And scary." Hameeda looked into her lap and sighed deeply.

"I know you had to go. For the family. Thank you. Do you know my mother came here with my sister Suray?"

"Really? How did it go?" asked Hameeda, trying not to bite her lip.

"Awful. Lots of silence."

"Rather go to his funeral than yours," Hameeda said suddenly, a defiant look on her face.

"Oh, Hameeda, I've missed you so much." Shireen teared up.

"Now stop that. You'll be home before you know it. Put things to rights."

"Don't think I can go home. Mother said I could but—"

"Shireen, you must. And you can. Now that *he's*—"

"Hameeda, you can say his name. Farouz. Say it. He does not frighten me anymore."

"Farouz, Farouz! But I don't believe you were ever scared of him." Hameeda spoke with pride.

Shireen squeezed her friend's hand, then asked about school. Her eyes widened as Hameeda gushed with stories and gossip and goings-on.

"But now—serious face." Hameeda smiled. "We have computers back. And Miss Jezar has come back. And—"

"And?"

"Boys! We might go co-ed!"

Then came the screams. Vertical plunge, roller-coaster screams that brought guards bursting into the room. They looked around and saw nothing but two girls in a fit of snorty giggles. The young soldiers grumbled incoherently before leaving, pickle-faced and a bit angry. The girls burst out laughing again as the door slammed shut. It felt good to laugh again.

A few days later, Shireen laughingly told Micah about the incident. "We apologized. Later, you know. Wow, Mates, you should be there!"

"Glad I wasn't." Micah squirmed in his seat.

He had arrived about half an hour before. Uncle Bernard had been okay about driving him back to the Medical Center in

Beersheba. More than willing to mooch about and give Micah some "private time," as he called it, somewhat condescendingly.

Micah didn't care as long as Uncle Bernard did not hover. He wanted to tell her about his concerns, his fears for her safety, but his resolve to tell her had dissolved when he walked in the room. Shireen didn't seem to notice his reticence. She went merrily on, unafraid and unconcerned. But Micah *was* afraid. For her.

Since he had last seen her, Micah's thoughts regarding Shireen's safety had only gotten darker. And there she was, prattling away a mile a minute, not a care in the world. He put on a doom-and-gloom face, hoping she'd notice and ask what was wrong. But she never did. She said she was to be released the next day and stay in a fancy hotel for a week. A hotel with a pool. In Jerusalem. She gushed on. Apparently "Mister Yossi" was setting up TV interviews, a photo shoot, appearances, and archival footage, whatever that was.

The prospect of umpteen media and public events finally prompted Micah to express his fears. He didn't like the idea of being the big bubble buster, but he felt he had no choice.

"Look, Shireen, I've been thinking." He took a nervous breath. "It's about your brother and how he got to the farmhouse, and—uh, look, I think you're still in deep yogurt. Dangerous danger."

"Mates? What are you saying?"

"Knock, knock," Yossi Chazoom entered without knocking. "Are we decent? Why, if it isn't young Mister Micah. Great news, Shireen, great news."

Shireen leaned forward and any thoughts of concern she might have had just flew away as Chazoom carried on. "It's the signing ceremony. For the Side-by-Side Accord. It will all take place at the International Convention Center. The site of the Eurovision song contests. I know, I know, how yucky can you get, but the I.C.C. is the home of the Israeli Philharmonic, and if it's good enough for them… But Shireen, the main thing is, your friend—" Chazoom took a breath and paused for effect, "your friend the PM wants you there. To give a little speech. Can you do that?"

"Me? Oh, yes."

Unbelievable, Micah roiled inwardly. It's like she never heard a word I said. Chazoom breezes in and I'm on the outs. Deep yogurt? What was I thinking of—dessert? And *dangerous danger?* I can't believe I actually said that.

"You can recite something if you'd rather," said Chazoom.

"Shakespeare?"

"Oh, sure. But no unleashing the dogs of war, okay? The theme will be 'growing together.' I see the stage set with desert grasses and fake rocks and—"

And on he went. Micah could see Shireen was totally caught up by the images Chazoom was conjuring. She looked positively energized.

"Hello, Shireen. Micah. Are you—?" Gilead entered the room.

"Eron." Chazoom clapped his hands together. "Shireen, tell him."

Shireen blushed. Gilead rolled his eyes as Chazoom told him about her speech.

Micah had heard enough. "She's still in danger. Don't any of you see that?" he said angrily, and then stormed out.

Micah tried to slam the door, but it wouldn't slam. Rats, he thought. Rats! He stomped down the corridor toward the elevators, but stopped halfway. He thought about going back, but instead he slumped down on the carpeted floor in a complete funk.

"Cheer up, Micah, you're worrying for nothing."

Micah looked up, and there was Gilead.

"Am I?" said Micah, pulling himself up. "It's *not* for nothing."

Gilead's usual smile was replaced with a look of wary caution.

"So, what is it? Come on, get it off your chest."

"I think someone tipped off that guy in the Old City," Micah said.

"The coin dealer?"

"Not him," Micah said impatiently. "I think that was just coincidence. The guy with a knife…it wasn't Farouz."

"How do you know, did you see him?"

"No, but that's why it couldn't have been Farouz, he wouldn't have done it secretly. He wanted her to see him, for honor and all that crap. So that means someone, someone *else*, wanted her dead. And he's still out there."

"Micah, you don't know that it wasn't—"

"And what about in the desert? Farouz got there long before you lot did. Remember?"

"The bus had a tracking device; he must have put it there."

"Why? If he knew Shireen was on that bus, he would have attacked right in the car park." Micah was unconvinced and getting angry.

"We believe the knife guy in the Old City was Farouz. And Farouz is dead. Micah, let it go."

The elevator opened and Uncle Bernard stepped out.

"And here's your uncle."

"This a private party or is anyone invited?" Bernard chuckled nervously. "Want to say good-bye to Shireen? There's time Micah, we have time." Bernard pointed to her room.

"No. I'll send her a text or something." Micah was incensed at being so easily dismissed.

"He's been through a lot," Bernard said to Gilead as if Micah wasn't there.

"Leave it, Uncle Bernard, just leave it." Micah snapped more harshly than he meant to.

Bernard shrugged a smile. Kids. What can you do?

"And here's the elevator again," Bernard announced with some relief.

As the doors closed, Micah fixed Gilead with an angry, disappointed stare.

# Chapter 63

"Oh, please, Uncle, go on, please. Can I see them?" Micah pleaded.

He could see his uncle was beginning to cave. Micah only called Bernard "Uncle" when he wanted something. And he wanted this particular something very badly, so he had been going on about it since they'd left the hospital in Beersheba.

"I need to see them, just for a few minutes. Just to say thanks, really, and see how they are. I mean they did protect me and everything. Please, please? Me?"

Micah's pointed reference to Bernard's musical era helped sway him.

"All right then, I suppose it's not too far out of our way."

"Thanks, Uncle, you're the best. Yeah, yeah, yeah," he sang.

"All right, don't push it." Bernard tried not to smile.

When they got to the Baka District, Micah found a tree-lined neighborhood replete with old Arab-style mansions, neighborhood cafés, bike paths, and corner parks overflowing with flowers. And more cats. But better cared for than those in the Old City. Food and water bowls had been left out for them.

Bernard dropped Micah off and said he would return in half an hour.

"Thanks, Uncle, you're a good egg. Honest," said Micah.

Bernard bowed slightly. Smiling contentedly, he drove off in pursuit of a cappuccino. Micah walked up a lush garden path to the front door of the big old mansion Rianne had called a *"petite pension."*

He found Yimca and Colonel Jack playing poker, staring each other down like a mongoose and a snake. The hand of cards was quickly concluded, followed by heartfelt hellos. The troupe had gone back to Jerusalem as soon as they could. They were all itching to work again and tourists were flocking back to the ancient capital.

Both ladies, Micah learned, were on a shopping expedition. Then they would pick up Walloo from his physical therapy session. Apparently he was bored; a good sign, said Yimca. The arterial graft had taken and Walloo was on the mend. Yimca told Micah that the tourniquet had saved Walloo's leg and possibly his life.

"Scout stuff," Micah said dismissively.

*"Good* Scout stuff," Jack corrected him smartly, but then grinned through an uncombed mustache.

The colonel was still in a wheelchair. Felt spiffy, he said, refusing to let it get him down. And if Jack felt spiffy, Yimca certainly looked it. A silk dressing gown was draped over his shoulders, covering his bandaged arm. Micah noticed his shock of black hair was no longer as shockingly black, but apart from that he was looking dapper and the mischievous gleam was back in his eye.

Without more ado, the ever-perceptive Yimca asked what was up. So Micah spilled the proverbial beans and gave them his take on events.

"I just know Shireen's still in bloody danger," he ended dramatically. "And Eleni knows it, too. But I can't tell Eron Gilead about Eleni's warning. He'll just give me adult smile, you know?"

"We know. And we are also knowing enough to never be dismissing Eleni, even when we don't know what she is on about," said Yimca.

"Of course, she's a funny old thing, if you get my meaning, but her predictions—they come true more often than not." With some difficulty, Jack leaned forward. "Trouble is, this Gilead thinks like a policeman. The crime is over. The brother is dead. Shireen is alive.

Case closed. But I understand your concerns. Somehow he got the tracking device on our bus, but *how* in itself is not important. What *is* important is the timeline."

"The timeline, Colonel Jack?" Micah was intrigued and grateful that he was at last being taken seriously. "Go on, go on."

"If the bastard brother believed you were on the bus, you're right, why wait till you were miles out of town before attacking? Not so easy to melt away in the desert. Much easier to attack in an urban area. Places to hide, people to hide you. Could have got you in the parking lot, when you were on the bus. But I think Shireen's brother didn't know you were on board—"

"—until *after* you telephoned your uncle from the desert," finished Yimca.

"That's when he found out where we were?" Micah spoke uncertainly. "How?"

"Tipped off. By who?" Jack looked at Micah. "Did you call anyone else? Think!"

"No. But before the phones went dead, Shireen called a girl in her village. She didn't want anyone to know about it. She said she didn't tell her friend or anyone where we were. But she must have done."

"When did Shireen make this call?" asked Jack.

"During the storm. When I was covering up the windows with Walloo."

"During storm." Yimca mulled this over. "You called Uncle Bernard many hours *before* Shireen made her call. But the brother showed up at our farm *soon* after the storm."

"So if Shireen did tell her friend, and the friend did tell the brother—" Micah narrowed his eyebrows, then looked up. "How could he get to the farm so quickly?"

"Quite so, said Jack. "It's quite a drive from Jerusalem to here.

Brother Bastard must have been on his way when the storm hit. Must have known you and Shireen were already here."

"Farouz is knowing where you were *before* Shireen is calling friend. So her friend is in the clear."

"And something else," Micah sighed. "Who knew that me and Shireen would be at the Jaffa Gate? I mean, apart from my family. How did the knife guy know we'd be there? Gilead thinks the knife attack was also Farouz."

"You don't?"

"It wasn't Farouz, I would've seen him. And besides, he'd want Shireen to know…you know?"

No one spoke for a moment.

"So there is another bastard out there who is out for Shireen," Jack said.

There was another silence.

"It gets back to who is doing the tipping off," Yimca said finally. "Who knew where—"

"Who indeed," said Jack.

"Hang on a bit," Micah said. "The cab driver, Mehmet. *He* knew we were in the Old City. I mean, he drove us there. I thought he was looking at us funny. Maybe he followed us and tipped off the bloke with the knife? What do you think?"

"Could be a lead," said Jack. "But get Gilead involved. This Mehmet could be a bad actor."

"Does this Mehmet have a last name?" Yimca raised a quizzical eyebrow.

"Not that I know. And I can hardly search online, must be millions of Mehmets—"

"You remember what he is looking like?"

"Yeah, I'd recognize him if I saw him again. But—"

"If only he could see him again. Well, well." Jack grinned knowingly.

Micah looked from one to the other, confused. Yimca grabbed up a clipboard and perched it on his bony knees. Then he magically produced a pencil.

Micah smiled. "Thumb palmed?" he asked.

"And for the longest time," Yimca admitted with a shrug.

"He used to draw caricatures in restaurants," Jack explained.

"Really?" Micah sat up in his chair.

"But I must not think caricature. I must see this man as you see him, Micah. Now tell me as much as you can. I need details." Yimca twirled the pencil like a wand.

"Thin face. Thick hair—close-cropped to his head. Big forehead. Mid-twenties. No chin. And teeth. He had teeth too big for his mouth. They stuck out," Micah said.

Yimca's hand moved nonstop, keeping pace with Micah's description. Words were transformed into graphite lines and a remembered personality became shaded into life.

"Eyes?" Yimca was carefully crosshatching. He looked up, one eyebrow raised inquiringly.

"They were round. Not bulgy but set back, dark-like. And he had ears."

"Everyone is having ears. Big ears?"

"Longish ears."

"Beard?" asked Yimca, without looking up.

"Not exactly. But stubble, you know."

"I think I know," Yimca said, shading in his sketch. "Thin lips, fat lips?"

"Not fat. And he had a bit of a nose, big but not pointy."

Yimca stabbed dots, created thin lines, and then paused before sweeping the page once more with careful, more delicate strokes.

"Like this?" Yimca slowly turned the clipboard around for the big reveal. It was Mehmet.

Micah started to applaud. "It's like you know him!"

"Should I sign it?" Yimca asked innocently.

Jack smiled wearily. Just then, Micah heard a car honking. He looked out and saw his uncle. He also saw it was raining.

Rats, thought Micah, just like England.

Carefully Jack placed the artwork in an envelope, and then in a plastic bag. He suggested making copies and circulating the sketch, but again urged caution. Micah insisted he would do nothing risky. Nothing. Not a thing. He hooked his friends a big thumbs-up, then took off.

Yimca and Jack exchanged looks as their game resumed. Micah was an endearingly bad liar.

## Chapter 64

Bernard tsk-tsked at the rain as he drove. He talked non-stop as Micah tried to peer out the window, trying to think.

"Your Aunt Gilly won't like this. Hates to cook in this weather. We should pick up some take-away. Gilly will love that. We'll all love that, what'd you say, eh?"

"Can you get Indian food here?"

"Of course you can. But I don't. Too spicy. Jippy tummy, can't be helped." Bernard quickly looked down at the expanding oval of his stomach. He looked up, smiling. "Falafel?"

"Falafel? Falafel! Uncle, you are a genius. You are brilliant." Micah's face brightened.

"I am?" Bernard rather took to the praise.

"I know this brilliant falafel stand, near where the magicians park their bus when they're doing shows, and the vendor probably knows all the cab drivers, and—" He stopped abruptly.

"Cab drivers? And?"

"Well, you know, I meant cab drivers know this falafel man. They know all the good spots, don't they? Cabbies. They always seem to, you know—" Micah backtracked as best he could.

He felt like kicking himself for almost blurting out about looking for Mehmet. Fortunately his uncle had visions of chickpea fritters in mind, and not images of a might-be treacherous cab driver.

"Sells good falafel, does he?" Bernard seemed to be answering his own question.

"Yes, fresh, makes it fresh, I saw him. Are we near the Jewish Quarter?"

"Driving right past it. Glad you like falafel." Bernard grinned. "Make a local of you yet."

Apart from the illuminated ramparts, most of the Old City was in rain drenched, icky darkness. Uncle Bernard pulled up at the lot, gave Micah some money, and wished him luck.

Micah was wet through by the time he took shelter under the awning of the falafel stand.

"A customer. Praise be," the vendor shouted to be heard above the rain exploding on the corrugated metal roof. He threw Micah a few paper towels. "Here, no charge."

Micah nodded his thanks as he wiped his face and hair.

"I was here a week ago. Had a great sandwich. Five please. Falafel."

"Five? Serious? Very good, very good. I make fresh for you."

Micah watched the vendor drop mounds of falafel mixture into the deep fryer, then he pulled out the plastic bag and slid out Yimca's drawing. He spread it on the counter.

"Mehmet, you say? He is ugly as this?" The vendor looked closely at the sketch.

"He's no oil painting, but he's a friend. I'm looking for him."

"A cab driver, huh?" The vendor drained the crispy balls on brown paper.

"Yes. I left something in his cab. School stuff. Anyway, if he shows up—he might come here, and if he does, give me a call, okay?" Micah wrote his name and phone number on a takeout menu. "This guy, he'll remember me as 'Shabbos Boy'—that's what he called me."

"Here's your falafel, Shabbos Boy. If I see him—"

Micah thanked him, then hopscotched puddles back to the car with the food.

The vendor watched him for a second or two before scanning the overhead awning. It was peppered with countless business cards. He grabbed one with a red border.

"Mehmet Drives!" the card proclaimed in large type.

# Chapter 65

THE NIGHT RAIN HAD FADED INTO GHOSTLY WISPS of steam and the day broke on a clear blue sky. Shireen was driven in a well-appointed SUV from Beersheba to a fancy hotel in Jerusalem. The plan was to keep her there, sequestered and protected, until after the signing ceremony.

Her suite was large, with panoramic views of the Yamin Moshe district and the ramparts of the Old City. She smiled, happy to be alone for a moment. And it was just a moment. Before she had even unpacked, Chazoom was hurrying his young charge out of the hotel into another waiting car.

Ten minutes later, they met with Singer and Gilead in front of what appeared to be a hospital. But it was like no hospital Shireen had ever seen. It was, in fact, part of a converted monastery on one side of Mount Scopus, in northern Jerusalem. The high fence and concrete barriers surrounding the ancient buildings seemed out of place. But inside, the grounds evoked a sense of peace that harkened back to more tranquil times.

They told her it was called the Puzzle Palace. For spy stuff, they said. Electronic spy stuff. Monks' cells were now home to Magic Lantern operatives, hackers, counter-hackers, sniffers, decoders, virus doctors—cyber warriors on the battle lines of electronic and wireless communication.

The Huddle Room was oddly named. Shireen had expected something small, but they entered a large, open room. Topographical maps were projected onto enormous flat screens. Two analysts were seated behind control panels. Hands moved across keyboards like squirrels burying nuts.

A young analyst waved the group forward but kept his eyes on the screen. He had a long face and ears to match, and was appropriately known as Gun Dog. Singer stared at him, appalled by his disheveled appearance. The other analyst was a young woman named Leah, a graphic artist and specialist in composite images.

Using Shireen's description, Leah drew a digital diagram of the terrorist hideout. In half an hour, they had a dimensional representation of the villa and grounds. Then Shireen was asked to look at photos of terror suspects. She identified several, including Anwar, the creepy tailor. Flipping through pictures on a screen was more tiring than she ever would have imagined. At one point, she almost nodded off. Then a photo of the Oily One snapped her to alertness again. He looked a bit thinner, younger, but it was definitely Jamal. Quickly Shireen passed on to the next shot. She had not flagged him. Then a man with bulging eyes and a large mouth appeared on the screen. She looked up.

"This one. He came near us. By the Old City gate. I saw him."

"Did he have a knife? Did he attack you?"

"I saw him. Perhaps, yes." Shireen shrugged.

Gilead studied the image very carefully. He recalled what Micah had said. Perhaps the attack was not as simple as he had imagined.

# Chapter 66

Everyone nodded to Micah as he slouched across the school yard. Students, teachers, even the school secretary seemed more solicitous. Micah was amazed. He only hoped his new, polished profile would help with "Operation Mehmet," as he called it. He had brought two dozen copies of Yimca's drawing to school to show around. Jakey said he would help during break.

Just before his first class, Micah had his picture taken for an ID card. It was all part of the new safety measures the school was implementing. Micah was told not to smile by an awkward-looking security guy in his twenties, with red lips and cheeks that made him look as if he'd just gotten out of a hot bath. His name was Udo. Just to be contrary, Micah grinned for his picture.

"Ha, ha," said Udo wearily as he handed over the plasticized card.

On his way to class, Micah's phone vibrated. He didn't recognize the number but hoped it was Falafel Man.

"Hello, Shabbos Boy."

"Mehmet!" Micah exclaimed with great relief.

"So you look for me?" Mehmet laughed. "Some guy say you left something in my cab?"

"Nah, nah, it's my dad," Micah lied. "He's coming to Israel, to Jerusalem, and I thought you could give him a tour. He'll pay you and everything."

"I give him ultra-best tour. Come over, we figure out route, yes?"

"Sounds great."

Mehmet gave him the address. Micah wrote it down.

"I'm in school now. About four? That okay?"

"How about early? At one. I have to work. If you can't make it, we pick other time, yes?"

"No, no, I'll be there about one, or just a bit after. Okay?"

"Okay, Shabbos Boy. I play the Turkish music you love so much. Remember?"

"Oh, no. Not that. Anything but that, Gordon Bennet."

"I know, I was just funning with you. See you later, Shabbos Boy."

Micah called Gilead. Straight to voice mail. He sent a text. He pocketed his phone just as the school bell stopped. Micah ran to his first class, which stretched out like a wad of gum mixed with glue. Finally it ended. He had three minutes before the next one started. Micah went to the water fountain. And there was Udo.

Micah darted around the corner. He looked back and saw Udo again, hovering, pretending to read outdated stuff on a notice board. Micah seethed, convinced the security guard was shadowing him. He went outside and propped himself against the wall.

Again, he called Gilead. Still no luck. He was getting beyond worried. He backtracked to the portable classrooms. He scrolled the numbers on his phone. Colonel Chazoom? The big signing ceremony was that night, and Chazoom was orchestrating it, and Shireen's appearance, and who knew what else. So he called him.

A metallic voice announced that Micah was not calling a valid number. Not a valid number? Then Micah remembered—Chazoom must have a new phone. Nice of him to give me the number. And where was Eron? At lunch? On break? On a hike?

Right, okay, that's it, Micah thought, that is it! Enough is enough. He decided to call the police. He pressed for English and waited. Someone answered. He tried to explain what he knew. The dispatcher transferred his call. At last, he thought. Then a computer voice asked him to select a language. He requested English.

A few seconds later, another metallic voice said to leave a message. He didn't bother.

"What are you doing here?" Udo had suddenly appeared.

"I've got to go to the loo." Micah gripped his stomach and ran to the bathroom. Udo looked momentarily confused but followed. Locking the cubicle door, Micah leaned against it. He flushed the toilet with his foot, then made yet another call. He crossed his fingers.

"Colonel Jack!" Micah was relieved to hear his friend's gruff voice. He explained the situation. Jack asked where he was supposed to meet Mehmet. Micah gave him the address.

"That's in Silwan. South of the Old City. Not a good place. And this Mehmet suspects nothing?"

Micah explained about pretending to hire Mehmet for a sightseeing tour. Jack sighed, said Gilead should be reached before doing anything. Jack even volunteered to help track him down.

"Micah, I wish I could help, but beyond making calls, I'm in no state to gallivant about—"

"I don't expect you to, Colonel Jack. You've done enough. All of you. I just wanted to talk to someone. Need some advice, I suppose."

"My advice is to wait. You can't wander about Silwan alone. It's too bloody dangerous. Micah, you understand me?" Jack was trying to be patient. "You must wait for—"

"Wait for what? For Shireen to get killed? That ceremony is tonight. I can't wait."

"Yes, you can," said Jack emphatically.

"You don't get it, do you? None of you get it!"

Micah put away the phone, roiling mad. Did Colonel Jack think he was stupid? He wasn't going to start anything with Mehmet. That would be nuts, and he knew it. But he could talk to him. Use his phone, record a bit of audio. He could do that. Get the ball rolling. But oh, no. He had to wait. Wait for an adult. Micah growled bitterly. If he and Shireen had waited for adults, they would both be dead by now. Dead! He slammed the toilet door so hard it rattled the other cubicles.

"*Zuh-heeroot?*" asked Udo.

He spoke more Hebrew that Micah barely understood and then, in halting English, he said he'd wait in the hall. That's where Micah pushed past him, railing against the world.

Jamal had been overseeing the shutdown of the secret village. He intended to leave some equipment. Something for the enemy to find. The specialists, the mentors, and those preparing for martyrdom were already gone. The Brigade would rise again. But Jamal regretted leaving that which could not be taken: the intricate system of tunnels and trenches. Above ground, all had looked uninhabited and barren; beneath, the insurgency had pulsed unseen.

"You wait for the Jewish?"

It was Anwar, the tailor. For effect, he had a grenade pin sewn into the measuring tape that hung around his scrawny neck.

"I wait for the wind." Jamal stared at the emptiness, the sad beauty of it all. He turned away and headed for the villa on the opposite hillside.

Jamal needed to be alone. He entered the villa. Even here, much had been cleared away. It looked ramshackle. But some things remained. He unlocked the rooms where Shireen had stayed. He was shocked at what he found. The place was like a camel's trough. Everything thrown everywhere. Clothes, CDs, stuffed animals. A mess. All new, all for her. Just left. She took nothing. He bristled with the prickliness of a stern uncle.

Fool, he thought. Fool! Why would she take these things? How could she? She had been groomed for Heaven, not for shopping malls and wicked dancing parlors.

For a tiny moment, he almost smiled, and then his pocket rang. No number appeared on the phone's obsidian panel, but he knew who was calling.

"The evacuation goes well, Leader. The task is almost complete." Jamal walked out of the room onto the lush, plant-filled courtyard.

"The girl was shown a picture of you, Jamal." A sharp intake of breath. "But she did not bring this to the attention of the Jewish."

"Perhaps she has not turned against us. Or our cause." Jamal was pleased—at least somewhat.

"She identified Khalid."

"A pity we could not have dealt with her before. Now we must wait." Jamal felt oddly dejected.

"I do not wait. The wheels are set in motion. It will soon be over."

"Apologies Leader but I assumed, with the so-called cessation of hostilities that it would be impossible to take action for at least—"

"You assumed? Oh Jamal, how you disappoint me, even now."

The line went dead. Jamal pocketed his phone. Could it be? The Rafah Brigade at odds with the higher-ups? Jamal knew the political leadership in Ramallah was going along with the Side-by-Side ceremony, for now anyway. As an act of conciliation, all paramilitary operations and civilian attacks had been suspended. And yet his leader was clearly planning something.

He sat down on the stone seat in the garden. He stared at the pond and pondered the possibilities.

# Chapter 67

"Am I a genius, or not? You can admit it. Go on." Chazoom grinned shamelessly.

"Maybe." Shireen held up the halter-top dress, metallic and shiny like a beaded costume. She looked at it with a critical eye. She laid it down, picked up a seamless, velvet black leotard and held it against herself. Then she picked up the dress again.

"Fashion show. I want to see. Go change, go on, go on."

She rushed into her bedroom. Chazoom sank languidly into the sofa, more than a little pleased with himself. Shireen's outfit would satisfy his politically sensitive bosses, Islamic sensibilities, as well as his junior prima donna. Three for three. He hoped.

Chazoom recalled when he last broached the subject of what she should wear for the event. He had handed Shireen an Egyptian magazine filled with the latest fashions for young Muslim women.

"Pick something," he had said, "anything." But Shireen just threw the catalog back at him.

"Just look, look! Body bags with slits. Me? Never."

Chazoom shuddered at the memory. But that was then, and this was now. The American president's visit had snowballed the signing ceremony into a bit of a circus. Cynically he knew nothing much would change. Whatever the outcome, he would be there. Shireen would make a short speech. Perfect. A natural, she's a natural, he thought.

He got to his feet when Shireen reappeared. He was speechless. Apart from the lump around the cast-like bandage, the leotard fit perfectly. The flowing top made of strands of diamond-cut beads shimmered like the surface of a sun-skimmed lake.

The dress was padded very slightly in the appropriate areas, skating the thin ice of propriety. But it worked. Even though she moved a bit self-consciously, Shireen looked stunning.

"Perfect. That outfit is going to bend a few mullahs out of shape, but my, oh my, who cares?"

"Montsees! Why are you still here?"

Micah almost jumped, startled by the science teacher in the doorway of the lab.

"Just leaving, sir." He hustled out with his books and a tissue box containing ingredients he had "borrowed" to make fire pellets.

If things with Mehmet got out of hand, he would drop a fire pellet somewhere in the apartment. Maybe in a trash can. An ashtray. Once the pellet caught fire—instant diversion. Easy-peasy. Then he'd leg it. Micah had it all planned out. He headed to the locker room, where he'd arranged to meet Jakey to explain how his cousin could help him.

"It'll work. I've done it before." Micah was emphatic.

"A lot can go wrong," said Jakey, trying not to sound anxious.

"I know, but I've got to get proof Shireen is still in danger. No good after she's dead."

"Udo will find out, and you—" Jakey slapped his hands together like he was washing his hands of Micah, of the whole escapade. "You will be done."

"Udo'll never know I've floated. You will help, won't you?"

"I said I would, and I will."

Micah smiled his thanks and got down to business. He removed the science lab materials from the tissue box. Using a dropper bottle he dripped glycerin into an inverted half-capsule, which he jammed into another half-capsule containing potassium permanganate. He pushed another half-capsule on top to seal the liquid in place. The dry, purplish chemical and the glycerin were still separate, both held within a capsule not much bigger than a headache pill. Micah made two more pellets, then uncoiled three safety pins.

"What is that for?" Jakey asked, fascinated.

"They're triggers. I'll put them in later."

"What is going to— What're you planning?"

"You really want to know?"

Jakey shook his head.

From his locker Micah pulled out his extra-long red-and-white Arsenal scarf and a pair of scissors. He paused for a moment, took a breath, then cut it lengthwise. Micah had brought the scarf over from England, a prized possession.

"I never thought I would see you do this," Jakey said. "I know this means a lot to you."

"She means more. Now listen..." Micah explained what to do, and Jakey took off with one half of the scarf in his pants pocket.

Micah waited a couple of minutes before emerging from the locker room with the other half of the scarf around his neck and bouncing a practice soccer ball. He waved to Udo, who was standing just outside the locker area. Udo waved back. Micah turned away. He kicked the ball along the school fence. Then he kicked it gently through the main gate and followed it. For just a second, he was out of Udo's sight. Udo started for the gate but stopped when the scarf-wrapped boy darted back into the schoolyard, again kicking the ball along the inside edge of the fence. Udo stayed back but kept an eye on the back of the boy, unaware Micah was long gone.

It had been a simple switch.

Micah had kicked the ball toward the school gates. Jakey had waited, unseen, behind one of the brick columns on which the gates were hung. When Micah passed him the ball, Jakey kicked it back into the schoolyard and followed it in. From a distance, with everyone dressed virtually the same, a red-and-white scarf and a ball were enough to differentiate Micah from the other students. And of course, Udo had kept his eye on the ball, as Micah had known he would. Everyone looks at a moving object, a waving hand, a coin spinning, a ball rolling…

Mehmet looked across to the corner of the room.

"He is coming. If God wills it…I don't want to be here when he shows up. Okay, boss?"

No answer. Mehmet wanted to leave his apartment but had been told to stay. At least they had returned his cab. But why did the spider in the corner sit there like that, cross-legged on the floor? And why was the other one smiling? He remembered them from the first meeting in the café. And then in the car. Especially the one with the knife. The withered hand. And those eyes. He was supposed to scare the boy.

He scares me, thought Mehmet. They both did. This was not turning out the way he had imagined.

# Chapter 68

The journey was taking longer than Micah had expected. He was walking down a one-way street; cabs sped past him, too fast to be hailed. He held up his hand, the way he would in London. But he was not in London, and no one stopped. He'd forgotten to point to the pavement. When he did, a Mercedes pulled up and took him to the entrance to The City of David, in the al-Bustan neighborhood of Silwan. Two communities just outside the Old City, one Jewish, one Arab. Both shared the same glorious views of the Dome of the Rock, but little else.

The cab driver would not go farther. Micah would have to walk the rest of the way. Not really knowing where he was, Micah ventured down a steep street, past uncollected garbage. A lot of the buildings looked ramshackle. Boarded windows. Graffiti. Micah was nervous but continued walking. He held out a map, tried to look like a lost tourist. In a way, he was.

A few men had gathered on a crumbling sidewalk. Micah noticed them eyeing him suspiciously, but he went up to them anyway. He showed them the address he'd written down.

They spoke no English, pretended not to understand his Hebrew. Hand gestures, shrugs, and jabbing fingers were twisted in the air like bits of human origami. Micah seemed to be heading in the right direction.

*You're late, Shabbos Boy…*

Mehmet's apartment building was a breeze-block cube built on a rubble-yellow landscape with faded bits of shrubbery. Micah wasn't sure it was the right place until he saw Mehmet's cab parked outside. With a sigh of relief, he took out his phone and plugged in Mehmet's number.

"Hey, where are you, Shabbos Boy?"

"I'm here. Outside. Downstairs, actually. Sorry I'm late."

"Its okay, Shabbos Boy. Look at the third floor window. I see you, you see me, yes?"

Micah glanced up and there was Mehmet, waving and grinning through his too-big teeth.

"In my apartment—I play the Turkish music. Your favorite!"

"Oh, not that. I told you, I hate it." Grinning, Micah waved a fist up at him.

*Oh, Shabbos Boy, you are not understanding. So I must do more?*

"Shabbos Boy, you must—" Mehmet yelled into the phone, beyond the window, beyond consequence. He sounded scared. But he said no more.

Micah looked at his phone. The signal was gone. He glanced up at the window. Mehmet was gone.

Okay, he thought, a bit odd, but—

Micah entered the rain-stained building. Tiny shadows were thrown by the puckered concrete skin that covered the inside walls. Micah heard the hum of machinery. A phone chimed. Children cried. Someone yelled. A door was slammed, but no one appeared. Then silence.

*I call him Shabbos Boy; it's just a name. I mean nothing by it, please—*

Micah found the elevator. He pressed a button in the greasy brass surround. He waited and waited, annoyed at his own laziness. He realized he should have taken the stairs. Finally the door opened. The metal box smelled of pee and sweat. Dirt was caked up in the corners. A dim light bulb was imprisoned in a metal grille.

The elevator door opened onto a small landing. Micah looked around. No one was in sight. He sat down on grimy concrete and inserted a safety pin into the top of each divided fire pellet. He would only have to push the pins through to the bottom half of the capsules to start the reaction. The glycerin would drip through onto the permanganate and the pellet would ignite. The time it took to flare up depended on how small the crystals were ground. Micah figured he would have a minute. Time enough to run if he needed to.

A few thumping beats of music came from an apartment along the hallway. Turkish rap. Micah knocked on its blue door, splintered with age and neglect. No answer. Micah pushed on the door and it stuttered open. He called out to Mehmet. No response. Peering inside, he saw a pile of clothing in one corner.

"Hey Mehmet, your laundry, it's starting to pong a bit."

Micah tried to smile. Maybe he's in the loo, he thought. The air was warm and smelled sour, like rancid meat in an outdoor market. Micah joked about the music, how he hated it, how Mehmet should turn it down, how—

The door slammed shut behind him. Micah turned around. Standing there was a wiry-looking man with a knife clenched in his fist, angled low. Not Mehmet. Micah started backing away. He turned again, saw another, taller figure. A bug-eyed man with huge lips and a withered hand. Micah wanted to call out, but he was too scared. He backed up and didn't stop until he hit a wall. He looked around. And then he saw it. A body, lying there, ungainly and awkward, necklaced by a seeping collar of blood. Micah couldn't see the face but he knew who it was.

"Oh, Mehmet." Micah could barely speak.

Micah looked at the door but that escape route was blocked by the smaller of the two men.

Micah pressed himself against the wall and started slowly edging his way around the room. He could see the one with the withered hand moving slowly, so slowly, towards him. He saw a smile on the large lips, and those eyes. Suddenly a knife appeared in the man's good hand, but he didn't seem eager to use it.

He's playing with me, thought Micah, toying with me. If I can just get to the window, I'll jump, I'll jump.

Micah's crazy notion of jumping to freedom, of somehow melting through a closed window was taking hold in his panicked brain. The wiry man said something that made the withered one smile more. Then the smile froze. Micah dove across the floor, just missing the sweeping blade by a mere knife point. More laughter. As Micah landed, he brushed against Mehmet's body. The head lolled over, and Micah saw the blanched and jagged face of death. And that's when he found his voice. He screamed for something beyond help. For Mehmet, for himself. A scream that fused with the discordant music that still filled the room, a ghastly coda to the song, to Mehmet's spent life, to his own impending murder.

The withered one was closing in. Then something cut through Mehmet's noisy music: the sound of splintering wood. The withered one spun about as the door burst open. A loud battle cry poured through the opening. Micah heard grunting words in Arabic. Then a high-pitched scream, followed by a creaking, painful groan.

It had happened so fast. Micah saw the wiry one was pinned to the wall by a three-pronged cane, the type seniors used to get around. But the person wielding this particular cane was no senior. Just a very angry man. A very *big* angry man.

# Chapter 69

"Walloo!" Micah called out just as Walloo pulled the cane away from the wiry man's chest.

The guy slid to the floor in a puddle of pain and shock. The one with the bad hand prowled this new adversary like a jackal looking for a weakness in its prey. He found it as Walloo reached down to help Micah rise.

The jackal sprang.

Walloo pushed Micah clear and swung his arm up to protect himself as a small blade ripped into a bicep. A lion-like roar of pain gave way to a growl of triumph as Walloo hurled his attacker aside. The man ricocheted against the opposite wall, but within seconds scrambled back into a crouching, fighting stance.

Walloo pulled the knife from his arm and flung it aside. Blood flowed, dripped down, but he paid it no heed.

Micah could see the normally smiling face was set granite hard. Mesmerized, he watched the ongoing duel.

The man with the withered hand was smiling. Walloo lifted and moved the outstretched cane in a small arc. As if drawn by it, the attacker mirrored the sweep of the cane. Walloo tried to move forward to finish the fight—but then he stopped.

Micah was shocked as his friend faltered. He tried to get up to reach him, but Walloo gave him a quick, enraged look. *Keep down*, he seemed to be saying, *keep down.* But Micah could see Walloo was fading fast. He grabbed hold of the table and pushed with all his might.

The attacker glanced down for a second then looked up just as quickly, barely distracted. Again Micah pushed on the table, hoping to get it between Walloo and the knifer. While he shoved he saw Walloo fumble the cane in his uninjured hand.

The table skidded and Micah turned it over. It clattered on the bare floor. Now Micah had the attacker's attention. He looked at Micah and smiled. The small knife was now gone. From nowhere he had produced a long, curved blade, turning it in his good hand as though admiring its brilliance.

"You are barely worthy of my khanjar…but it will teach you not to interfere in the affairs of men."

With frightening speed, he spun around the upturned table and closed in on Micah.

That's when Walloo charged.

The three-pronged cane had become a lance, and Walloo was both knight and destrier, moving as one unstoppable force. The rubberized prongs connected and the attacker was pushed backwards. His feet skimmed the floor. Micah could not believe how quickly and effectively Walloo had mounted his attack.

Then Micah heard the sound of breaking ice as Walloo threw the bug-eyed man into the window frame. Attacked by breaking glass, the killer screamed as searing pain needled his senses and punctured his skin. Like a martyr in a stained glass window, he hung there, pinned and imprisoned.

One more push would send the man flying through the window, stabbing at air.

"Don't do it," Micah said as Walloo leaned forward on his cane.

Walloo snarled, then nodded reluctantly. He slumped against the wall as Micah began calling the police.

"You were brilliant, Walloo, bloody superb." Micah was talking loudly, trying to keep Walloo awake and engaged.

"Thank Colonel Jack. Told me to come here. Wanted eye kept on you…I have big eye."

Walloo tried to smile but it turned into a painful grimace.

"I've called for help. Just hang on, Walloo."

Walloo nodded. While Micah made another call, he looked about.

"Gone! Look! The other one, where is he?" Walloo whacked his good arm into the wall.

"Must have snuck out, I didn't see…"

Micah carefully picked his way around the room. Suddenly he saw the figure of a man. Micah recoiled, then relaxed.

"Oh, it's you," he said with relief.

Eron Gilead was standing in the opened doorway.

"What happened here? Don't touch anything, don't—

"I won't," said Micah wearily.

"So 'ow did he end up there?" Gilead pointed to the man stuck in the window.

"Walloo skewered him."

"His name is Khalid Omalah. He's the one who tried to kill you at the Jaffa Gate. Shireen identified him for us. And this one? This is Mehmet? The cab driver you were looking for?" Gilead indicated the body on the floor.

"Yeah, it's him, poor chap," Micah said. "I think he tried to warn me but I still don't get why he was tied up with the others— Oh, and there was this other bloke. But he got away. He just—"

"I'll need a description. You okay with that?"

"Yeah, I'm fine. Right as rain." Micah shuddered, then pointed. "And you know Walloo. If he hadn't shown up when he did— Well, anyway, here we are."

The comforting wail of approaching emergency vehicles drew their attention.

"Walloo has the big hurt. Not good," Walloo mumbled.

"Hear that, Walloo? The cavalry's coming. You were brilliant, the way you faked him out. Faked me out, too, bloody hell." Micah stood by his big friend, feeling very proud of him.

"Now listen, Micah, I must ask something. Very important. You do for me. Yes?"

For the first time, Micah saw fear in Walloo's eyes.

"Yes, of course. What is it? Anything."

"Don't tell Eleni!"

# CHAPTER 70

THE APPROACHING SIRENS RATTLED Khalid from his tortured stupor. He felt a tingling numbness. His eyelids fluttered. He saw the khanjar on the floor. Then he saw the big curved knife in his hand. It felt strangely sharp and painful. Good, he thought. Good. What I feel is nothing to the pain I will inflict upon my enemy. Oh, the curving pain of the khanjar. He felt it.

There was a wheezing sound, a hard, sharp, tearing noise as glass tumbled and smashed.

Micah saw him first, staggering toward Walloo, a long glass shard in his hand. Blood was seeping through his fingers.

"Walloo!" Micah screamed as Khalid lunged. Then every other sound in the room was obliterated, and every action and reaction was stilled on a heartbeat.

Gunfire.

Khalid spun around and collapsed in a heap of twisted flesh and glass. Seconds later, Gilead was standing over him, a semiautomatic still trained on him. He lowered the weapon.

"Clear," he said.

The apartment was cordoned off, and the forensic team moved in. Downstairs, Walloo was helped into the ambulance, where his arm was temporarily treated. Micah didn't look or feel too good either. His teeth had started to chatter and his face was white as flour. Gilead swiped a blanket from the ambulance and put it on Micah's shoulders.

"I'm fine. Honest," Micah lied.

"Big gulps of air, big breath, I think," Walloo said. "And Micah, don't forget—"

"Don't tell Eleni. I won't forget."

Micah held onto Walloo's big paw for a second or two, and then gave him a strong-fisted wave as the medics closed the ambulance door. Micah and Gilead watched the vehicle pull away.

"How did you find me?" Micah asked.

"I was at the I.C.C., in meetings. But I got your message. Finally. Called your Colonel Jack. He had Mehmet's address. Mind you, he didn't tell me he sent in the big guy. Glad he did."

"Me too."

Micah called Colonel Jack, and in one breath told him what a daft-arsed twerp he had been, and that he was dead right about everything, and Walloo had been totally brilliant.

They were soon out of Silwan on the highway skirting the Old City walls. But instead of heading north for French Hill, Gilead turned west toward the New City. Micah thought of Mehmet. He tried to imagine what he might have done differently. But nothing came to mind.

"Aren't you taking me home?" asked Micah.

"I will, but I want to see someone first; you all right with that?"

"Yeah, okay, but I'm a bit of mess and I feel sick."

"If you feel like throwing up, I know just the person to do it on."

# Chapter 71

"Oh, my, Mister Micah!" Chazoom shot a worried look at Gilead. "Is he okay?"

"He's fine," said Gilead.

"Really?" Chazoom raised an eyebrow but said nothing.

"Oh, Mates. Are you—" Shireen could neither express her concern nor hide her fear. Micah looked as if he'd just returned from a war zone. Despite the blanket, she could plainly see the smeared blood on Micah's clothes.

Micah mumbled hello. Behind the ebullient colonel were three guards in suits and sunglasses, constantly scanning the hallway as if they were expecting someone. One muttered into his sleeve. Either used to servants or to security personnel, Chazoom ignored them completely.

"If Micah is now a target—" Gilead looked intently at the senior officer.

"Got it." Then, with a grudging smile, "And I'm sure Micah has lots to tell us?"

The suite doors were open and music poured out like bathwater down a drain. It sounded like people barking in German with bits of music thrown in, or so Micah imagined. Chazoom bristled as he pulled sodas from the mini-fridge.

"It is recitative. Eighteenth-century rap," he said dryly.

Micah and Shireen stared at each other, totally bewildered.

"*The Magic Flute*. Mozart?"

"Oh, yeah, right. A little night music and all that stuff. *Amadeus.* Saw the movie."

"He saw the movie." Chazoom looked at Gilead in disbelief as he turned the music down. "So! What happened? Tell us all."

Shireen and Chazoom looked anguished as Micah's frightening tale was retold. Relief softened some of their distress as Micah recounted Walloo's unexpected arrival. But Shireen had been betrayed. That was now irrefutable.

"Why they go after Micah?" asked Shireen.

"I don't know. Maybe they figured we might end up believing him."

"Believing Shireen is still…in danger?" Chazoom stared blankly.

"I am now convinced she is," Gilead said, admitting they had dropped the ball.

Chazoom turned and spoke in Arabic. Shireen looked confused, answered in kind. She sounded angry. Micah needed no translation to know what had been said.

"The PM will be disappointed, but under the circumstances," Chazoom reverted to English, a tight smile firmly in place. "It's too dangerous, Shireen. I am sorry. We have to keep you safe."

"I am not coward. Not." Shireen was fuming. "I was invited, by Prime Minister, to go. I will go." Now she looked as stubborn as she was mad.

"Shireen, are you listening?" It was Micah's turn to be mad. "I almost got killed today. You just want to be in a bloody spotlight—"

"Not true. That is not truth."

"You want to be a star," he yelled as if hurling an insult. "A stupid starlet!"

Her blue eyes froze over with cold rage, but Micah knew he had hit a chord. She was yelling now in coarse Arabic, and Micah shouted back in ripe Cockney. It was Babel. Only louder. Chazoom flapped about, trying to calm them down.

She switched back to English. "You think I do for fame. For red carpets? You are not Mates!"

Shireen ran into the bedroom. Doors slammed, drawers rocked.

Micah was almost out of breath from yelling so hard. The three exchanged nervous glances. Everyone looked drained. Shireen unexpectedly came back out, and went right up to Micah.

"I am the worst friend in all the world. I am…you still Mates?"

"Don't be stupid."

Her face crumpled, blue eyes now a melted wave of shock and distress.

"Of course I am. I'm just worried sick about you, you twerp," Micah added quickly.

Despite his bloody clothes, Shireen hugged him as tightly as she could.

# Chapter 72

ENTERING HIS MODEST APARTMENT, Jamal locked the door, flopped down, and reached to the side table. Without even looking, he pulled out a burlap bag. Hidden inside, a bottle of malt whiskey.

He poured a large drink into a glass tumbler enclosed in a metal cup holder, the kind used for tea. He dropped ice cubes and mint leaves into the glass. The amber liquid looked like strong mint tea. He smiled to himself. Even here, quite alone, subterfuge never ended.

The buzzer rang. Jamal looked out the window. A delivery man was holding a pizza box in one hand while pressing, with the other, every bell on the side of the building. It happened all the time. He buzzed the man in.

Jamal sat on the edge of a well-worn armchair and nursed his drink. He let the aroma of the whiskey waft around his nostrils. He sipped the scotch.

Where to go? Did it matter? He knew it did not. The journey would determine his destination. He looked around the place he called home. He would leave it, and he would miss it. Silently he slipped out of his apartment.

The delivery man rang the bell of Jamal's apartment and tried the door.

The noise of a shot ricocheted around the stairwell as the bullet ripped the man's insides. The delivery man dropped like a stone. The pizza box fell from his grasp. And with it the concealed gun. Jamal stepped over him.

"I knew it might come to this. Who sent you?" Jamal whispered politely.

Blood bubbled from the man's mouth and obliterated the reply. Along with his life.

Jamal reentered his apartment, picked up his case, and walked out into the alleyway toward the waiting cab. No smell of pizza! Jamal should have known faster. A gun in a box. So clumsy. So obvious. He felt pleased with himself, but also angry that he, Jamal, was now a loose end.

Someone would pay for this, he mused. One day.

# CHAPTER 73

MICAH WENT UPSTAIRS TO HIS ROOM to shower and change while Gilead recounted the day's events to the Rothners. Sighs were sighed. Angry glances exchanged. Worried looks thawed only slightly when Micah came back down. He explained as best he could.

"We never even got a text, let alone a phone call." Bernard turned to Gilly. "Did we?"

"Micah, why did you go to a place like that? And to go alone and, and—we would never have known. Because nobody told us." She turned accusingly to Jakey.

"He told me," said Jakey. "He asked me not to say."

"I did not know anything of this," Zeke shrugged.

"What is the matter with you boys? I've just...had it. With all three of you!"

"Sorry, Aunt Gilly. Honest," Micah said nervously.

Instead of throwing her hands in the air, Gilly smacked them into her lap. She looked up, her mouth a set line. "Your heart may be in the right place, Micah, but your brain—"

"I suppose." Micah didn't know what to say.

"Come here. This instant," she commanded.

Micah just stood there feeling awkward. Gilly got up and gave him the biggest hug.

"Goes without saying. Goes without saying." Bernard patted Micah's shoulder and winked at Captain Gilead, who smiled. He got up to leave but Gilly insisted he should stay for coffee.

Bernard padded after Gilly into the kitchen. Micah was glad Gilead had stayed; his presence had helped smooth things over with the family. And things, he thought, were already getting back to normal. Except for Zeke, but nothing ever was normal with him. Micah could see he was absorbed with his coins again, trying to be deliberately uninterested in just about anything that was going on.

"Zeke, can you make a bit of an effort, darling?" said Gilly as she returned with the coffee.

"What's that, Ima?" Zeke asked innocently.

Bernard came out of the kitchen with plates. "Focus on the family for few minutes, Zeke. Put the coins away, son." He spoke with a smile but Zeke got the message.

"Focus on the family? You mean I should focus on Micah?" he snickered.

"I do not like your tone, young man." Bernard sounded sterner.

"Everyone is making such a big deal about another one of Micah's misadventures. I mean, what is the big deal?"

"Do you know what almost happened to your cousin today?" asked Gilead quietly.

"Yeah, I heard. I was listening," Zeke sneered. "Ask me if I care."

"Care about this." Micah smacked the tray of coins off the coffee table. The coins splayed up, bouncing and jangling around on the floor.

"You moron!" Zeke shouted.

"That is enough out of you, young man," Bernard said.

"He lost my coins." Zeke was scooping them up from the floor, feverishly counting.

"Don't get so worked up. We'll find them," Bernard stormed back, but got on all fours with his son. "Jakey. Micah. You can both help, too."

Soon the coins were accounted for. Except one. The missing coin was very old, Zeke said in a voice near panic. He crawled around the carpet, hands outstretched like a salamander, feeling for coins. Jakey and Micah started looking under the sofa cushions.

"Is this it?" Micah held up a small, shiny disc.

"Can I see? Years back, I did some coin collecting," said Gilead.

Zeke held out a hand for the coin, but Micah handed it to Gilead, who held fast to it and went on with his story.

"Fell into it by accident. You know, hiking. You find things. This place. Israel. It's one big archaeological site. Did you find this one on a dig? Zeke?" asked Gilead.

"Probably dug it out of a coin shop, right Zeke?" said Micah pointedly.

"Can I have my property back now? Sir?" Zeke sounded snippy. Hand held out.

Gilead took out his phone, zoomed onto the coin and photographed it. "You don't mind, do you? A beautiful coin like this. From the Roman period. The time of Masada, perhaps." He plugged in some numbers and transmitted the photo.

"Masada!" Bernard shook his head, amazed. "Well, well!"

Even Micah knew about Masada, the hilltop fortress where Jewish rebels held out against the Romans in AD 70. When all hope was lost, they killed themselves rather than be crucified or enslaved. He knew it was a big deal in Israel, representing the nation's fighting spirit.

As Zeke fumed on the couch, Gilead sat down and handed the coin back to Micah. It had an embossed chalice, with spiky letters dancing attendance around the rim. On the reverse side, a three-leafed flower was embossed in the center. The coin shimmered and seemed alive in his hand.

"Minted during the Israeli occupation," Zeke added with some authority as Gilly arrived with cake slices. She sat down next to Zeke.

"Judean," Gilead corrected gently. "This was Judea then, ay? Perfect impression. Silver, yes?"

"Yes. It is, all the way through," Zeke said in a patronizing tone.

"Almost two thousand years old. Passed around all that time ago." Gilly nudged him. "It's wonderful. Why didn't you show it to us? And have some cake, Zeke."

"Jingling in a leather purse, from souk to souk," Bernard speculated. "I'll have some cake," he enthused.

"I doubt that. Look at it. Mint condition, hardly ever been used. Right, Zeke? The inscription. Hebrew, I suppose...*shin*...I don't know what it means. Do you?"

Zeke shrugged again. He took the coin from Micah.

Gilead's pocket buzzed. Two texts had come in.

"Shin is a letter. The rest of the markings apparently represent numbers. Year five of the Jewish Revolt. Very rare. Only a handful in existence." Gilead looked at Zeke. "So how much did you pay for it, Zeke?"

"Can't remember."

"You can't remember because you didn't pay for it. This coin is priceless. But you knew that, Zeke. Didn't you?" Gilead stood up.

Everyone looked at him, stunned.

# Chapter 74

"I knew it. He stole it," said Micah.

"Someone did. I just got confirmation. This coin is one of five stolen from a museum of antiquities here in Jerusalem. So how did you get it, Zeke?"

"This guy."

"Does 'this guy' 'ave a name?"

"Captain Gilead, please. This is sounding like an interrogation." Bernard sidled over to Zeke protectively. "My son collects coins. It's just his hobby. Tell him, son."

"This is a national treasure, Mr. Rothner. One of the rarest coins found at Masada. We figure the Rafah Martyr's Brigade stole it. No direct proof, but we're pretty sure. They sell artifacts for cash. They like coins. Coins are valuable. And portable. Been doing it for a while. Funds various activities. So tell me, Zeke, what 'guy' gave you this?"

"Zeke, where did you get this coin?" Gilly angrily demanded.

"I did nothing wrong. I bought it."

"Why are you lying?" Bernard hauled Zeke to his feet. "I know when you're lying."

"You never bought this coin," said Gilead. "Unless it came up on the black market. But I don't think you're on the ins with that crowd. So where did you get it?"

"It was sent to me." Zeke paused for a moment. "I've got the envelopes."

"Envelopes?" Micah picked up on that. "You got more?"

"I'll get his coin box." Jakey sprinted upstairs.

"No-o-o!"

Zeke tried to follow him, but Micah stepped in and pushed him back down onto the sofa. The nagging suspicions, the freaky coincidences weren't freewheeling around in his mind anymore. They were coming together in the shape of his rotten rat of a cousin.

Jakey returned with the chest Zeke had grandly shown off when Micah first arrived. The box without a lid, without a lock. The box Micah had opened. Jakey handed it to his father, who reluctantly handed it to Micah. Zeke raged, but everyone ignored him.

Micah held the box at the opposite corners, pressed in, and pulled. The box came apart, as it had before, revealing not just Zeke's regular coins, but something else, tucked beneath the inset shelves. Micah found three small envelopes which he handed to Gilead. He opened them and revealed more coins. One was gold, the others were silver and bronze.

"From Masada?" asked Bernard.

"These are different—" Gilead sounded uncertain. "Possibly older, maybe from the Second Temple. And if they are—"

Bernard was incensed. "How did you get these?"

"Those coins are mine." Zeke squirmed.

"You could be arrested for receiving stolen property, you know that?" Gilead shook his head.

"I was spying. For us. For our side." Zeke looked at his dumbfounded family.

"Who? Who was it, on our side?" Gilead asked. "I'm not clear."

"I was recruited to the Israeli Intelligence Service. The I.I.S."

"Unbelievable." Micah barely spoke the word.

"The I.I.S.! Impressive. And the coins? They were payment?" Gilead played along with Zeke's story, even though no such group existed. "Payment for informing against Micah and Shireen?"

"You ratted us out for coins?" Micah felt sick.

"You make it sound bad. But my handler said the Arab girl was dangerous."

"A handler? You think you're in a spy movie?" asked Micah sarcastically.

"You betrayed them, and for this, our stolen heritage—oh, Zeke," said Gilly despairingly.

"I didn't know they were stolen," Zeke snapped. "My handler knew I collected coins. Spies often get paid in silver or gold. Known fact."

"So tell me, who do you report to at the I.I.S.?" Gilead asked.

"You're fourteen, Zeke. You can't work for Mossad—or anyone," Bernard said.

"It's the I.I.S., Dad. Israeli Intelligence Service. Get it? Keep up."

"He's dreaming, dreaming—" Bernard sank back on the chair, shaking his head.

"Why didn't you tell us?" Gilly had tears in her eyes.

"My handler told me to keep it secret, Mother." Zeke sounded disdainful.

"Who was it?" Gilead hadn't meant to yell but his sudden loudness silenced everyone.

"He's your boss, too." Zeke had regained some of his bravado.

Micah could see that Gilead was momentarily thrown. Then Zeke mumbled a name. Gilead asked him to repeat it. Zeke said the name again. In fact, he shouted it.

# Chapter 75

"Singer? Colonel Raphael Singer?" Gilead stared at Zeke, willing him to falter.

"Colonel Singer. Yes. He came to the house. With you, and the other one. Gave me his card."

"His card?"

"Don't believe you," said Micah.

Zeke tossed the business card on the floor. Micah picked it up. Singer's name, his rank, his contact information were all on the card.

"So, did you—" Gilead stopped, almost sighed before going on, "did you call him?"

"No. He called me. On a secure line." Zeke smiled smugly. "Strictly hush-hush."

"Hush-hush?" Gilead paused, then asked, "And you're sure it was him on the phone?"

"Of course! Why not? He sounded as he did when I met him, even above the din."

"Din?" asked Micah.

"Noise, I guess, not sure. He had to shout. But I could hear what he said." Zeke elaborated further. "He told me he was trying to rescue Micah. Said the girl was bad news. And he said there was a traitor where he worked and he wanted to stay one step ahead of him. That's it."

"Yes, that *is* it. Now go to your room." Bernard pointed forcefully to the stairs.

Baffled, Zeke shook his head, then headed upstairs. Gilly looked imploringly at Gilead as he headed for the door, a phone to his ear.

"Gilead." Bernard waved vaguely at the stairs. "He's a boy, easily led. How could he know?"

Gilead nodded. "We'll deal with the coins and the rest of it. You deal with Zeke."

Micah watched Gilead leave. He suddenly felt very alone. Helpless. He heard Uncle Bernard saying it would be all right. But it wasn't all right. It was all bloody wrong.

Micah ran out and slammed the front door, shutting out the sound of his aunt imploring him to stay. But he had to get away. He ran down to the street, just as Gilead was getting in his car.

"Take me along," Micah said. "I'm not staying here. Not now."

They drove in silence for a few minutes. Micah could see that Gilead was preoccupied, so he kept quiet. At least Shireen was not going to be there tonight. At least she would be out of it. He handed over Singer's business card.

"You'd better have this," he said.

Gilead took the card and screwed it up in his fist.

"Why? Why?" Gilead sighed deeply. "But the bloody thing is, it fits. It all fits. The colonel is old-school. An Arab Christian. Pessimistic. Hates politicians. Always thinks the military is getting the shaft. Maybe he was against the current peace talks, and 'ated the idea of more concessions. I dunno."

"Will you arrest Colonel Singer?" Micah finally asked.

Gilead didn't answer. He turned on the radio. Rock music blared. Very loudly.

"Do you think he wants to kill her?" Micah almost shouted to be heard.

Gilead's earpiece started buzzing. He checked his phone. He knew the number, knew who was calling. He switched off the radio and pulled over. The phone buzzed a moment longer, then Gilead answered on speaker.

Singer asked where he was, why he had taken so long to answer. Gilead explained there might be a breach in security. He remained deliberately vague. Singer seemed cool and unfazed, said to stop wasting time and head over to the Convention Center. He would meet him there.

"Didn't know you were going there, sir." Gilead was surprised by the new order.

"Nor did I, Gilead. Nor did I. But I'm going now. And you know why?" There was a pause, then Singer dropped his bombshell. "It was the PM. Interceded personally. Wants the girl—Shireen—wants her there. At tonight's event. Can you imagine, after the attack on the boy?" Singer sighed gruffly then, almost whispering, "He sounded as superficial as Chazoom. It's PR, Gilead. All they care about."

Micah couldn't believe what he was hearing.

"They should be landing soon," Singer added.

"Landing, sir?" asked Gilead.

"Yes—that's why I'm going early. Our beloved Prime Minister sent a helicopter for Chazoom and the girl. Couldn't take a chance on the streets. The air corridor is 'uncompromised,' he said."

"They're at the I.C.C. now?"

"I assume so. They all believe the girl will be safe. Fools, they are."

"Excuse me, sir, a question…did you give a business card to one of the Rothner kids?"

"What? Might have given one to the father, but—why?"

"Nothing really. But one of the Rothner kids, he had one of your cards."

"What has that got to do with anything?" Singer sounded annoyed.

"Are you a numismatist, sir?"

"Am I what? Oh, for God's sake, Eron, just get to the I.C.C. and do your job."

Gilead deliberately put the phone away and pulled the car back onto the road.

"He had no idea what *numismatist* means. He's not a coin collector. And, and he didn't..."

Micah leaned in. "He didn't what?"

"He did not *yell* at me. Even now. He was angry, but he didn't yell. Never does."

"Well, he did when he was talking to Zeke, because of the noise. Remember? Zeke said he was shouting over the din. Like when you just had that music on. I had to yell to get you to hear me."

"I like loud music. But—" He looked at Micah.

"Your boss doesn't like loud music?"

"That's just what I'm saying." Gilead stopped the car again. Seconds later, he was back on the phone, on speaker.

"Mister Rothner. May I speak once more to Zeke?"

"What is it?" Micah asked.

Gilead didn't answer. A long moment later, Zeke came on the phone.

"Yeah, what?" he mumbled.

"Hello, Zeke." Gilead sounded conciliatory, almost friendly. "This is important. You can help yourself here. You understand?"

"Yeah."

"Tell me, you said Colonel Singer was yelling at you. Why was that?"

"No, I said he was yelling to be heard. Because of the noise. It was weird. People were singing but not singing. Like a lot of people talking. And loud."

Gilead ended the call, turned to Micah. "He wasn't yelling at him, just shouting to be heard," he repeated. "Because of the noise. People were 'singing but not singing.' That's what he said."

"Singing but not singing?" Micah was as perplexed as Gilead.

"And loud. And people talking. He was in a restaurant?" Gilead shrugged. "Background noise? Background music?"

"It's a riddle." Micah's frowned. "Wait, remember at the hotel? In Shireen's room. What was Chazoom listening to?"

"Some kind of opera stuff. He's always listening to that guff."

"Eighteenth-century rap, that's what he called it, and he called it something else. Like 'reciting' or something, but foreign."

"Recitative?" said Gilead.

"That's it! Singing but not singing. And that's what Zeke heard!"

"Chazoom!" Gilead pounded his fist on the dashboard.

"He's with Shireen right now," said Micah.

"I know, I know. You want to be useful?" Gilead started the car, not waiting for a reply. "I don't have a siren. So you, my young friend, you punch the horn. And keep punching it, okay?"

"Okay. What will you be doing?"

"Speeding!"

They went through red lights, through a cacophony of blaring cars and shrieking, angry people. Finally Gilead slammed into an ear-splitting skid by a side entrance to the International Convention Center. Police and army personnel ran toward them.

Micah fell back in his seat, inhaling the stink of burnt rubber. As soon as they parked, an army sergeant and two secret service officers crowded the car and started briefing Gilead. A helicopter had landed safely on the roof. Chazoom and Shireen had been aboard.

Gilead ordered another sweep from the auditorium at the mezzanine level and up and ran into the building.

Micah had a job keeping up. Police and the military were everywhere. Anyone entering the building was screened. Even Gilead and Micah were scanned. Micah felt reassured by the security. How could anything bad happen?

# CHAPTER 76

WHEN THE HELICOPTER HAD LANDED with spectacular precision on the rooftop helipad of the I.C.C., neither passenger was screened. Chazoom and Shireen had been greeted by two officers brought in for the occasion. One noted that Shireen had a bag over her shoulder and Colonel Chazoom was carrying a large black attaché case. They had entered the building unhindered. Chazoom had since then been unaccounted for. He had disappeared.

"And the girl?" Gilead asked.

"Backstage, sir. Where Colonel Chazoom left her."

"What a surprise." Micah felt more relieved than he sounded.

They followed the soldier into the bowels of the theater through an entryway covered in white cloth like a billowing tunnel.

"Hello, Mates." Shireen was glowing.

The anxiety that had knotted Micah's stomach began to unravel. There she was, standing in the dressing room, safe as could be. The large room was decked with flowers and teddy bears, but Micah was just staring at her.

"You like?"

Shireen pointed to her dress, which appeared to be made of flowing strands of glittering red diamonds. Underneath, she wore a neck-to-foot, skintight black leotard. Micah could barely recognize her. She looked so grown-up, so alluring, but then she beamed her big happy grin, and within that smile was the spunky girl he knew.

"Yeah, you're not bad."

"Not bad?" Shireen twirled around and stuck her hands on her hips. "Just not bad?"

"Yeah, not bad—for a girl." Micah shrugged awkwardly.

"For a girl? Tuk, tuk, tuk!" She glanced over at Gilead. "What you think, Mister Eron?"

"Great." Gilead nodded distractedly. As he turned away, he looked at Micah and said quietly, "Not a word. Be right back."

Gilead left the room. They were alone.

"He's got something to tell you—" Micah felt flustered.

"Well?" Shireen was only listening for compliments. "And I am covered, my head, you see? I am…what is word…*accessorized.* Yes, accessorized."

Shireen opened her matching clutch bag and took out the only thing inside, a fancy new phone. She showed him its myriad features and apps.

"Does it take calls?" Micah asked with a slight smile.

"Yes, Mates, of course. You bet."

Micah figured she didn't get his sarcasm, until he noticed a sly smile. He was, she said, the first to have her cell phone number. Micah entered it into his own phone and captioned it with her picture.

"You want to call me?"

"Now? Don't be daft. Anyway, my battery's almost out."

Gilead returned with three soldiers, who began going through everything in the dressing room, including the flowers, the plush teddy bears, and the other gifts. Shireen's mood faltered. Gilead told her to sit down. Reluctantly she did as he asked but shot Micah a look.

"Look, Shireen, there's no good way of saying this but—" Gilead shook his head.

"He wants you dead. Chazoom. He's planning to kill you. Here. Today. Tonight." Micah spoke quickly, glad to get it off his chest.

Shireen stared in disbelief and anger. Anger at Micah for suggesting such a thing.

"He's right. Chazoom is planning something," Gilead added. "We don't know what though. So we 'ave to find him. Quickly. As of now, he does not know we're onto him. That's our only advantage."

"What are you saying?" Shireen looked confused. Then she shook her head. "No. I do not believe this. When you find Mister Yossi, you find him innocent. He is my friend."

"Like the Oily One?" Micah asked quietly.

Shireen stared at him as if she had been slapped.

"Wasn't he your friend?" Micah pressed.

"Hameeda told me he came to your school," said Gilead.

"Hameeda? She told you?"

"He was in the photo files at the Puzzle Palace. But you didn't flag him," Gilead said. "I took some pictures to Hameeda. She said he was the one who took you away from your family, your friends, to be what? A martyr? A killer? Which was it, Shireen? Do you even know?"

Silence.

"The man you did identify was a hired killer called Khalid Omalah. He was the one who almost killed Micah this morning."

"He was probably sent by that Jamal geezer," Micah jumped in. "Your 'oily one.' And who do you think his boss is? Yeah, you've got it, it's your friend, 'Mister Yossi'—that smarm."

Shireen said nothing. Gilead muttered something about Stockholm Syndrome, but Micah didn't know what that was. Or care. But he could sense Shireen's inner turmoil and confusion. When he spoke again he tried to sound less angry.

"Maybe you feel bad because Jamal and Chazoom, they're clever at not looking rotten. Like bad eggs. Bad eggs always look good until you crack them open."

The ice fire in Shireen's eyes betrayed the pain of accepting the truth. Finally she took a deep breath and unloaded. Yes, she had not flagged Jamal. Yes, he had planned her suicide and the destruction of a busload of schoolchildren. Yes, he must have worked with Farouz to track her down and kill her. Yes. Yes. Yes. She knew. She knew everything. But she felt like a traitor, disloyal to a cause whose tactics she had rejected.

"What I felt then—what I feel now matters more." Shireen turned to Gilead. "He said—Mister Yossi said—he had to see music director. In back of theater. Light box, he said. You understand?"

Gilead nodded his thanks and told her to stay put, with Micah. The door closed behind him.

"So we have to wait here. Could be worse." Micah could see how upset she was.

"Mister Yossi told me to wait here, and then—go on stage. Be a star. You are right, Mates. I wanted to be on stage, to strut like a puffed-up peacock. For what? For nothing. But I believed all he told me. Because I wanted to believe." Shamefaced, she sank back into herself.

He didn't know how to respond. So he said nothing. Silence grew between them like a stale cloud. Micah could almost taste it. He got up and looked aimlessly about. The he spotted something. He plucked a typed page fastened to the dressing room mirror and began reading it.

"'I must keep faith with my belief. Yet, I must find another path. A path that will not tolerate cruelty and barbarity. A path that will not glorify evil actions. A path that will not veil me in the darkness of ages. I will find a path filled with light. I will find a path to God.'"

Micah had spoken her words back to her. It was as if she was hearing them for the first time. "That wasn't puffed up. That wasn't nothing. That was you. Good stuff. And for what it's worth, your written English is better than mine—almost." Micah tried for an encouraging smile.

Shireen gave a long, exasperated sigh. Suddenly loud thumps filled the emptiness in the room. Startled, they looked up. Footsteps were pounding above them.

"Is on the stage. Let's see, you want?" Shireen's glum mood magically spun itself out.

"No. Can't get out anyway, there's soldiers—"

Before he could argue, she pulled back the long drapes near the dressing table and was gone as fast as a ferret down a rabbit hole. He wanted to yell at her, but decided to save his breath and follow instead. He scrambled through a small opening and found himself on a tiled floor that smelled like a swimming pool. No sign of—

"Boo!" Shireen jumped out from a shower stall.

"Gordon Bennet!" Micah jumped, eyes and mouth wide open.

Shireen thought he looked very, very funny.

"Don't do that again, you."

"Tuk, tuk, tuk." Shireen was laughing.

She took off through the shower area yelling "Gordy Bennet"—knowing it would drive Micah nuts. And it did. She flew down a passageway and up a flight of steps. Micah was charging right behind her. Within seconds came noise and lights, and smells of perfume and mothballs and feet. They were on an empty stage. Micah blinked. Shireen bowed to an imaginary audience. Soft bursts of sidelights plumed into life, burning away a faint smell of ancient dust. Crashing sounds came from above as floodlights were switched on. And then Shireen spoke, in near-perfect English.

"'When I consider everything that grows, holds in perfection but a little moment. That this huge stage presenteth nought but shows, whereupon the stars in secret influence comment…'"

"More Shakespeare?" Micah groaned, but his anger was fading.

She acknowledged his guess with a slight bow. Micah watched as she strutted happily about the stage. Her leotard fused with the shadows cast by the curtains and scenery. It was like watching the old black-art trick. Apart from her hands and face, all Micah could see were the shimmering beads of her dress catching the light. It looked like a magic trick, but to Micah, *she* was the magic.

# Chapter 77

GILEAD RAN BACK into the crowded auditorium. He stopped when he saw Shireen.

"Get off that stage!" he yelled, then turned to the back of the hall. "And you up there, kill those lights!"

Running down the center aisle, Gilead sprang onto the stage. Grabbing Shireen by the arm, he marched her back down the stairs. She flailed about and shouted in Arabic and English, but Gilead did not let go. Micah followed but wisely kept his distance.

Gilead flung open the door of the dressing room and pushed Shireen inside. He told one of the soldiers on duty, a female corporal, to go inside and stay with Shireen at all times. He closed the dressing room door and took a call, then told Micah the briefcase had been found. They hurried back up onto the stage and met Singer in the back of the auditorium.

"The girl was his Trojan horse. She got him inside the building undetected, with this."

Singer showed them the attaché case Chazoom had been carrying. It was customized to hold a high-powered rifle assembly. The case was empty.

"So where is he?" asked Micah.

"He must know by now that it's over. We're clearing the building." Singer sounded confident. "He will be found."

"But he's got a bloody rifle," Micah sighed. "And I bet he is a good shot."

"Yes. He is," Gilead said.

Citing a severe threat level, Singer left to adjourn the signing ceremony. An evacuation of the building began, but no details were made public. No mention of a suspected terrorist roaming the building. No mention of a high-ranking FARD officer gone rogue.

The sudden postponement of the ceremony sparked rumors that one or both parties had pulled out. Many believed the "severe threat" story was just that: a story. To help quell the rumors and avoid bad press, the three heads of state agreed to remain in the building until a joint statement of commitment to the peace process could be issued.

Meanwhile, the gantries, air vents, and stairwells throughout the I.C.C. were checked again. But nothing was found.

"I need to think," Gilead said unexpectedly. He flipped a theater seat and sat down.

Micah sat beside him, but not for long. Awkwardly he stood up again. "I've got to go."

"Don't worry, we'll get you home. I'll arrange a car. All right?"

"No, I mean, I gotta go. The loo. I'm busting."

"Oh. That. First on the—wait! I'll get someone to go with you."

"Go with me? You must be joking," Micah walked away.

"For security, you twit. Hey, wait there," Gilead called out.

Not listening, Micah headed up the aisle to an exit, pushed down the metal bar, and stepped through the door. He was in a concrete shell. No more carpets. No more colorfully draped walls. Where was the men's room? He looked around. The door snapped shut behind him. Desperately he tried opening it, but it was sealed. He was trapped.

And Yossi Chazoom was still one step ahead.

# Chapter 78

"Help! *Hatzilu!*" Micah yelled.

Failure. He shouted louder. Silence. He walked down the oblong concrete tube. No loo. Nothing. A bit farther along, a metal door broke the concrete monotony, but there was no handle, just a thick metal sheet overlapping the doorway. A fire door. And he was on the wrong side of it.

He slammed his foot against another metal door and yelled "Idiot!" but that didn't help. Walking faster, he nervously followed the corridor as it twisted sharply to the right. Beyond his own footsteps, he could hear nothing. He was surrounded by cold grayness and scary silence. He had to find a way back into the auditorium. Must be one. Micah's thoughts became jagged and apprehensive. He suddenly remembered his phone. He tried to call Gilead. No signal. No signal? Where was he?

Micah replaced the phone in his pocket, felt the fire capsules still there. He had transferred them from his blood-splattered school jacket, unused, useless. Why had he bothered? What had he been thinking? And Chazoom was out there. Somewhere. Where? Close by? Micah gulped. For a split second, he thought about turning back but he went on, trying to outrun his fear.

The corridor took a sharp turn to the left, and he saw streaks of late-afternoon sunshine. He ran up a zigzag of stairs, pressed down hard on the metal bar across a door, and pushed forward.

He was out.

Micah stopped to get his bearings. He was in a parking lot. But where? Loud street traffic came up from below and behind.

Momentarily disoriented, he peered through the gap in the concrete slats. The International Convention Center was across the highway. Micah realized the bleak gray tunnel was an underground walkway connecting the I.C.C. to a multilevel parking lot.

Turning back, Micah saw, with some relief, a restroom sign near a stairwell. A long way from the one Eron had suggested, but at least it was there. When he came out, he darted toward the stairwell, then stopped. Music. He could hear it above the traffic and the throb of the giant air conditioning units. The sound came from deep within the lot.

Crouching slightly, he zigzagged between rows of cars. The closer he got, the more distinct the music became. He could hear a woman's voice. It was gentle, delicate almost. His mum would have loved it. Micah knew only one other person who liked opera.

Then Micah saw him.

Yossi Chazoom. He was sitting in his little yellow car, one hand on the wheel while the other waved gently, conducting an imaginary orchestra, oblivious to anyone and everything. Micah stopped and tried to think. What could he do? Nothing rash. Not again.

The car started up, moved gingerly from the parking space. No time to think. Jumping out, Micah waved and smiled as if nothing had happened. Chazoom braked. He registered surprise, then beckoned. As Chazoom rolled down the side window, he rolled up a smile.

"So! It's young Mister Micah. Hang on," he shouted above the music. "Hate to turn it down, it's the 'Flower Duet' from *Lakme*. So ethereal. Do you know it?" Chazoom finally turned off the music, reached for a box of chocolates on the dashboard. "Chocolate? They're very good."

"You tried to kill me and you're offering me chocolates? And now you're trying to kill Shireen." Micah's words sounded clumsy. Something out of a bad movie.

"Me?" Chazoom sounded almost hurt.

"They found the rifle case," Micah blurted out.

"A rifle case? What's that got to do with me? I'm here. In my car. And now I'm leaving."

"No, you're not, because I found you. And if I found you, the others will, too. It's over."

"Is it? Well, I guess you did find me, you clever little fellow. How did you manage it?"

"What?"

"Oh, do tell. I'm so impressed by your detective skills. So much better than Tintin."

"You tell me what's going on. And I'll tell you how I found you."

"And why not?" Chazoom smiled smugly. "But, by the by, you must believe me, I didn't want you dead. Just scared. Threatened. You see, I couldn't have us going through Singer's security net. Had to override it somehow. Once you were attacked, everyone knew Shireen would be next. So I pulled her from the big event. I gambled that once word got back to that old sentimental windbag of a prime minister, he would step in. And he did, bless him. 'Oh, Prime Minister, if only we could avoid ground transportation, so dangerous for Shireen,' etcetera. Eventually he suggested the helicopter. 'Master stroke, Prime Minister,' I said. So thanks to him, we leap-frogged the security wall old Singer had erected. Worked out perfectly for us. Your turn."

Chazoom stared in eager anticipation. Micah held his gaze as he reached into his pocket and pushed the pin into the lower chamber of one of the fire capsules. He leaned onto the car door.

"You said 'us.' what does that mean? Was Shireen part of this?"

For a split second, as though bored by Micah's questions, Chazoom rolled his eyes. Micah dropped a primed pellet among some papers in the side panel of the door. The action was unnoticed.

"I don't get it. You were going to shoot her."

"Nothing so crude."

"They found the gun case."

"Mere distraction. Shireen is a key part of it all. Still is." Chazoom's face darkened. "She just doesn't know it yet."

"I don't believe you."

"You will. Now it's your turn." Chazoom was smiling again.

"Okay. Well. I needed to pee. I was looking for a loo. I took the wrong door. Ended up here."

"Don't insult me, you lying little bastard! You—"

The car screamed into reverse, then accelerated straight at Micah. Stumbling backwards, he half rolled between two parked vehicles just before Chazoom came towards him again. As Micah struggled to his feet, he caught a glimpse of Chazoom's angry face.

That's when Micah saw it: a tiny plume of smoke.

# Chapter 79

Chazoom couldn't pinpoint the source of the growing stench of burning plastic and paper. He drove on a few feet but the smell did not clear. He realized, too late, that it was coming from inside the car. Translucent gray smoke wafted up from the side of his seat. He stopped the car and stared in disbelief. Pencil-thin yellow curls appeared and disappeared in the shimmering heat and curtained the window. Yelping with fear, he stamped his foot as orange threads ignited around the car floor. Fatter flames curved around the roof, reaching out for more of him.

A piteous scream of terror rose on a sudden gush of air as the door was pulled open. Hands grabbed Chazoom and dragged him clear. He was flopped onto the ground like a giant fish. Stinging smoke needled his eyes. Whooshing sounds filled the air and he felt a jet of some cold substance soaking his leg. The lower half of his pants were still smoking, but the flames were out.

Micah trotted over for a closer look at the still-smoldering car, and the prone and handcuffed Chazoom.

A police officer was spraying the inside of the vehicle with white foamy stuff. While he was occupied, Micah decided to take a running kick at Chazoom.

"Back off!" It was Gilead.

"I just wanted to help him up," said Micah.

"With your foot? You're funny." Gilead pulled Chazoom up.

"He set my car on fire. Imagine!" Chazoom sounded mockingly disgruntled.

"Shut your face," Micah said.

The police on the scene wanted to take Chazoom into custody. Gilead patted the air with his hand.

"Come on, lads, cordon off the area, give me a moment with him." He smiled at the uniforms.

The police officers exchanged glances, hesitating. One officer took off, but the other stayed nearby.

"So you found me," said Micah.

"Figured you took the wrong exit. Just followed you 'ere. How did you firebomb his car?"

Micah took out the remaining capsule.

"Flared right up in thirty seconds. Just pressed in the pin. Spontaneous combustion."

"And this one?"

"It's a dud. The pin fell out."

"But he doesn't know that, does he?"

Micah smiled. They walked back over to Chazoom.

"The boy firebombed your car with one of these. Clever." Gilead held up the capsule. "What they teach you in school, ay? Right. You. Down. On your knees."

Chazoom obeyed. Gilead grabbed him by the collar and pushed him forward, then stuffed the capsule down his back pants pocket. Chazoom reared up like a frightened toad. Gilead shoved him back down on the pavement.

"Take it out of my pocket. Eron. Please. We are professionals, after all."

"Micah! What did you call it? Random explosion?"

"Spontaneous combustion," Micah said helpfully.

"Spontaneous—yeah, that's it." Gilead peered at Chazoom. "At least it'll be quick. Quick-*ish*."

"Please remove it." Chazoom sounded calm.

"You saw what it did to your car, eh?"

"Especially in an enclosed area," Micah added.

Chazoom shouted to the policeman hovering nearby. He screamed torture. The officer looked on uncertainly, but Gilead glanced at him and shook his head, patting the air with his hand again. The officer smiled. He understood.

Gilead leaned down to his captive.

"Micah, how long 'as he got?"

"About thirty seconds."

"Just 'ope I can get the extinguisher going. Mind you, I'll probably break the bloody thing—"

"All right. Giving it up. Giving it up. Get it out of me!" Chazoom howled fearfully.

Gilead leaned over and pulled the capsule from Chazoom's pocket. Micah smiled. Gilead would make a good magician. Or con man. Micah wasn't sure which. But the trick had worked.

"Let me try and explain…" Chazoom said, shaken but still trying to cling to his charming persona. "Just wanted to disrupt tonight's event. Glorified civil disobedience, nothing more."

"Tell me about the rifle."

"The rifle?" Chazoom sighed wearily. "Can you see me entering a concert hall, guns blazing?"

Gilead grabbed him by the back of the neck and yanked hard.

"All right! I was going to shoot the PM. Or the American. Or that West Bank flunky. Hadn't made up my mind which one."

"Then what's Shireen got to do with any of this?" Micah asked with mounting anger.

"I don't get it." Gilead was shouting again. "Wasn't this Side-by-Side thing worth a chance?"

"No. Never," said Chazoom.

Gilead pushed Chazoom hard against the side of the car, cutting short his sneering chuckle.

"The Rafah Martyr's Brigade, you part of that?"

"Part of it? I *am* the Rafah Martyr's Brigade. But that's another story. Meanwhile, my great plan is foiled; so sad—" he said mockingly.

"Liar! He's lying," Micah said. "Shireen was part of it. A key part of it. And still is, he said."

"You misheard me, boy. She's an innocent." Chazoom did his thin-lipped smile and shrugged.

Micah stared at Chazoom. The image of Shireen on the stage came back to him. She had spun and swirled to the music in her head, dancing in and out of the stage's deep shadows, almost disappearing within the blackness of the leotard. Her head and hands were visible, but when she turned around, all that remained was the shimmering, sparkling outer costume, looking like a bright shadow.

A bright shadow.

He suddenly remembered Eleni's strange prophetic words. Something about a bright shadow bringing death. Whether prediction or perception, to Micah it was becoming as clear as clear could be. On the bus, Shireen had worn a custom-made vest. On stage, she was wearing a custom-made dress. Micah saw a horrifying connection.

"It's in the dress, isn't it? It's going to happen this time, isn't it?"

Silence. No come-back. No funny quip, no disparaging glance.

"That's why you're not over there. In that convention hall. You don't *need* to be there. Shireen's going to do it all for you. It's what you planned for her. She just doesn't know it—that's what you said.

"You said Shireen was a 'key part' of your plan, she '*just doesn't know it yet.*'"

No response. But Micah saw it. The imperceptible twitch of an eyebrow. Chazoom's eyes still shone with disdain. But he said nothing.

"Yeah, she's *an innocent*, but she's a key part of it, all right. You bastard. It's in the dress, isn't it? A bomb." Micah pressed him.

"Her dress?" Gilead was stunned.

"That's how you planned to kill her and everyone else. Wasn't it?"

That was it. No more words were needed. As the police took Chazoom into custody, Micah heard Gilead screaming into his phone.

"The device is in the dress! But she does not know. Repeat, she does not know!"

Smashing back the exit door, Micah and Gilead jumped stairs. In seconds, they were on the street level, running across. Micah suddenly stopped.

"Wait! I've got her number." He fumbled in his pocket.

"Call her. Call her now."

Micah nodded, took out his phone. He began scrolling for Shireen's number. He saw her name imprinted on the black marble-like screen. Then it disappeared. Darkness stared up at him from a bottomless square. The battery had finally died.

## Chapter 80

SHIREEN WAS BORED. She didn't know what was going on. She glanced over her speech and sighed. The soldier assigned to protect her was not one for conversation. She was not unfriendly, just reserved and striving to be professional. Shireen wasn't in a mood for talking anyway, so she paced like a caged lion.

The door of her dressing room suddenly opened. The duty soldier stood to rigid attention, and a few nonmilitary types in dark suits filed in.

"What happens now?" Shireen spoke slowly.

Without a word, the men fanned out around the room to create a protective phalanx. Then the battle line opened and Shireen was relieved to see a familiar, friendly face. The Israeli Prime Minister ambled toward her, smiling broadly. Shireen was neither overwhelmed nor overawed. To her, he was her big, silver-haired teddy bear, and she rushed him for a hug. He chuckled and hugged her back.

The Prime Minister said the renegade security officer had been apprehended. Shireen asked about the signing. He told her that the public event would not take place—a logistical problem, whatever that meant. But he assured her that the accord had been signed by the three parties. Shireen expressed delight and tried to suppress her personal disappointment, then cheered up when he asked if she would like to meet the president of the PNA. Shireen was happily speechless.

The suits began to part to allow the Palestinian president through. Shireen suddenly felt very hot. A bit woozy. She tightened her grip on the Prime Minister's hand to steady herself, but the nausea wouldn't go away. *"There is no sure foundation set on blood, no certain life achieved by others' death."* Shakespeare's words unfurled across her mind like a banner. Why? Why now?

The Prime Minister asked if she was unwell, if she wanted to sit down. She tried to smile, but the feeling would not go away. Deep in the pit of her stomach. She looked around. Concerned faces. People talked. People moved. Shireen turned away, said she was okay. But she was not okay. She felt so sick. She had to get away. Words bounced around her head. And the words hurt. Made no sense. Had to get away. But from what?

She headed to the locker room behind the dressing room. Someone followed. A voice, a kind, caring voice called out, but she waved it away. She needed to be left alone because it was happening again. The feeling. The sweating. The physical manifestation of all she feared before was writhing within her once more. And yet it made no sense. She was not wearing death, not—

# Chapter 81

CHAZOOM WAILED about the big misunderstanding. About the apologies that would be streaming his way. But meanwhile, he just wanted to make a call. One phone call. One of the officers said he could make a call when they arrived at headquarters. He knew that, he said, as he gleamed a smile at them. Could they do him a tiny favor?

His aging mother lived with him. She's a doll, but she worries. How she worries! Does your mother worry you to death? Chazoom seemed genuinely interested. He leaned into the grille of the police vehicle as if it wasn't there and they were just three pals out on a jaunt.

Chazoom explained that his mother couldn't sleep when he was on assignment or working late. "She likes me to check in," he said.

The policemen grudgingly smiled. They understood. They had mothers. Mothers worry, especially in Israel. So would it be okay to call and tell her he was all right? No? Well. Chazoom understood. Perhaps one of the officers might call, on his behalf, just to say he'd been…delayed? Chazoom smiled from one officer to the other.

Well, it did not seem much to ask.

# Chapter 82

Shireen closed her eyes. Almost stumbled against the wall. Her face was burning hot, the cool tile felt good. She didn't want to open her eyes but she did. She had run into a shower stall.

Surging up, the vomit gushed from her mouth. It splattered up from the floor and onto her feet. Even the handbag she was still clutching. She reached out, feeling, not seeing.

What had she done? Was she mad? A hysterical girl? Stage-struck one minute then filled with stage fright the next? Yes, that was it. Stage fright. That was all. She felt like laughing and crying but nothing came. She couldn't close her eyes. Or crawl away from the consequences. It was a wide-awake, humiliating nightmare. And it was all hers.

Then Shireen's phone rang.

# Chapter 83

Holding his badge above the crowd like a herald, Gilead pushed forward, yelling to people to stand clear. Micah kept close, but progress was slow as they fought a way through the foyer filled with impatient guests trying to leave. The departing ticket holders turned angry as the now frantic Gilead and Micah pushed and jostled to get through. They were finally in the empty auditorium, running toward the stage.

Micah pulled himself on top of the guardrail separating the deserted orchestra pit from the stage. Then he heard it.

The cracking noise blew out from below the stage, and Micah knew they were too late. Shireen's dress had exploded. A gauzy gray mass of smoke seeped up. Alarms were going off, Micah heard shouting, noise. People running. Sprinklers turned on. He rushed toward the stairwell but was yanked back by Gilead.

"Don't! Don't go down there. Wait here."

"No!" Micah spun his arm free.

Gilead grabbed him again. "Stay here, Micah. It will not be her. I've seen it before. It's nothing you can imagine. Nothing. Stay here."

"I'll see her."

"For God's sake, she's gone." Gilead pushed Micah against the side wall. "Wait here. She won't—" He suddenly started coughing.

Covering his mouth, Micah pulled away and staggered down the stairwell, then stopped. He could hardly see through the smoke. He stumbled but Gilead caught him and dragged him back up. They sat together at the top of the steps. Neither spoke. Micah felt his face was hot and wet with tears. He buried his head in Gilead's shoulder.

The older man held him for a moment, then let go. Micah slumped forward, head down to his knees, arms hanging by his side. He looked up briefly to wipe his face, his eyes welled up again.

"Must be the smoke," Micah said softly.

"Must be. It's bad. Can barely breathe, and it stings. Come on, let's get you out of—oh, my God." Gilead was on his feet, staring.

Micah looked up. A shape was held in place by dust and smoke, clinging to the bottom of the steps like elegant brushstrokes on a gray background. Like lines coming together in a Japanese painting. A figure in black was being drawn into life. He could barely see beyond the liquid-like canvas, but when he did, he gasped. Then, an almost inaudible voice…

"Mates—"

She was pale and wet. Face devoid of line or shape or color. Slowly she staggered up the stairs. Smoke streamed her eyes with tears. Wet hair framed her ashen face like a shroud.

But she was alive.

Micah almost tripped as he moved toward her. Gilead smiled as he pushed a phone to his ear. He was told the VIPs were safe. Miraculously no one had been hurt by the blast. The shiny dress was gone, turned into a million tiny razor shards of glittering death.

Shireen coughed and coughed as she tried to speak. Micah helped her out of the blanket of smoke that hung in the stairwell.

"Look at you. Look pretty awful! You do, really," Micah said.

She couldn't stop coughing. He tried patting her back but it didn't help. A medical team arrived and gave her oxygen. As soon as she was breathing normally, she pulled the mask from her face, asked for water. She drank greedily before explaining.

"I was feeling bad, sick. I knew it was coming, Mates. Like on bus, remember? So I ran. I ran out of the dressing room, into locker room. I felt myself bad, inside. And outside of me, so very hot. My skin felt burning and my beautiful dress felt so heavy, closing in on me. So I threw it off. And then sick like before. After that my new phone rings. I answer. And the great noise came. Sharp. Crack. And then more hot." She shook her head, hardly believing what she had somehow survived. "A wave of heat. Other noises. And…"

Her voice crackled and she gasped on a rasping cough. Micah gave her more water. The coughing stopped and she began breathing quickly, as if she had just run a long race.

"Sorry, Mates." She looked exhausted.

"Ah, come here, you." Micah pulled her close.

# Chapter 84

The medical emergency team wanted Shireen to go to the hospital. But she was adamant. Not again. She asked if she could go back to the hotel for a few days. Gilead made the arrangements.

She spent the following day taking stock. She thought about home. Home! As evening approached, she headed for the hotel rooftop. She sat by the pool, dipped her toes in the water and dove into *The Tempest*. Shireen spoke a verse aloud, as if words so full of magic could loosen the bad memories she longed to set free.

Hearing her name made her look up, startled. Micah and Gilead were walking toward her. She put down her book of spells. Bravely she smiled and said hello. She was pleased to see them but Micah could see the quiet despondency in her eyes. He thought a punch on the shoulder might help but decided not to test his theory.

"You are to tell me what happened, yes?" She smiled sadly.

"You can't blame yourself," Gilead said. "Your lack of experience, your innocence, they were counting on that. It was all part of the plan. We've found out a lot since yesterday."

"You can tell me, yes?"

Gilead explained that a small quantity, about 100 grams, of pentaerythritol—PETN—had been mixed with a soft plasticizing agent and injected into the bra area of the dress to create a false but unsuspicious form.

"Made me look more than I am," Shireen said.

"It was well made, by all accounts."

"The tailor of death. They called him that. He—" She shuddered. "Go on, please."

"The beaded top you were wearing was connected to a wireless detonator. Chazoom engineered a call from the back of the police car. When you answered, it set off the explosion."

"I was so stupid." Shireen stood up, annoyed.

"Not as stupid as the police who made the call for Chazoom. The call signaled the MH2 transmitter, which detonated the explosive. If all had gone as planned—" Gilead looked at her, reluctant to spell it out. "You left the room at the right time."

"I was sick inside." She sounded almost apologetic. "I had to leave that place. I knew I was carrying the sickness again. Somehow."

"If you hadn't left the room, your president and the Prime Minister of Israel would have been blown to pieces," Micah said. "Along with you, of course."

"I did not believe— How could Mister Yossi—?" Her blue eyes iced over. "Chazoom. Evil sat on his shoulder and whispered in his ear. But I did not hear it, did not see it."

"He fooled us all," Gilead admitted. "He's been a double agent from the beginning. Always hated Israel."

Gilead explained that Chazoom had patiently waited for the perfect opportunities. His status and reputation had grown with each successful attack—but he had turned on his leaders when they had turned toward peace. He planned his last, most audacious attack independently.

"We found the tailor," Gilead added. "And Mahmoud, one of the bods who killed Mehmet. We think Jamal got away. Someone was shot dead outside his apartment. Maybe he was sent to kill Jamal."

"So Jamal is free. He looks for me?" asked Shireen.

"We're not taking any chances," Gilead said. "You'll be placed in protective custody."

"How long?" Micah asked.

"Until it is safe." Gilead sounded firm.

He looked at his watch and said he had to go.

"Don't stay up here too late, you two." He said it with a smile, but they knew what he meant.

It was time for good-byes.

Apart from two security guards at the far corner of the roof, they were now alone. They looked out onto David's Citadel. The floodlights illuminated and appeared to warm the ancient ramparts of the Old City, but not them. They didn't say anything for the longest time.

Uncertainty clouded Shireen's thoughts and muddled her feelings. No words of Shakespeare came to mind, but her heart was filled with her own. She wanted to tell Micah how she felt about him, but the words stayed deep within. She just shook her head.

"Oh. I almost forgot. One last magic trick."

Micah took out a handkerchief. He reached beneath its folds and produced a box, the size of a pack of playing cards.

"Prospero Boy!" Shireen exclaimed with delight.

"Dunno about that, but anyway, this is for you."

Micah handed the box to Shireen. Her eyes widened along with her smile when she opened the gift.

"Oh, mates." She was unable to say more.

Then Micah took off. A good time to make an exit, he reckoned.

But as he got to the glass door, he saw Shireen's reflection. The hand-rolled silk scarf he had bought for her was fluttering, twirling through her fingers like a shaft of pure gold. Micah watched as she draped it around her neck and over one shoulder. The scarf was the color that dappled Jerusalem's ancient precincts. Her color. Her city. He turned back. Shireen's smile ran deep and her blue eyes held a morning sky filled with promise. And they held him.

Slightly shy and a bit embarrassed by things unsaid, Micah almost looked away again but did not. Could not. Shireen held his gaze with arms outstretched, fists strong, thumbs cocked. Micah grinned as he returned her salute.

That's tight, he thought, bloody tight. He would see her again. He just knew it.

# Epilogue

"My dear Micah, I knew you would be making it! Sim sala bim!" Yimca was in grand form.

The entire troupe—even Eleni—stood to greet Micah and his dad. Paul had flown to Israel to pick up his son, but he also wanted to thank the magicians for all they had done. Besides, Micah wanted his dad to meet them, knowing they would like each other. Hugs all around. Then everyone sat around a couple of tables at the outdoor café on Ben Yahuda Street.

"And now our *petite soirée* can begin, *non?*" Rianne beckoned a couple of waiters.

"Feed!" said Eleni, in her usual manner.

"Drinks first, old darling." Colonel Jack puffed contentedly on his cigar.

Moments later, beverages and plates of food started to appear. Yimca insisted the wine be placed in champagne buckets as it was in Paris. He got the ice buckets but had to settle for rosé wine from the Hills of Galilee instead of the Cote de Provence. Oh, well. It would have to do.

Soon, everyone's glasses were filled. Micah got a splash of wine with lots of fizzy water. Walloo was more than happy with a milkshake. They all drank to life, to friends, and to Micah and Shireen.

"And to Micah's mum. A brave lady with a brave son. May she get all better, very quick." Walloo raised his milkshake above his head. Paul thanked him. Micah's mother was now back home, he said. The Montsees family would soon be back together.

"Talk to me about yourself, Mr. Montsees," Eleni commanded.

Paul spoke with her for a bit, but there wasn't much she didn't already know. Soon, everyone was bantering about Micah and Shireen and their shared exploits. More toasts were made. Paul reveled in the affection in which the troupe held his son. They had risked their lives for him. But each time Paul tried to express his gratitude, he was interrupted by a laugh or another tall tale.

The late-afternoon sky took on the color of the wine they had quaffed, crystal pink, full and fresh. Paul grabbed the tab and insisted on paying. Everyone thought that was a splendid idea.

Time to go. E-mails, other numbers and addresses were exchanged. Walloo wrote in a little notebook. "Paper does not end up in the black holes," he said cannily.

"I have much more to teach you, my boy. So much more." Yimca tried to smile as Micah hugged him, but his voice cracked. "Now get going. We'll be visiting—you can be counting on it."

Paul put his arm on his son's shoulder and they turned to walk away. Micah looked back.

The table, the chairs, the debris from the afternoon remained, but his friends were gone. Disappeared. Magicians! Paul squeezed his son's shoulders and the fizz in Micah's throat began to settle. They walked on, quiet and happy, enjoying being together.

"That Eleni character," Paul said slowly. "She said Mum won't be sleeping through your tricks anymore. Didn't know Mum slept through your tricks. Does she?"

"Yeah, when she's tired."

"I see." Paul nodded, then added, "So what did she mean by that?"

"It's a riddle, Dad." Micah grinned broadly. "But I think it's a good one."

# Acknowledgements

IN THE COURSE OF MY ADVENTURE writing a contemporary thriller for teens, several people rallied around to help me through. I am grateful to you all. Particular thanks go to Nancy Hargrave for her willingness to re-read and re-proof the manuscript with great care and enthusiasm. Thanks also to Dan Snodderly for insightful character suggestions; and to Annabel Sebag-Montefiore and Andy Zvara, who are always in my corner.

I would also like to thank my daughter Kate Lipman, for whom I wrote the book in the first place—it just took a little longer than I imagined. Also, close to home, I must give a heartfelt thanks to my lovely wife Frances Erlebacher, who edited every draft of the book, always offering fresh insights and ideas, and showing great patience with, at times, a very crabby writer. Thanks also to my junior reading team, led by Kate and wonderfully assisted by Hannah Johns, who wrote the first glowing review for *Striking Terror.* I have it still.

For medical assistance I must thank Dr. Jim Ronan, who helped ensure my heroes and villains didn't suffer beyond the realms of possibility. For rock climbing assistance, thanks go to Marty Terwilliger. And what would I have done without the insider help of anti-terrorist specialist Matt Hudren, my very own Quartermaster! Regarding weaponry, thanks to Bob Kaylor and Mike Walker for helping me get the feel of things in the armament department.

On a personal note, I would like to applaud all the real-life "Shireens" of this world, who bravely stand up to tyranny, reject terror, and work for peace.

Lastly a word of remembrance for my cousin John Carpenter, who gave me my first box of magic tricks; and Dick Scott, a grand old performer and magical inventor who years back taught a young lad how to cut and restore a piece of rope. And yes, it did take five weeks to learn.

For more information, please visit DenisLipman.com.